Praise for Sonya Lalli

"From yoga studios to finding oneself in trips abroad to online dating, Lalli gives readers a wonderful novel about love and belonging and [the] meaning of happiness and home."

—Soniah Kamal, award-winning author of *Unmarriageable: Pride and Prejudice in Pakistan*

"Anu's struggle to find herself is wrought with obstacles and sometimes frustrating, but the resolution of her story is both satisfying and realistic. A moving look at one woman's journey between her family and her desire for independence."

—*Kirkus Reviews*

"Sonya Lalli offers up a tale of familial pressures, cultural traditions, and self-discovery that is equal turns heartbreaking and hilarious. . . . Lalli tears down stereotypes with humor and warmth."

—*Entertainment Weekly*

"An engaging love story that delivers on the promise of true love forever. . . . *The Matchmaker's List* comes through in spades (and hearts)."

—NPR

"Lalli's sharp-eyed tale of cross-cultural dating, family heartbreak, the strictures of culture, and the exuberance of love is both universal and timeless."

—*Publishers Weekly* (starred review)

Praise for *The Matchmaker's List*

"Bright and vivid, and fresh and funny—I was utterly charmed by this insight into Raina's struggle to be the perfect Indian daughter. A delightful debut."

—Veronica Henry, author of *How to Find Love in a Bookshop*

"A riotous odyssey into the pressures of cross-cultural modern dating that will chime with every twentysomething singleton."

—*ELLE* (UK)

"A funny and moving exploration of modern love."

—Balli Kaur Jaswal, author of *Erotic Stories for Punjabi Widows* (a Reese's Book Club pick)

"Absolutely charming." —*Woman's Day*

"A warm and refreshing look at cultural identity, unexpected romance, and unbreakable family bonds." —*Kirkus Reviews*

"Lalli's debut is a delightful, multicultural romantic comedy full of humorous banter and loads of life lessons about family, happiness, love, honesty, and acceptance." —*Booklist* (starred review)

"A knockout romantic comedy debut."

—*Washington Independent Review of Books*

BERKLEY TITLES BY SONYA LALLI

The Matchmaker's List

Grown-Up Pose

Serena Singh Flips the Script

Serena Singh Flips the Script

SONYA LALLI

BERKLEY · NEW YORK

BERKLEY
An imprint of Penguin Random House LLC
penguinrandomhouse.com

Library of Congress Cataloging-in-Publication Data

Names: Lalli, Sonya, author.
Title: Serena Singh flips the script / Sonya Lalli.
Description: First edition. | New York: Berkley, 2021.
Identifiers: LCCN 2020045201 (print) | LCCN 2020045202 (ebook) |
ISBN 9780593100936 (trade paperback) | ISBN 9780593100943 (ebook)
Classification: LCC PR6112.A483 S47 2021 (print) |
LCC PR6112.A483 (ebook) | DDC 823/.92—dc23
LC record available at https://lccn.loc.gov/2020045201
LC ebook record available at https://lccn.loc.gov/2020045202.

First Edition: Februray 2021

Printed in the United States of America
1 3 5 7 9 10 8 6 4 2

Cover art and design by Vikki Chu
Book design by Ashley Tucker

For Jay

Winter

"Is it Singh Time, *beti*?"

Slowly, I craned my neck to the side. Uncle Singh, one of the many Uncle Singhs in our community, was towering over me. I'd been making eyes again with the hot photographer, whose name I kept forgetting, and hadn't noticed the uncle make his approach.

"*Singh* Time?" I asked, feigning ignorance as I stood up from my chair and stalled for time.

"It is time to sing, *hah*?"

Party hosts in our community knew to allot one, even two hours for Singh Time, during which various uncles took over the microphone and serenaded the room with their off-key renditions of Punjabi folk songs. But my baby sister, Natasha, who had married a white guy and had mainly non-Indian guests at her wedding that night, had given me strict instructions to withhold the microphone "by any means necessary."

I snuck a glance to my right, down the length of the head table. She was sitting happily next to Mark in her bedazzled gold *lengha*, flanked by both sets of parents, and then the wedding party. I had been mildly disappointed when Natasha asked the two other bridesmaids, her closest childhood friends, to give the toast to the bride instead of me, but I suppose she needed me up here as MC to fend off the uncles.

"Where is microphone?" I heard Uncle Singh ask. I turned back, beaming at him as a lightbulb went off in my head.

"Uncle," I whispered, as if I had gossip to share. "Natasha specifically asked me not to let you sing tonight."

He gasped, and I squeezed his hands in my own.

"Because she has something more special in mind for you."

He narrowed his brows, the two thick bushes above his eyes merging into one long one.

"You, Uncle Singh, are her most favorite uncle."

"I *am*?"

"Have you not always felt a special bond with our family? With our sweet little Natasha?"

He glanced over at her curiously. Even though we shared the same, extremely common surname, we weren't related to this Uncle Singh. To be completely honest, our families didn't even know each other that well, and if Natasha wasn't dressed up like a bride, I doubt the uncle would have been able to pick her out of a lineup. But if fourteen years in advertising had taught me anything, it's that Uncle Singh didn't want the microphone to sing. *No.* He wanted the microphone to feel admired, even loved.

And that's all the information I needed to make the sale.

Within minutes, I'd convinced Uncle Singh that it was tradition for the bride's favorite uncle to ask her to dance during the reception and that she'd be waiting for him after the DJ started later that evening. (Thankfully, he didn't grill me too much on the alleged custom, accepting my answer that it was something *goray*—white people—liked to do.)

It was just before nine p.m. by the time he returned to his seat, and according to the Google spreadsheet Natasha, her treat of a mother-in-law, Mrs. Hartshorne, and their team of organizers had prepared, it was nearly time for me to make the introductions for the final round of toasts. I grabbed the microphone from where it was hidden in my purse, not wanting to wait a moment longer in case another uncle or auntie cornered me, and walked up to the podium, my heart beating in my stomach.

It's not that I was nervous. Far from it. I loved public speaking, and I was good at it, too. But presenting a pithy, original advertising campaign to get a client on board with the idea, and then consumers on board with the product, was *very* different than MCing your baby sister's wedding.

Your baby sister's *Indian* wedding.

I surveyed the room as I gathered the courage to start. Everyone seemed to be having a good time, chatting and laughing, shoveling in forkfuls of the chocolate lavender wedding cake Natasha and I had spent hours picking out. And the room was gorgeous. We'd decorated it to be the exact winter wonderland Natasha had imagined.

But it was strange to see the room divided into brown and white—except for the four or five tables closest to the bar full of Natasha and Mark's friends, beautiful people in a rainbow of ethnicities that would have been perfect as extras on the sportswear campaign I'd been working on all winter.

Up near the front sat Mark's family and his parents' friends—the stuffiest, most highbrow residents of Washington, DC, or Bethesda of the "old money" variety, including one senator, two House representatives, and three directors of one federal agency or another. (I knew this because Mrs. Hartshorne had demanded I give them a "warm welcome" yet said we didn't have time to thank all of our relatives who flew in from the UK and India.) Most of the men were in tuxedos, and the women in gowns—although their diamonds, pearls, and general decadence didn't outshine the sparkle coming from the back of the room, where our extended family and community was seated. The uncles were in kurtas or western suits, the aunties in saris or *salwars* in true gilded Punjabi glamour.

A group of particularly glitzy aunties caught my eye halfway toward the back. They were gawking at me, and even from here I could see the pity on their faces. I tried not to roll my eyes, imagining what they were saying about me whenever I was out of earshot.

Already thirty-six, and to have a younger sister married first?

What ever happened to that nice boy Jesse? Did she scare him off?

She is not too old yet, nah? *My cousin's nephew has a job now. I will make the arrangements!*

"Now *that* is what I call butter chicken," I said loudly into the microphone, cutting off their voices in my head. The whole room laughed. I'm not sure at what exactly.

"I hope everyone's having a wonderful time!"

A table near the bar cheered and clinked their glasses, and I gritted my teeth as the rest of the room joined in, and Natasha and Mark stood up for a chaste, tasteful kiss for their fans.

My chest ached, but I wasn't jealous, even though it would be easy to think as much.

I was genuinely, wholeheartedly happy that she had found someone to spend her life with.

I was also happy that one of the Singh sisters was finally married, checking off the "good Indian girl" box, which meant I didn't have to.

Five hours later, I found myself in the happy couple's honeymoon suite, trapped on a sectional between Natasha and one of her giggly friends. I yawned, hiding it with my palm. Natasha had assigned me with last-minute wedding tasks that week because she didn't fully trust the planner, and I was exhausted, but I knew it would look bad if I left early. Leaning forward, I checked to see if there was anyone else I could talk to. The groomsmen were pouring another round of tequila shots in the kitchen. They were nice enough guys, all thirtysomethings with fancy jobs in government or law or medicine, but they drank like fish whenever they were off the clock. I turned my head toward the deluxe king-size bed, on top of which Mark and his sister, Bethany, and a handful of their friends were dancing up a storm. Their shoes were still on, and I felt even more exhausted just watching them.

I sighed silently, sinking back into the couch. Just a few more hours, and I could crawl into bed, close my eyes, and the wedding would be over.

Finally.

Today had felt like a long, *long* time coming, if only because Mom had been fantasizing about it since the day Natasha brought Mark home.

Do you think he'll propose, Serena?

Do you think they'll have a Sikh ceremony, Serena?

Do you think your sister will pick the red jai malas, *Serena?*

I'd been fielding these sorts of panicked, overexcited calls for years, but I didn't mind in the slightest. As much as Mom adored her new son-in-law, I freaking *loved* having him around. Not only had Mark proven to be a great buffer at tense family dinners, but ever since he entered the picture, Mom had stopped hounding me about the fact that *I* wasn't married.

I glanced around the room at Natasha and Mark's friends, suddenly nostalgic for my own group, whom I'd hung out with every single day from grade school to high school graduation. We'd been like this once. Big groups of us sitting around, dancing, telling one another the same old stories that had defined our friendships, built their foundations. But things were different now that we were older.

Just a few years ago, I could count on scores of dynamic, caring women in my life, from school or college or whom I'd met at work. But one by one, they'd gotten married and had families. And one by one, their commitments to our friendship took a backseat. Our movie nights, weekly phone calls, or Saturday dinners became less and less frequent, morphed into forty-five-minute catch-ups at a Starbucks near *their* apartments, when *their* spouses were at the gym or out of town. They'd forget my birthday or to ask me about the new client I'd scored, but they'd text to remind me I still hadn't RSVP'd for their baby showers or housewarmings an hour and a half away in suburbia.

Most of them kept their careers after having children, so it was understandable that they never had time for their single friends in the city. That those few precious moments between working and commuting, bath time and story time, were dedicated to their partner, their hobbies, their own mental health.

I wasn't a robot. They were my friends, and I got it. But I didn't have to like it, and I was certainly allowed to resent it.

"You awake?" I heard Natasha ask me, and a split second later she elbowed me in the ribs. "Are you ever going to tell me why I had to dance with that random uncle to 'Mundian to Bach Ke'?"

I started to explain to her the Singh Time situation, but then she grabbed my shoulder and cut me off.

"Look who it is!"

I followed her eyes through the crowd toward the front door of the suite. It was the photographer I'd been flirting with the whole day. Suddenly, I didn't feel so sleepy.

"I told him to drop by." Natasha shrugged nonchalantly. "I wonder why he came."

"Free booze?" I ventured.

"I saw you two chatting today. A *lot.*"

"Like when?"

"Like, right before the ceremony. The cocktail hour. The *reception.* Becket is so into you!"

Becket. So that was his name.

He hadn't seen us yet, and I watched him hover awkwardly in the kitchen and shake hands with the groomsmen, and then obligingly down a tequila shot. He was wearing a checked shirt and tie beneath his suit, and his black hair—which I'd noticed earlier had a few grays, too—swooped adorably across his forehead, like a surfer.

"Go talk to him."

I shook my head, even though I couldn't stop smiling. It had been a while since I'd felt attracted to someone like this—eight months or so, the UN Swahili translator I'd briefly dated—and the thrill of something new sent a shiver up my spine.

I knocked my knee against Natasha, in thanks. She was shameless, but she was also my best friend. I mean, she noticed who I was giving the eyes to on her own wedding day. Maybe I didn't need my other friends. Maybe it didn't matter if everyone else in my life had started to drift away.

"Serena, if you don't go over there—"

"Chill, OK?" I caught her eye, and she made a face at me. "Please don't make this awk . . ."

I trailed off as I suddenly realized that Becket had left the kitchen. He was standing in front of us.

"Hey," he said, his hands in his pockets.

I was about to speak when Natasha intervened.

"Becket!" she squealed, standing up. "I'm so glad you came. You've met my big sister, haven't you?" She pushed him into her spot on the couch, and I felt his thigh rub against mine as he sat down.

"Can I get you a drink?" she asked him.

"Sure. I'll—"

"No, don't move." She shook her head furiously, took a swig from her beer, and then pressed the bottle into his hand. "Here. Take mine."

You call that chill, Natasha?

Becket smiled at the half-drunk bottle of beer. He took a sip, catching my eye just as he raised the bottle into the air, and we held each other's gazes as Natasha and her giggly friend disappeared into the background.

"So what's your story?" I asked, after they'd left. We were the only ones left on the couch.

He finished swallowing and brought his beer back down to his lap. "Do you want the abridged version or the full monty?"

"The full monty."

When you get to a certain age, when you've dated a certain number of people, you learn how to cut to the chase.

"The full monty," he repeated, sighing through a smile. "Do you have time? This might take all night."

God, he was flirty, but there's nothing I liked more than some innuendo.

By the end of the evening, we'd learned where each other had gone to school, what neighborhood the other lived in, and where the other worked. (Or in my case, was about to start work.) He'd set his hand on my knee, and when I walked him to his Lyft, he grazed my ear with his lips as he whispered in my ear.

Lightly, I kissed him, and it didn't matter what the kiss meant or what he had whispered. It didn't matter that we were both thirty-six, and if this—whatever *this* was with Becket—lasted six more minutes, months, or even years. Because the truth was, for me, dating was just that. *Dating.*

I didn't want to have a family. I didn't *want* to catch myself a husband #lovehim #blessed.

I just wished people believed me.

SANDEEP

Six years earlier

"Natasha, I can't afford to buy in Georgetown." Serena brought a fingerful of *chole bhature* to her lips. "Maybe a studio. *Maybe.* But then there wouldn't be room for you—"

"OK, OK. Columbia Heights it is!" Natasha elbowed her older sister, giggling. "I guess that's where all the yuppies are going."

"So I'm a yuppie, huh?"

"Yep. And I'm going to be one, too, in six months, roomie!" Natasha squealed. "Can you believe it, guys? Only six months until I'm done with college *forever* and out in the real world. Living in the freaking *city*!" She threw back her head with such fervor Sandeep thought it might fall back onto the kitchen floor. "I can't wait to get out of here."

An awkward silence followed, sending chills down Sandeep's spine. A moment later, Natasha smiled sheepishly.

"No offense, Mom and Dad."

"None taken, *beti*," Veer answered.

Sandeep glanced over at her husband. Veer was chewing thoughtfully on his food. She spotted a crumb above his upper lip in his whiskers, and she resisted the urge to rub it away. When they first married, she wasn't fond of his full beard or turban, but it suited his features, his frame, and she very quickly found it irresistible. She still did.

Veer was strong but silent. Frustratingly silent. Sandeep cleared her throat, nudging him under the table. He didn't budge, and she wondered what it would take for him to offer anything further to the conversation, if he understood the term "yuppie," or perhaps might even reveal to his daughters that it had been their dream, too, to buy a place in the city. But in front of Serena, he stayed quiet on all important matters—such as his view on her not yet being married, the hideous tattoo on her neck, and now her decision to buy an apartment on her own. Only later, as they settled together beneath the quilt, would he reveal to Sandeep how he truly felt.

"Are you OK, Mom?" she heard Serena ask. "You've barely eaten."

Sandeep looked back at her elder daughter. Serena had switched to Punjabi and was smiling at her. She offered her hand across the table, and Sandeep accepted it, squeezing.

"It's nice to have you here," Sandeep said quietly. "I'm just happy you're home."

Serena didn't answer, and Natasha resumed babbling about her plans after graduating university.

It was like "pulling teeth" to get Serena to come home sometimes, or so the American phrase went. Even for her birthday. Would Natasha follow her lead and disappear when she left home that summer? Just the thought of it ruined Sandeep's appetite.

After dinner, Veer and Natasha disappeared into the sitting room, and Sandeep relished having Serena to herself. She was always more forthcoming when it was just the two of them, and Sandeep enjoyed learning more about her daughter's mysterious life through anecdotes and passing comments she let slip without realizing it. Tonight, there was one particular piece of information she was determined to retrieve, and she waited for a lull in the conversation for her opportunity.

"It's a big birthday this year." Sandeep sighed, watching her daughter spoon leftover chicken curry into an old yogurt container. Natasha was the outright beauty, but Serena was uniquely striking. Her intense eyes and lovely lips. Even her short hair suited her graceful cheekbones and neck—if only she hadn't ruined it with that tattoo.

"The big three-oh," Serena said dryly.

"Do you have special plans for tomorrow night?"

She held her breath, waiting. Serena turned her gaze.

"*Special* plans, Mom?" Serena paused. "Why yes."

Sandeep's heart sang. "*Acha?*"

"My friends are throwing me a birthday party. You remember Jenna, right?" Serena snapped the lid on the yogurt container. "She's going. The whole school gang, and my city friends, too. I'm looking forward to it."

Serena's eyes were piercing.

"It's been a while since I've seen some of them."

Sandeep swallowed hard, forcing a smile. For weeks, ever since Serena announced she wanted her family birthday dinner to be held the night before the big day, Sandeep had been convinced. Surely, it meant she was dating someone. Surely, on her thirtieth birthday, she would only put a boyfriend above her family.

"Sounds like a fun party," Sandeep answered finally.

"You look disappointed," Serena said. Her eyes were uncompromising. "Was there something else you were trying to get at?"

Sandeep thought she'd been subtle, but apparently not.

"I've asked you so many times not to push me, Mom." Serena's voice had changed. "I have no 'special plans' tonight, tomorrow, next year. Not ever. Do you understand?"

"*Hah,*" Sandeep answered, out of instinct. "I understand."

"No, I don't think you do. Because every time I come home, you show me some random guy's *bio data,*" Serena scoffed, imitating Sandeep's accent. "Or badger me about who I'm dating, or just *assume* that anything special in my life has to do with a guy!"

Sandeep bit her lip, frustrated. "I am not pushing. I am *suggesting.* I know finding a good match is a problem for educated women."

Serena groaned, but Sandeep persisted.

"Let me *help* you. You are so busy, working so hard." Gently, she patted her daughter's cheek, trying to articulate her next thought: that she knew Serena and knew what she was looking for. What she needed. A man who understood the way the world worked now, who was strong, and above all else, was strong enough to accept Serena as his equal.

It's what she meant to say, but instead, her words failed her. Instead, she said, "I will find you a man that accepts that you work."

The moment the words left her lips, Sandeep knew they were the wrong ones, that they hadn't reflected what she truly felt. Her intentions had jumbled up as soon as she spoke, and now it was too late. Serena was enraged.

"I just can't believe you sometimes!" Serena spat, tears in her eyes. "You don't get it at all, Mom."

"*Beti—*"

"But maybe I haven't been clear enough." She seemed to be chewing her words, slowly. "I do not want you to find me someone. Because I do not want *anyone*. OK? I am never getting married and having a family."

Sandeep's ears rang. Serena had hurled out these angry words before, and here it went again.

"Why don't you believe me?"

"You were so close to marriage with—"

"That was years ago. Before I had a career, before I knew what I even wanted. My priorities have changed."

"No husband? No *family*—"

"Why," Serena said, icily, "exactly should I get married, Mom?" She gestured to the pile of dirty dishes in the sink and then toward the sitting room. To her father.

"Explain it to me."

Love could not be explained or reasoned with. Neither could Serena. She was stubborn, just like her father, and often it seemed like nothing Sandeep said or did would ever change her mind.

Something spiteful, and harsh, sat on the tip of her tongue, like a sour lozenge. Sandeep was about to spit it out when Natasha waltzed into the room, oblivious.

"Oh my god, *guess* what's on TV . . . *Mrs. Doubtfire*!"

"Really?" Serena's features softened.

"Remember how we used to watch it every weekend?"

Serena smiled. "Because we had the VHS."

"Mom, have you seen it?" Natasha asked.

Sandeep hadn't seen the movie in years, back when her English was much poorer, and she hadn't understood why Robin Williams had spent the whole movie dressed like an old woman until later that night, when Veer explained the plot.

"I'm not sure," Sandeep answered, turning back to the sink. "Should we watch?"

"I'll make popcorn!" Natasha swung open the pantry door

and then lowered her voice. "So what's the dress code for tomorrow, by the way? I can't *believe* I finally get to meet John."

Sandeep's ears perked up.

"Tash . . ." Serena hushed. "Not now."

"You did invite him, right? I won't grill this one, I promise—"

"Shh!"

"Just gotta make sure they're good enough for you, sis . . ."

The two daughters chattered like small sparrows as they set to work on the popcorn, speaking in hushed voices. Sandeep couldn't understand much of what they were saying—their English was too rapid, too colloquial—but she'd heard enough.

She heard there was a "John."

So Serena *was* dating someone; she just didn't want to admit it. She didn't want to get her heart broken again.

Sandeep smiled, wondering if John was Sikh or even Indian, and was surprised to find that she didn't really mind. The question that had seemed so pivotal when Serena first became a young woman had paved the way for more important ones.

Was he educated? Would he respect Serena's strength of character?

Would he love and cherish her daughter the way she so dearly deserved?

By the time Sandeep was settled into the love seat next to her husband, Natasha had pulled out the cupcakes she'd baked and hidden in the garage. She'd also arranged for paper plates and napkins patterned with "30" in gold and black, and handed a plate to each member of the family. One cupcake and a fistful of popcorn each. After, she hopped on the other couch with Serena, nuzzling into her the same way she had as a girl.

Sandeep loved how close the girls were. Serena babied and Natasha worshipped, and suddenly the thought of them living together in the city made it a bit more bearable that she'd soon have no children at home. Her daughters were grown-ups. Well, at least Serena was a grown-up. As infuriating as she could be, Sandeep was proud that she'd raised her to be strong-willed, and never compromised from being anyone but herself.

Sandeep was the same. It's the reason they frequently collided.

Had Natasha not interrupted them in the kitchen, Sandeep's argument with Serena would have escalated. It would have turned into another fight, another reason for Serena to storm out. Another months-long stint where she refused to come home. Sandeep was grateful. If she didn't want to lose Serena for good, she supposed she had to be grateful.

She also had to accept her as she was, but Sandeep was still learning how.

3

I stood up as the door opened, pulled my shoulders back, and smiled. It almost felt like my first day of high school, except this time I wasn't wearing an outfit that Mom found in a thrift store bargain bin or received as a hand-me-down from one of the affluent families at our *gurdwara*. Today, I had ironed my favorite black trousers and paired them with bold red heels and a crisp white collared shirt. I had worn contacts for all of Natasha's wedding functions the week before because she'd begged me to, but I hated poking at my eyes, so I was relieved to be back in my glasses. Today, I'd picked out my favorite pair of gold-green cat eye frames. I felt fabulous.

"*You* must be Serena Singh," a woman said, pushing through the door.

"Hi," I said, extending my hand. "You must be Tracy."

Tracy, my human resources contact, nodded at me, taking stock of me as she shook my hand. I could tell I was not what she expected as her eyes fixated on my neck tattoo.

"Did you find parking all right?" Tracy asked. "I can validate it until we organize your pass."

"No need," I said. I didn't have a car. "I took the bus."

Tracy nodded vaguely and then waved her arm at the office behind her. "Well, this is it! Let's have a tour, shall we?"

The office took up half of the second floor of a building a few blocks south of Dupont Circle. It was open concept and had lots of natural light, and there were touches of the infamous Deborah Kim style everywhere. The warm leather lounge chairs and hanging plants in the lunchroom. Trendy acrylic desks organized into eye-pleasing pods. A gallery wall full of art from some of her most successful advertising campaigns, as well as staff and family photos. I wanted to pinch myself. I couldn't believe I was *here*.

I'd parlayed a college internship at an advertising agency infamously known as a "boys club" into a junior copywriting role after graduation and had worked hard to climb the ranks. But there were only so many times I was willing to tolerate having a male colleague take credit for my work or being passed over for a promotion into a leadership role. I had been quietly interviewing around town for six months when I received an e-mail from none other than Deborah Kim, Korean-American advertising legend who had left the helm of one of North America's largest agencies to go solo a decade earlier.

"I've gotten too big. I can't run the accounts and the campaigns," she'd said when we met up after hours at a restaurant far away from my old office. "We're a small team, Serena. Agile, socially ethical, none of those ridiculous old-school traditions weighing us down. And I need a creative director who gets that."

My heart started beating so loudly I could swear the whole bar could hear it.

"I've seen your work." Deborah sipped her cranberry juice. "Nicely done with the McMichael campaign."

I hesitated, and then she laughed.

"I know you were on the account, and that means you did the work—even if that fucker Iain took the credit."

My old boss Iain *was* a fucker. It felt good to hear someone else say it.

She'd tapped her trimmed, unpolished nail on her wineglass hard enough that it clanged. "Sell this to me," she said, so I sold it to her, and three hours later she offered me the job.

My *dream* job.

On the tour, Tracy showed me where everyone sat: operations, HR, finance, accounts, business development, purchasing. Each department had its own pod of desks, and I couldn't stop admiring how beautiful the office was. How friendly it felt.

Tracy stopped short at a pod at the far end of the space, pointing. "Our digital director, Ainsley, sits right here with her team—website, analytics, all that fun stuff I don't understand. She's on vacation right now . . ."

I nodded, following Tracy's hand as it flicked to the opposite pod. "And your team sits here. The *creatives*, as we laywomen like to call you."

Your team. I couldn't help but smile. I was finally running my own team.

After thanking Tracy for the tour, I sat down at my desk, powering on what looked to be a brand-new MacBook Pro. There was a stack of business cards next to the mouse.

Serena Singh. Creative Director.

More like: *Serena Singh. Creative Director. Badass Brown Girl. Advertising Ass-Kicker.*

A beat later, the clacking sound of heels made me look up. Victoria West, my senior copywriter, was walking toward me. I'd Googled everyone who would be working for me, and just flicking through their social media, I knew we'd make a great team. Who knows . . . maybe we'd even become friends.

"I'm Serena," I said brightly, standing up. She walked right up to me, but she didn't smile at me. If anything, her expression turned to a snarl.

"You're in my seat."

I froze. My hand, which I'd been about to extend to shake hers, began trembling.

"That's where I sit. I've sat there since I started four years ago."

There were six desks in the creative pod, and Tracy had clearly pointed to this one on the end, closest to Deborah's office. Hadn't she?

My computer sat on it. My business cards, too. Well, *this* was awkward.

I looked back at Victoria. Her face was unreadable, and I was both aghast at her manners, and at myself, because it had been a full eight—nope, *nine*—seconds since either of us had said anything.

"Uh."

Good god, Serena, say something! You're her new boss. You're Badass Brown Girl, and Advertising Ass-Kicker, remember?

So much for this not being like the first day of school. This felt exactly like the first day of school, and I had just met the Mean Girl.

"Vic!" Someone called, breaking the silence. We both turned to look in that direction. It was Tracy, her head popping through the kitchen door, as if independent from her body. "Thought I heard you come in. You're going to switch seats with Serena. Cool?"

"Totally!" Victoria exclaimed happily, giving Tracy the thumbs-up. My eyebrows narrowed.

"OK, then," Victoria said, brushing past me to a seat farther down the pod. "*Welcome.*"

Welcome? I sure didn't feel welcome. As Victoria shrugged off her coat and rummaged through her purse, I knew I needed to say something, but *what* exactly? Did I need to assert myself? Salvage the situation? Invite her out to lunch?

"So you must be Victoria," I said, finally.

"Vic," she said, without meeting my gaze. "Call me Vic."

"What did Becket's text say again?" Natasha asked.

"He was in the area and would I like to grab a bite."

"Verbatim?"

"About, yeah." I sighed. "But it's been a long day. Maybe I'll just go home."

I could hear her typing on the other end of the line. A day and a half into domestic bliss, and she was already cataloging the wedding presents into an Excel spreadsheet.

"I shouldn't go, right?" I asked.

She didn't answer, and I thought briefly about telling her about my first day on the job.

It was a great first day. Well, it was *good*.

OK, fine. It was mediocre. At best. And I didn't really feel like talking about it yet.

"What if I suggest Thursday night for a date?" I asked Natasha, refusing to dwell. "Maybe—"

"You're free tonight," she said, interrupting me. The clicking of the keyboard stopped. "You haven't eaten yet. He's a good kisser. So can you just stop pretending you're not going to go, and save us both a half hour?"

I pouted into the phone, even though she couldn't see it.

"Should I take that as a yes?"

After Natasha grilled me on my OOTD, which she approved

and then asked to borrow, I hung up the phone and texted Becket back.

We met at a sports bar on Connecticut Avenue I'd been to once or twice before, and I found him in a cramped booth at the back. I could smell his cologne from where I was sitting across the table, but I didn't recognize it.

"We probably should have ordered champagne," he said, after the waiter left with our orders. (Beer for Becket. Ginger ale for me. Loaded nachos for both of us.)

"I don't really drink," I said, even though I'd already told him as much the night we met.

"What about on special occasions?"

I smiled. "Well, sure, for a toast—"

"Well, I think we should have a toast to your new job. If that doesn't deserve champagne, I don't know what does."

I smiled coyly, rubbing the paper napkin between my fingers. "It's not a big deal, really . . ."

"It is a big deal. You just got a job at Deborah Kim's boutique, and according to *Forbes* magazine"—he made a silly face—"she's *kinda* a big deal."

"Did you go all stalker on me?" I laughed. "How? I'm not on social media."

"I have my ways." He leaned forward on the table. "And you're her new creative director? You never told me *that*, Serena. That's incredible! You must get asked this all the time, but is your life anything like *Mad Men*?"

"Exactly like *Mad Men*. I even have a hot ex-wife who's a dead ringer for January Jones."

"*Really?*"

"Really," I deadpanned, and it took Becket about five minutes to figure out I was kidding.

It was one of the better first dates I'd been on in the past fifteen-odd years. I never expected much on dates—a nod toward chivalry, a token amount of interest in my life and not just their own. Becket rose higher and higher in my books as the evening went on, as we ordered another round of beer and ginger ale, when he told me rather convincingly that he was "man enough to be proud of my success." By the time we got the bill (we split; I always insisted), I knew there would be a second date and, very likely, a few more after that.

It was surprisingly warm for early February, so we decided to walk home. We didn't live far away from each other.

"If it was colder," Becket said quietly, "I would have an excuse to wrap my arm around you."

In response, I reached up and wrapped my arm around his shoulder, so tight that he had to hunch over to walk alongside me. He didn't say anything, and about ten steps later, he craned his neck awkwardly to look down at me.

"What, aren't you man enough for this?"

He grinned, and he looked so cute—so damn kissable—I put my other arm up around his neck and kissed him. He'd said he was strong enough for a woman like me, hadn't he? If that was true, which I still wasn't sure was the case, he could handle me initiating the kiss.

Becket's lips caught mine with just the right pressure and warmth. He wrapped his large hands around my waist and held me there, firmly, and I let myself melt into him for a moment before pulling away.

"Jesus." He licked his lips, breathing hard against me. "If it wasn't a Monday night, I'd ferry you away back to my place."

"And if I was easy, I'd let you."

"You have a high-powered job and don't put out . . ." He dropped his hands from my body. "This is never going to work between us."

I laughed, gently tugging on his arm. As we waited for the walk light, my eyes flicked away from him and across the street. Cars whizzed down Massachusetts Avenue, slamming on their brakes as they rounded Dupont Circle and made way for pedestrians and joggers. I watched them admiringly. I never could run outside in the winter; it made my lungs burn.

Suddenly, a flash of cherry red caught my eye. A burst of neon green. My eyes skirted past the jogger with the uncoordinated outfit as he ran on the spot waiting for the walk light opposite us, but there was something about him that made me take a second look.

The man had dark hair poked out over his ears and the nape of his neck. He turned to the side slightly, and my stomach twisted at the familiar profile. His forehead. The bridge of the nose. The shape of his lips.

It couldn't be *him*. Could it?

"Did I offend you?" I heard Becket ask. I turned to face him, my heart still beating wildly. "I was only joking."

"Right. I know . . ." I trailed off. I glanced back toward the jogger just as the walk light changed, and the blur of red and neon picked up speed.

"What are we looking at?" Becket asked.

"I think that was my ex-boyfriend."

Becket put his arm around me as our own walk light changed color, and we continued on our way. Why had I told him that? I hadn't meant to. The question had come as a surprise, and the words simply came out.

"Was it a recent ex-boyfriend?"

Oh boy. This was becoming a thing. A conversation. I racked my brain for the easiest answer.

"A million-years-ago ex-boyfriend," I said finally.

"My favorite kind." His hand slipped from my shoulder to my waist. "Why did you break up?"

"Well, we met in college," I said slowly, surprised by how difficult it was becoming to string words together. "We were . . . too . . ."

"Young?" Becket finished, and I nodded, even though that's not what I was going to say. I wasn't sure what I was going to say.

"I don't miss being that young," Becket said, after a moment. "The older I get, the more I realize how little I know."

He moved off the sidewalk to tie his shoe, and when his eyes were down I scanned the crowd, sneaking a look behind me. The jogger had crossed paths with us, but I'd missed it. There wasn't a red tuque or neon green athletic jacket in sight.

"You ready?" Becket asked, standing up. I nodded, slipping my hand back into his, and we continued walking forward.

It was the only way to go.

4

My mouth watered as I scanned the menu. Gumbo and corn bread. *Quadruple* cheese macaroni. Spicy fried chicken.

"I should have worn stretchy pants." I tugged on the waistband of my high-rise jeans. "What are you going to order?"

"The gumbo," Natasha said. "Definitely. It's their specialty."

"If I order the chicken, will you let me try some of yours?"

Natasha threw me a look. "*Obviously.*"

I held her gaze for a beat, smiling, before returning to the menu. I was pleased that Natasha had suggested dinner for just the two of us. Before the wedding planning had taken over both of our lives, we used to spend most Friday nights together. Mark tagged along at least half the time, and usually our hangouts consisted of takeout and teen Netflix dramas featuring sixteen-year-old characters who had as much sex as either me or Natasha. (OK, definitely more than me.) But tonight she'd vetoed my suggestion that we gorge ourselves on dumplings and watch reruns of *The OC* and insisted we try a new restaurant she'd dubbed "Louisiana comfort meets Rihanna." (I gathered that the food hailed from the South, while the funky decor and upbeat music was in tribute to our favorite star.)

We both ordered the freshly squeezed blueberry and pawpaw juice, and after Natasha took a Boomerang of us toasting and posted it to her Stories, I reminded her that she still needed to pick up the rest of her stuff from her bedroom at my apartment. I even offered to help her move it, and she grunted noncommittally. Natasha had been unofficially living with Mark at his parents' town house in Georgetown for a while now, only spending the occasional night at mine. Most of the stuff she'd left behind, I gathered, she didn't really need.

Natasha was in a surprisingly unchatty mood, so I gave her the lowdown on my first week. I'd been dreaming about being creative director of an advertising agency like this for so long, and these past five days had been everything I thought they would be. Well. *Nearly.* The only thing that made it less of a dream job and somewhat of a nightmare was "call me Vic," one of the five women who now reported to me.

I'd given her the benefit of the doubt and tried to turn over a new leaf after our first awkward encounter, but Vic—whom I'd started referring to as Ginger Spice because of her red hair and temper—simply did not want to get to know me. We sat right next to each other, and she only spoke the bare minimum required of us to do our jobs and didn't even look me in the eye.

"What do you think I should do?" I asked Natasha, crossing my legs beneath the table. (Natasha was an expert in navigating complicated social situations. I'm not saying she was a Mean Girl in high school, but from the stories I heard, she was definitely Mean Girl *adjacent*.)

"Everyone else likes me. Should I just take Ginger aside, pull rank, and tell her off?" I sighed. "Although, that rules out the possibility of us ever being friends."

"Well, you're her boss, right?" Natasha played with her juice straw. “And if she’s a bitch, why would you even *want* to be friends with her?”

“True . . .” I hesitated, hoping I wouldn’t have to resort to conflict just yet. I’d never formally managed a team before or had to have tough conversations with someone who reported to me. Just the idea of it made me sweat.

“I might wait a few weeks and see if she comes around,” I continued. “Maybe she’ll warm up to me on her own.”

“Yeah,” Natasha said blandly. “Who knows.”

I caught her looking at something behind me, so I glanced in that direction. She was gawking at a rather fabulous-looking couple sitting at the bar.

“Do you know them?” I asked, turning back around.

“No,” Natasha said. “But she’s an influencer. I follow her. I wonder who that guy is.”

I sipped on my juice, and a chunk of something came up through the straw. I chewed it, hoping it was just the fruit.

“So there’s a reason I invited you out tonight,” Natasha said suddenly. “I have to tell you something.”

My heart fell. She sounded serious.

“Sure,” I said, trying to keep my tone light. “What’s up? Everything . . . OK?”

“Everything is perfect, actually.” A dreamy look washed over her face and then vanished an instant later. “I . . . I am . . .”

I laughed nervously. “OK, what is it? You’re freaking me out.”

“Sorry. I guess I’ll just spit it out, then. I . . .”

“Spit away. Just not in my food.” I laughed. “I mean—”

“Serena, I’m pregnant.”

I froze, and a huge pit formed in my stomach. I opened my mouth. Nothing came out.

Oh.

Oh, *fuck*.

Natasha was pregnant? My sister, who had been married a grand total of *six* days, was already knocked up?

Timed slowed down. I knew in that instant I couldn't let my feelings betray me. I *had* to say the right thing. I pushed out my cheeks into a smile, baring my teeth in a wide grin.

"Are you sure—"

"What do you mean, am I sure?" she snapped. "Why the hell would I *tell* you if I wasn't sure."

I grimaced, stalling. I guess I hadn't chosen my words carefully enough.

"Then, *wow*." My breath caught. "Congratulations!"

"You're mad," she whined. "I *knew* you'd be—"

"Mad?" I laughed, shaking my head. "I'm so happy for you!"

Was I selling it? I could sell anything else—name the product, the service, and I could figure it out—but *this*?

"Serena, I know how you feel about all your friends who are busy with mommy clubs—"

"Natasha." I swallowed hard, suppressing the acid rising in my throat. "Stop. This is about you, and this is . . . wonderful news. Mom is going to so happy!"

At least that was true. The silver lining was that a grandchild would make Mom smile, something she hadn't done enough in her life.

"I only went off the pill over Christmas." Natasha said. For a moment, she seemed as shocked by the news as I was. "I didn't realize I'd be so . . . *fertile*."

I reached across the table and squeezed her hand, and then forced out a laugh. "This is so exciting, I'm going to be a *massi*!"

Natasha beamed, repeating the Punjabi word for "mother's sister" back to me.

"I'm so *excited*, Serena. We've wanted this for so long, you know?" Suddenly, Natasha was back to herself: a babbling brook of smiles and giggles and infectious lightness. And as she was talking, it hit me: This wasn't an accident. Natasha and Mark had been trying for a baby, and she'd never even told me.

I swallowed the hurt, attempting to listen as best I could, to be excited for her the way I should have been. Why was this news coming as such a surprise? I'd known all along that my dear, sweet sister would want to have a baby.

So why hadn't I prepared myself?

"The timing *is* a bit inconvenient, though," she said, coming up for air. "Now I can't drink on the honeymoon."

I wondered if she also found it "inconvenient" that she had to literally grow a human inside of her, that in nine short months, her entire life would feel full of inconveniences.

"Mark's over the moon. We just took the test last night. We're going over to Mom and Dad's this weekend to share the news. We'll just tell family for now . . ."

I nodded my head as she continued chattering, and I was sure to make all the right noises and faces.

Natasha had already given up her name, gotten herself pregnant, and moved into her in-laws' house; what else would she be willing to give up?

I'm still going to make space in my life for my friends, my hobbies.

It's what all my friends had said, but I hadn't seen it happen yet. And it didn't matter that Natasha wasn't just another friend, but my very best friend and my own flesh and blood; I was suddenly scared shitless that it would happen to her, too.

Guess what," I said, turning the corner from the boardroom. "I . . ."

I stopped in my tracks. My pod was completely empty. I furrowed my brow, glancing at my watch. It was only four minutes past five o'clock.

Irritated my whole team had left without saying goodbye, I sat down in a huff and plugged my laptop back into my workstation. I'd spent the last hour in the boardroom with Deborah and the accounts team finalizing a handful of strategy documents, and I'd been looking forward to updating the Spice Girls and handing out the next wave of assignments. I was even thinking about asking them out for happy hour that evening.

My silly nickname for Ginger Spice had stuck, and in my head I was now calling the whole team by their pop star doppelgängers. My creative intern and youngest employee who worked with Ginger on copywriting was Baby Spice. The obvious choice for Sporty Spice was my social media specialist, who had again worn Lululemons to work that day, while I was calling our brand manager Scary Spice, not because she scared me but because I seemed to scare *her*. That left our graphic designer with Posh

Spice, which made sense, because I'd heard her talking about her boyfriend named David.

My computer powered on, and I tried to force myself to get back to work. I was flattered by the rate at which Deborah was onboarding me. (She'd already handed over complete decision-making authority on campaigns and creative strategies.) But it was only Tuesday afternoon, and already I felt like I was running on steam. Except for a quick date with Becket at my favorite local farmers market, I'd worked straight through the weekend, staying up late and waking up at the crack of dawn, trying to get myself up to speed on the new job and conquer my imposter syndrome.

Trying not to think about how Ginger Spice still seemed to despise me.

Trying not to think about my future niece or nephew.

It was too selfish to admit out loud, but I wasn't ready for Natasha to have kids yet. Not because I resented her becoming a mother for even a second, but because I didn't want to lose her the way I had all my other friends.

After seeing Natasha and Mark with their groups of friends, I'd gotten nostalgic and reached out to my own crew from school. Our WhatsApp chat group had been inactive for months, so I wrote a long update about Natasha's wedding and my new job—providing full details about the look on Iain's face when I told him I was leaving him for Deborah Kim. And then I asked if we could schedule a brunch soon. (Brunch was good for them because it was during daylight hours and allowed them the option to bring their children. Brunch was good for me because I loved eggs Benny, and after meeting up at our favorite gastropub in Fairfax County, I could swing home for a quick visit with Mom.)

Over the next few days, everyone else's replies and updates came in. There were new jobs, houses, or holiday plans. Just one new pregnancy. We created a poll for the next weekend we'd all be available, and my mouth dropped when I saw the verdict.

July.

That was more than four months away, and by then I wouldn't have seen any of them for nearly a year. Is that the type of friends we'd demoted one another to? God forbid, if I had a family emergency, or got *married*, I knew these women would be there for me in a heartbeat. But the truth was, I couldn't count on them anymore in my day-to-day life. We knew one another best, but in other ways, we didn't know one another at all.

Natasha. *She* knew me; we saw or spoke to each other every single day. And I only had to scroll through my text messages to appreciate just how big a role she'd started to play in my life outside of work. She *was* my life outside of work. In the months leading up to the wedding, other than colleagues, every single text message was from Natasha, her bridesmaids, her wedding planners, or . . . *Mom.*

I took a deep breath, trying to extract myself from the pity party swirling inside of me. I hadn't talked to Mom that day yet, so I swiveled my chair away from the rest of the office and called her.

Mom felt close to me by talking *at* me, so I went through my junk mail folder as she told me in rapid-fire Punjabi about the *pakoras* she was making for a dinner party, a fundraiser she was planning at the *gurdwara*, before seamlessly transitioning to the one subject I didn't want to talk about.

"Natasha and Mark FaceTimed us this morning. They are having a nice time in the Bahamas."

"Uh-huh," I said dryly.

"I asked about her plans for the baby shower, but she became very emotional." Mom paused. I could almost see her standing there in the kitchen, one hand on the cordless, the other propped high on her hip. "Has she talked to you about it?"

"No . . ." I actually hadn't heard from her since she'd left.

"She will let me host, *hah*? She refused to discuss the subject."

"Well, maybe she thinks it's too early to start planning anything," I suggested. "They only just found out about the baby."

I trailed off when I felt a tap on my shoulder. I swiveled my chair around and looked up to find a woman I didn't recognize towering over me. She was my age or slightly older and was wearing a campus sweatshirt and ripped jeans. Her brownish-red hair was tucked away behind a yellow bandanna, and when she blinked in surprise, I noticed how blue her eyes were.

"Shit," she whispered, taking a step back. "You're on the phone. Sorry!"

I held up my finger to signal I just needed a minute.

"Mom, I've got to go."

"*Hah.* Come home soon."

"I will," I said, still speaking Punjabi. "I love you."

I put my phone away and turned back around. The woman was perched against Sporty Spice's empty desk, her arms crossed in front of her, looking at me intently, like she was trying to solve a complicated math equation. Who was she? I tried to place her as I stood up, but I couldn't figure it out.

I extended my hand, and she offered hers in return.

"I'm Serena."

"I love you."

I froze, dropping her hand.

"Pardon?"

"I *love* you?" she repeated. "Right?"

I paused. Was that a question?

"Sorry. Jesus, look at your face!" The woman laughed. "I'm Ainsley. Ainsley Woods. The digital director."

"Right." I smiled awkwardly, taking a step back. "Ainsley. *Hi.*"

"I don't love *you,*" she said, loudly. "I mean"—she chuckled—"you seem great. I'm sure you're very lovable. But I'm learning Punjabi. Did you just say 'I love you' on the phone?"

"*Oh.*" I nodded, laughing as my body unclenched. "Sorry. Yeah. I was talking to my—"

"Mom, right?"

I nodded, and Ainsley pumped her fist.

"And did you say something about a"—she repeated the word in Punjabi—"baby?"

I saw her glance down at my stomach, and I crossed my arms in front of it. "Eyes up here, Ainsley. My sister's the one having a baby."

"My bad," Ainsley said sheepishly, and then in Punjabi: "I'm still learning how to eat Punjabi."

I pressed my lips together, trying not to laugh. "You're still learning how to *eat* Punjabi?"

"Shit. How do you say it?"

I repeated the phrase back to her correctly, and she practiced it again and again until she got it right.

"It's rather pathetic that I've been trying for two years," she said afterward, "and I can still barely string a sentence together."

"You're really good. It's a hard language. But I have to ask . . ."

"Why am I learning Punjabi? My husband's parents are from Amritsar."

I nodded, thinking she'd go into more detail, but she didn't.

"So, what are you doing here?" I asked, sitting back down in my chair. "I thought you were still on vacation."

"I'm officially back tomorrow, but I thought I would come in and grab my computer. I might as well catch up on e-mails tonight while I'm jet-lagged. We took our son, MacKenzie, to visit my parents. Have you been to British Columbia?"

I shook my head.

"Well, if you go, which you should, definitely check out Whistler. I may be biased, but I think it's the most beautiful place in the world."

"It sounds magical."

Ainsley smiled, then glanced at the clock above my head. "Are you ready to call it? My husband is on dinner duty, so if you wanted to grab a drink or something . . ."

I smiled, leaning back into my chair. "A *drink*," I said, stalling.

"Have you been to the Fox in Columbia Heights? Do you like beer? I don't. But for five dollars a pint, I'll drink it."

I laughed. The Fox was one street over from my local bus stop, and I wondered if Ainsley was my neighbor. "Five dollars, huh?"

"It tastes like piss."

"Piss. You're really selling this—"

"I know. It's almost like I should work in advertising."

I laughed again, and suddenly she was laughing, too. A part of me wanted to go. Ainsley seemed pretty cool, and I knew I'd have fun, and wasn't I just thinking, miserably, about how I didn't have any plans? How I didn't really have a social life anymore?

"I'm sorry," I said finally. "I can't tonight."

"Oh, OK. Sure."

She sounded disappointed, but you know what, I would be, too. I would be disappointed when we went to the Fox and I watched her work up the courage to awkwardly ask me about my partner, and then look at me with pity when I revealed I hadn't been in a serious relationship since my mid-twenties.

When she pretended to believe that being single, not having a family, was *my choice* and not a default.

"Another time," I heard Ainsley say.

"Another time," I repeated, knowing there would never be

another time. Ainsley and I lived in different worlds. Women with families like Ainsley asked someone for a drink and literally meant one drink so they could get home in time to put their kid to bed.

Would Natasha become someone who had time for only a quick drink—once a year—for her big sis, Serena?

I didn't want to believe it. I *refused* to.

6

"I'm not seeing anyone else."

I thought seriously about covering Becket's eyes with my hands and saying, *Well, you're not seeing me right now, either,* but he didn't look to be in the mood for one of my jokes.

It looked like he was about to ask me to be exclusive.

"Me neither," I said quietly, looking at our hands. His were folded romantically around mine as he spooned me beneath the covers. It was dusk outside, and the diminishing light cast a spooky glow around my bedroom. On the other side of the window, I could hear a group of teenagers laughing and hollering as they walked by down below, a bus, and then a bus driving the other way.

Was one month of dating too soon to be exclusive? I mean, I already was, and I'd assumed he was. It's not like I had the time or inclination to date multiple people, or would have slept with Becket for the first time thirty minutes ago if I had any intention of doing so. *Still.*

"I deleted my Bumble account weeks ago . . ." I heard Becket say, and then his loud breathing in my ear. "Are you still . . ."

"I don't have Bumble. Or any of the . . . 'apps,' as people say."

Tinder. Bumble. Hinge. I'd tried them all when they first

came out for the sake of it and had met a handful of people over the years, but I found the whole experience of dating and socializing on my phone overwhelming. I dealt with social media and apps enough on the job; I didn't want it clogging up my personal life, too.

"So," I heard Becket say, and I wondered why he was drawing it out. I rolled over, turning myself into him until we were nose to nose.

"So."

"We're both not seeing anyone else." He brushed the hair out of my eyes. "Do you want to see anyone else?"

I shook my head. "Except . . ." I waited until his cheeks reddened before continuing. "If I'm being honest, if Idris Elba asked me on a date, I would have a hard time saying no."

A grin spread across his face. "So how about we're exclusive, *except* for Idris Elba?"

"Works for me."

"So to be clear, because I don't want you to get mad at me later, this means we can *both* date Idris—"

Laughing, I cut him off with a kiss, and as I pulled away, I heard my phone buzz. My heart leaped as I reached for it on the bedside table. In another burst of motivation, I had messaged a handful of my old coworkers in a group text inviting them to dinner and a movie, as I hadn't seen them since my farewell dinner. Whenever someone left the company, we all promised to stay in touch, to transcend from more than merely "work friends," but it seemed I, too, was destined to lose touch with them.

I read the text alerts on my home screen. Every single one of them was busy.

"You better tell your other boyfriends you're taken," Becket said, as I set my phone back down. He'd said the word "boyfriend." I didn't realize to him that was the same thing as exclusive. I should have clarified.

"Was that Natasha?" he asked, and I shook my head. She'd gotten back from the Bahamas the week before, and except for the photos and emojis she'd dumped into the family group chat, I hadn't heard from her.

"It was an ex-coworker. I was hoping to go see that new Tiffany Haddish movie tonight, but everyone's busy."

"I'll go see that movie with you." He grabbed his own phone off the floor. "What's it called again?"

"You like rom-coms?"

"Who doesn't?"

"A lot of guys?" I shook my head. "Don't worry. I'm letting you off the hook. And didn't you say you have work to do later, anyway?"

"I *want* to see it with you, Serena."

"Yeah, but we've been hanging out all day, and I figured . . ." I trailed off when I realized I'd hurt him, and I blushed in embarrassment. I knew how I acted sometimes, and I'd been called out for my behavior by more than one ex.

Hard to get. Some guys loved it; all they wanted was someone to flirt with, to fuck, and then to leave. But the others, the more sensitive ones like Becket, made me feel like shit about it. But the truth was, I wasn't playing hard to get. Not really.

I was hard to keep.

"I'm sorry." I pressed my lips together in thought, trying to find the right words. "The truth is . . . I was really looking forward to seeing my old coworkers tonight."

"Really? Because if you want me to go—"

I shook my head, cutting him off. "This isn't about you," I said, and I wasn't lying. "This is about me and the fact that . . . I don't want to be the kind of woman who has nothing to do on a Saturday night but hang out with . . . her *boyfriend*."

As difficult as it was for me to say the word, at least Becket looked pleased. He put his arm around me.

"You're not, Serena. Look at you. Look at everything you have going on."

"I don't have a lot of friends." I grimaced, closing my eyes. "That sounded pathetic. I *do*. If you can believe it, I used to be pretty popular."

He laughed, brushing the hair out of my face. "Don't worry. I believe it."

I smiled, thinking fondly about the wholesome fun my high school friends and I used to have much later than our peers. Many of us waited until we were pushing eighteen to fool around or try alcohol and soft drugs. From childhood, everything new we experienced together, and then slowly, our lives diverged. Some of us went to college, others straight into a career. We charted out different paths that came with brand-new groups of friends, but we always made time and space for one another.

Always. And then even that started to change.

"I love my friends, but . . . we barely see each other." I shrugged. "So it kind of feels like I don't have any right now."

He nodded. Either he was a good listener, or he was trying very hard to be one, so I continued.

"It just seems like . . . people get married and have kids. And then they don't need me anymore."

"Serena . . ." Becket cooed. I averted my eyes.

"Natasha's pregnant." I was surprised by the emotion in my voice. I hadn't realized how badly I wanted to talk about it with someone who wasn't Mom. "Sorry. I know I should be thrilled."

"You're allowed to have mixed emotions, though. It's big news. Fast, too."

I glanced around my bedroom, which was the first room I decorated after buying the apartment. I'd saved scrupulously and bought vintage furniture from secondhand shops, styling it to my exact taste. Everything about it screamed Serena Singh, yet I knew that when Becket left—whenever he did leave—without Natasha around, I'd feel lonely, and I hated that.

"She was my best friend, Becket."

"Was?"

I nodded. "I know that she'll always be my sister—I'll always have her that way—but once she has this kid, we won't have time together like we used to. We used to talk or text every couple of hours, and now . . ."

Now? I didn't know. I'd been afraid to reach out since she got back from her honeymoon and find out.

"Everybody changes. Everybody moves on, whether they get married and have kids or not."

I nodded and let my head fall to his shoulder, even though I wasn't sure he was right. I wasn't sure I'd changed at all.

"I don't want to mansplain, but I think I have an idea."

"Go on . . ."

"Remember how I used to live in Ireland?"

I nodded. He'd told me on our first date how the best year of his life was the one he spent washing dishes at a Dublin pub.

"Well, I didn't know anyone when I first arrived. But then someone in my hostel recommended I join this Facebook group for expats. It was full of Americans, Aussies, Germans, Brazilians, Canadians—all of them new to Dublin. All of them looking for . . . friends."

I could tell where he was going with this, and I smiled gently, not wanting to turn down his idea straightaway. He looked so freaking optimistic.

"We'd drink together, go to movies, hiking, weekend getaways to the West Coast. We became buds instantly. Some of us are still buds." Becket propped himself up on his elbow. "What do you think? There's bound to be something like that here."

"That's a nice idea . . ." I said, squeezing his arm. "But I don't have Facebook."

"Well, I'm sure there are other websites that don't require you to have an account. Where's your computer?"

Hesitantly, I retrieved my laptop from the dresser, and after I entered in my password, Becket set to work. All it took was a few quick search terms like "make friends in DC" and "widen your social circle"—how dorky *was* I?—and a long list of options presented itself.

Did I want to join a book club? A recreational softball league? Or what about a salsa class?

There were websites to connect people around any and every interest, for social groups, however niche. Beer brewers. Wine tasters. *Literally* even candlestick makers.

I watched Becket scroll through website after website, trying to sell me on everything from Ping-Pong tournaments for thirty-plus women to Tuscan cooking classes to Bumble's BFF setting that allowed for platonic friendships.

"It makes sense, Serena," Becket said, trying to convince me to sign up. "We look for partners online. Why not friends, too? This way, you can even search for people with the same interests as you."

I quietly clicked shut my laptop, processing. He wasn't wrong. It did make rational sense, but since when did our hearts ever follow logic? Natasha and I had nothing in common, and it wasn't like my high school friends and I shared any of the same passions, other than one another. Our tastes and careers were as different from one another as Gucci to Joe Fresh, internal medicine to commercial real estate.

"I bet," he continued, "you could find someone to go to that movie with you if you really wanted."

I shrugged, thanked Becket for his idea, and told him I would think about it, even though I knew I didn't want just "someone" to go to a movie with for the sake of companionship. I needed to make my life feel full again, and warm bodies I found on the Internet weren't going to cut it.

7

I looked up from my screen as I heard the Spice Girls start to pack up their things. I yawned, smiling at them.

"Heading home?"

"Is that OK?" Ginger asked, coolly. "Check your e-mail. I've just sent you the revised copy."

"Thanks," I said, irritated by her defensiveness. "And that's not why I was asking . . ."

She threw me a look I couldn't read and then texted something on her phone. A beat later, I heard a ping to my right, and then Sporty Spice giggled.

Win her over, Serena.

Don't throttle her, Serena.

There's still a chance you can get along, Serena.

Three years earlier, I had taken a mindfulness course on a lark, and I stood up slowly, trying to employ the skills I'd learned. Trying to be the bigger person and give Ginger Spice a chance to come around. She was clearly the ringleader of their little group, and even though the rest of them liked me well enough, her disrespectful attitude was starting to rub off on them. Getting through to her was my new number one priority.

"Should we finally grab that drink?" I asked casually, looking at Ginger and then the others. I'd asked them once before, but maybe I'd seemed too eager. "It is Friday, after all."

"Can't," Ginger said dismissively. "I'm *wiped*."

"One drink—"

"*Can't*." She pursed her lips at me. An attempt at a smile. "I really gotta go."

I nodded, my face flushed in embarrassment as, one by one, everyone turned me down, grabbed their bags, and left.

As I sat back down, alone in my pod, a flurry of brownish-red caught my attention in the corner of my eye. It was Ainsley, the digital director, turning back around in her chair.

Had she been listening to our conversation? Momentarily, I felt bad that she'd overheard me ask my team out for drinks when I'd so blatantly blown her off the month before and, except for work meetings and small talk in the kitchen, hadn't made an effort to connect with her since.

My phone buzzing on the desk shifted my attention. It was Mom calling me back from that morning. I tried (and often failed) to call her every day.

"*Hah?*" she said, without saying hi. "I've been very busy today. We're raising money at the *gurdwara* for a new family that's just arrived. The poor couple. They have no family here. I remember what that was like."

I smiled. My mom was the kind of woman who spent every waking hour thinking about others, and I was proud of her philanthropy, her selflessness. It also made me want to shake her.

"You called?" she continued.

"Yeah," I said, walking toward the corner of the office, out of earshot from Ainsley and the others. "I was wondering if you wanted to come into the city tomorrow. Natasha and I are having brunch."

It had taken me a few days, but I'd finally worked up the courage to reach out to Natasha. She was my best friend, and I missed her. Yes, she was married now, and yes, she had a baby on the way, but we could still make time for each other.

"Brunch?" Mom asked, repeating the word in English. There wasn't really a Punjabi translation.

"Yeah. I know how badly you want to ask Natasha about planning the baby shower. It'll be fun. We can talk about it. We can even get a pedicure after. You can relax a bit."

"Uh ho." She sighed. "Your father has the day off. He'll be home . . ."

"So? Leave him—"

"Why don't you both come here? I can make you brunch, hot *aloo paratha*!"

I grimaced, tilting the phone away from me. "And exactly how will that be relaxing for you?"

Mom didn't answer. She often didn't.

"You are at work, my honey?" she asked, switching tones and gears entirely.

I nodded. "I am."

"I am so proud of you and your big job."

I wasn't sure Mom actually understood what my job entailed, or had ever asked me a more specific question than "How was your day?" but I thanked her anyway.

"And . . ."

And . . .

Do you have a boyfriend?

Do you have any "special plans" coming up?

Can I give your phone number to Mohan Uncle's Buaji's grandson?

Coincidence or not, her incessant nagging had trailed off ever since Mark and Natasha got together. Presumably, Mom realized that at least one of her daughters would be "settled." Still, she couldn't help leaving a pause like this in the conversation.

A place marker. Something to signal what was noticeably missing in her line of questioning and in my life.

A *husband.*

After we hung up, I made my way into the women's restroom, deflated, and sat down in the far stall. I couldn't get Mom out of my head, and my mind was racing. I peed and then sat there, thinking about what to work on for the evening while the office was quiet. I had a dozen campaigns on the go, not to mention pitches we were preparing for hopeful clients. I had a million options to distract myself.

Suddenly, I heard the door swing open and then footsteps.

"Is it here?"

"I know it's in here. I had it like two seconds ago . . ."

"There it is. *Knew* it."

It was the Spice Girls. I recognized all their voices.

"I would literally freak out if I lost my phone," Ginger Spice said. "Give me a second, guys. My lipstick isn't right."

I was about to stand up and flush when Ginger continued speaking.

"Do you think she's still here?"

She. I froze. By the tone, I could tell she was referring to me.

"Although, I mean, where else would she be?" Ginger laughed, and my stomach knotted as I put my hand over my mouth. "Can you believe she keeps trying to hang out with us? *Kind* of pathet—"

"Vic," said Scary Spice. "Cut it out."

"Is she married?" Baby asked. "How old is she?"

"She's thirty-six," interrupted Ginger. "But I don't think so."

"She's very impressive, especially considering how young she is." Was that Posh? "Did you see how many clients she's brought over from her previous agency?"

"We could have invited her tonight," said Sporty.

"As if. She's our *boss*." Baby laughed. "I don't want her to see me *drunk*—"

"She shouldn't even be our boss," Ginger snapped, her words echoing loudly against the tile. "It just pisses me off, you guys. I was basically Deborah's creative lead until she showed up."

I could feel myself sinking farther and farther into the toilet, my body tense.

"That should have been *my* job. I left *New York* to work for Deborah Fucking Kim," Ginger said, her voice echoing. "Not some . . . lonely middle manager."

"Vic, are you done yet?" snapped Scary Spice. "We're going to be late."

"One minute . . ."

My hands were trembling on my lap, and I moved to stand up, to go out there and say something, but I couldn't think of anything.

"Our Uber is here."

"Cool. Let's go . . ."

I waited for the footsteps to disappear, the door to slam, and then, like a zombie, I washed my hands and made my way back to the office. It was deserted except for Ainsley, who was staring at some *Matrix*-looking code on her desktop. Her headphones were on. I thought about speaking to her, but something stopped me.

I slid into my chair, angered by Ginger's words, but more so angry at myself for not confronting her.

Her confidence was astounding. Sure, she was good at her job, but she lacked experience—her strategy skills simply weren't there.

I shook my head. Why was I trying to justify Deborah's decision to pick me over Ginger Spice? Why did I care so much what some spiteful person thought about me? I deserved to be here, and everyone damn well knew it. Still, I couldn't stop ruminating. Ginger thought I was just some "middle manager." She thought I was . . . "lonely."

It hurt when the aunties said it, but it hurt more when it came from the mouth of one of my own peers. And maybe it cut so deep because they were right.

I'd tried and failed to keep my social circle alive, my passions and interests outside of work. Extracurricular activities were all well and good in school and university, but they were hard to keep up as an adult, as a woman of color breaking her back to try to make it in advertising.

Now it was safe to say I'd made it. I was here, at the helm, but there wasn't much in my life around the edges. Yes, I had Becket, and Natasha—who'd always be my sister at bare minimum. But what else? *Who* else?

Refusing to feel pathetic, I opened up an Internet browser and found one of the websites Becket had showed me. That very night, there was a book club at a nearby library—but I'd never read the memoir they'd selected. There was a board games group, which sounded interesting, but it was being held in somebody's basement. (And for all I knew she was a serial killer.)

I scrolled down farther, and just then, another option presented itself.

Cosmos and Conversation: Ladies night out with some new gal pals

I cringed, imagining Carrie Bradshaw on a bedazzled night out. Even though I'd never really drank, I'd had my fair share of nights out with the girls. That wasn't me anymore, but then again, who was I, really?

Not just some middle manager.

Not just some unmarried, lonely thirty-six-year-old set in her ways, too afraid to try to put herself out there.

The event started in forty-five minutes at a restaurant on the H Street Corridor, and without another thought, I grabbed my credit card and signed up.

After all, what's the worst that could happen?

Do you have a reservation?"

I squinted at the hostess. "I think so?"

"You think so?" She smiled at me. She didn't seem annoyed at all, but rather pleased a customer had a problem, one that she could help solve. "What's your name?"

"It wouldn't be under mine." I fumbled with my phone, racking my brain for the organizer's name. "Um . . ."

"Uma?"

I grimaced, putting my phone away. "No. Sorry. I don't know the name . . ."

"Oh." She beamed at me. "You're here for that make-new-friends dinner?"

Speak louder, wouldn't you? I don't think the guy outside heard.

"The"—her eyes flicked down to her podium—"Cosmos and Conversations thing?"

She took me to a back area of the restaurant, where I was presented to a large table of at least a dozen women.

"Hi," I whispered to no one in particular. Nobody heard me. Should I just sit down? There was a chair at the end, but would it be weird to just slip in?

I adjusted my glasses—solid-black square frames today—as they slid down my nose. Oh god. I was *sweating.* Why the hell was I so nervous? I dined with strangers all the time—various aunties and uncles, prospective clients, friends of Natasha and Mark's, blind dates.

"Hello," I tried again. This time, I spoke too loudly, and I cringed as my voice boomed across the table. Everyone turned to look at the same time, and I bared my teeth into what I hoped looked like a genuine smile.

"I'm Serena."

On cue, they all smiled back, waving, greeting me in return. I wasn't the oldest, although I certainly wasn't the youngest. They all looked very friendly, earnest, and while that fact should have put me at ease, it made me feel even more anxious.

"Take a seat!" called the woman at the far end of the table. She looked familiar, and then it dawned on me that I'd seen her profile online when signing up. *Cara.* That was her name. She was the organizer.

"Thirsty?" asked the woman across from me. She leaned in, filling my glass from a jug before I'd answered. "So what brings you here? I'm Lilly, by the way."

"Thanks," I answered, reaching for the glass. "Do you know what's in this?"

"Cosmos, duh."

"Right—"

"Ladies. Ladies!" Cara called from the other side of table, and we all turned to look. She had stood up, clipboard in hand. I heard Lilly snort.

Cara had us go around the table for introductions, and I tried my best to remember everyone's names and "fun fact," but the only one that stuck was Lilly's; she claimed she once climbed a cactus.

(While drunk, of course.) I was parched, and after finishing my glass of water, I took a sip of the cosmo. It was very good, sweet. I could barely taste the alcohol, so I took another sip. Drinking culture had never appealed to me much, although I had tried alcohol, of course, and always obliged with a few sips for a toast or a work cocktail. Once or twice, I'd even gotten tipsy. But I hated not feeling in control. How alcohol made me feel in general.

Cara had the waiter take a picture before anyone was allowed to eat anything, despite Lilly's rather vocal grumblings, and then wanted everyone's approval over how they looked in the photo, then the filter, then the hashtag. I dug into the cheese platter, feeling guilty for being happy about the fact I was seated far away from Cara, when I heard her call out my name.

"What's your handle, Serena?" she asked. No one else was talking. They looked as if they weren't permitted to speak.

"I don't have a handle."

"Your *Instagram* handle." She shook her head, smiling as if I'd just told a joke. "It wasn't on your registration form."

I set down my knife. "I don't have Instagram."

"Oh. *Good* for you." Cara nodded, returning to her phone. "I've been thinking about doing a social media cleanse. How's it working out for you? But like, as an influencer, I can't really afford to."

"No, I mean I don't have an Instagram account. I never have."

She gasped, audibly. In my peripheral vision, I could see Lilly laughing, and my cheeks immediately flushed. I tilted my head away so I couldn't see her.

"You're telling me you've *never* used Instagram."

"Not at all," I said, taking another swig of the punch. "I use it every day. I work in advertising. I just don't have a personal account."

This didn't seem to be an acceptable answer.

Cara didn't leave us alone throughout dinner, interrupting every natural conversation—which was surely the point of the whole evening—for the structured fun outlined on her clipboard, playing one get-to-know-you game after another. I tried to participate as much as I could, but I was having a blast at the other end of the table with Lilly. The cosmo really did taste very good, and I kept sipping at it. Every time, Lilly poured a little bit more into my glass.

"What's next?" Lilly whispered to me, as Cara instructed us to play Never Have I Ever. "Truth or Dare?"

"Shh!" I told her, patting my cheeks with the back of my hand. They felt hot. *I* was hot.

"Do you think Cara has any coke on that clipboard?"

I rolled my eyes at Lilly's joke. I *hoped* it was a joke.

"Stop it," I said. "We should join in. Cara just wants us to have fun."

"I'd have fun if Cara took a hike!"

I giggled and then felt terrible about it. I sat forward to take another sip of punch, but I must have moved too quickly, because my head started to feel dizzy. I steadied myself, and a moment later, the dizziness passed. How much had I drunk? Surely not that much. I glanced at my watch. Two hours had passed already. I hadn't even noticed.

"Never have I ever," I heard Lilly say, even though it was someone else's turn, "played this game as an adult."

"*Lilly—*"

"Never have I ever . . ." she said, even louder this time, "wanted to jump off a building in the middle of dinner."

I laughed, louder than I meant to, and when I sat back, everyone was staring us.

"Lilly," Cara said loudly.

Stiffly, Lilly made eye contact with her.

"Could we all, like . . . you know?" Cara pleaded. "It's a crowded restaurant. It's loud in here as it is."

I nodded, my cheeks flushing in embarrassment.

"It's just that"—Cara batted her lashes, pressing at the outside corners of her eyes—"I'm trying to find my bliss, you know? Empower myself with other empowered women—"

"Look," Lilly interrupted. "Cara, you need to—"

"*You* need to not speak over me!"

The table went eerily quiet. I swallowed hard as I tried to think of something nice to say, but I was finding it difficult to think clearly.

"I totally feel you, girl," Lilly said finally. "I'm sorry. I didn't mean to . . . obstruct you from finding your *bliss*."

Cara smiled, squeezed the hand of the woman sitting next to her. My stomach curdled. She had clearly missed the sarcasm dripping from Lilly's voice.

"I'm sorry, too, Cara," I said quietly.

"Serena and I are just talking about how we're *desperate* for a smoke." Lilly gripped my forearm, her eyes still on Cara. "Do you mind? I just can't seem to beat the ol' habit."

I felt unsteady on my feet as Lilly pulled me up from my chair.

"Of course! Go ahead," Cara said. "Should we pause the game?"

"Oh no, not at all! Keep the party going without us! We'll be quick. Won't we, Serena?"

I followed Lilly outside as I shrugged on my coat, grateful for the fresh air. The entire restaurant wobbled around me. I was tipsy, maybe even drunk, and I hadn't even meant to drink. The lightness I'd felt earlier transformed into a dense, dead weight in my chest.

"I've been at eighth grade birthday parties better than that," Lilly said, the moment we were out on the street.

As much as I hadn't enjoyed Cara's regimented idea of a girls' night out, Lilly was being pretty rude about a woman she didn't really know.

"It was interesting," I said, leaning back against the brick exterior of the restaurant. "That's for sure."

"Interesting? Aren't you in advertising?" Lilly laughed. "I thought you'd have a better word for it."

"Beguiling?" I offered.

"Ha! Mortifying."

I hesitated. "Eerie."

"*Pathetic.*"

I didn't respond. I thought about going back inside, but the cold air felt good on my skin.

"There's this party tonight . . ." She fished her phone from her pocket. "You should come with me. I'll call us a Lyft."

"Like, now?"

"Yeah."

"We can't leave right now . . . Dinner isn't over—"

"Why not? We already paid Cara online. Remember, we had to 'preorder' our fun?"

I laughed nervously, thinking about how rude it would be to disappear. I suppose it wouldn't be any worse than my behavior the whole evening.

"Our driver will be arriving in one minute." Lilly smiled.

"Lilly," I hesitated, feeling pulled in three directions. (Back inside, away with her, and, groggily, to the ground.) "We can't."

"We can," she said, gingerly. "And we will. But they won't let you in if you look drunk, OK?"

Did I look drunk to her? Maybe I was. It felt awful to think it. To be honest, it felt plain *awful.*

I didn't want to go back inside, but I didn't feel like being alone yet, either. So when a red sedan pulled up and Lilly crawled into the backseat, I got in after her. I closed my eyes as soon as I buckled up, and I must have fallen asleep because suddenly, I felt her hand on my knee, shaking me awake.

"It's just there." She pointed to a town house as we got out of the car. I blinked hard, looking up and down the street. I had no idea where we were.

"I used to come here all the time with my ex-boyfriend. Got the taste for it . . ."

Lilly linked arms with me as I half tripped over the flat pavement. She whispered something, but I couldn't make it out over the sound of blood rushing in my ears.

A bouncer let us into the house. Why there was a bouncer at a house party, I wasn't sure, but I wasn't in a state to question things.

"Do you want to get me a vodka tonic?" asked Lilly, once we were inside. She disappeared behind a beaded curtain before I had a chance to reply, so I took in the room. It was empty except for a bar with nobody standing behind it, and almost ghostly in its lack of decor or character. I could hear noises coming from somewhere else in the house, but it didn't sound like music. At least, no music that I'd ever listened to.

"Drink?" A head popped up from behind the bar, a young woman. I admired her neck tattoo, much bolder than my own, and then tried not to look too much at her top, which was so transparent I wondered if it was meant to be lingerie.

"One vodka tonic," I said, approaching her. "And a water? A big water."

She smiled at me, and I took a seat on one of the stools. I propped myself up on my elbows and let my head fall into my hands as my eyes closed. The whole room was spinning, faster and in wider circles. I don't know how long I was sitting there, but I was jolted from my reverie by a gruff voice to my left.

"First time?"

It was raspy, clearly male, and I sighed, still not opening my eyes. I hadn't heard anyone approach.

"Look, I'm not really in the mood for this."

"What aren't ya in the mood for, hon?"

"This," I said, rather curtly.

Did I really have to spell out that I was half asleep, and not really in the mood to get chatted up?

"I didn't mean to bother you. I'm simply buying my wife a drink and thought I'd be friendly. My apologies, miss—"

"Oh!" I opened my eyes, feeling terrible for making assumptions. "Sorry, I . . ." I trailed off when I turned and caught sight of the man sitting next to me.

He was old. Very old.

And very . . . *naked.*

I stuck my hand out in front of me to shield the view. "What the hell are you doing?"

"Pardon? I was just being friendly!"

"No, not that!"

"What's going on?" cried a voice to my left.

I turned. A woman, an older, naked woman, was standing next to me. She crossed her arms over her bare chest, waiting for the naked man to reply. It was a gesture of curiosity, not one of modesty; it was if she didn't even *know* her breasts were out.

"Harold," she snapped. "What are you doing? What did you say to her?"

"I didn't say anything!"

"I told you. We can't come here if you're going to be a *creep*!"

"I'm not a creep, Mary-Jean. I just said hello, and she got all hostile with me!"

"Hostile?" Now the naked woman's arms were crossed at me. She was the same height as me sitting down, and it was hard not to look at her nipples. "Why are you being hostile?"

I took a deep breath, trying to figure out if I was hallucinating. The bartender reappeared and set down the drinks I'd ordered. Even she was gawking at me.

"I . . ." I stammered. Why was everyone looking at *me*? I was the only one wearing real clothing!

"I'm really confused and don't understand why you're naked . . ." Just as I finished my sentence, Lilly appeared from behind the beaded curtain.

My breath caught.

Except for the nipple tassels, Lilly, too, was naked.

Where the hell was I?

"She looks lost, doesn't she, Harold?" I heard the naked woman say.

"I . . ."

I didn't finish the sentence. I lost my words and my bearings when I registered the scene behind Lilly, appearing and disappearing as strings of beads swung back and forth in her wake.

More naked people. A blur of naked people laughing, drinking. *Screwing.*

I was in a sex club.

No. The Twilight Zone. A naked Twilight Zone.

"So, what do you think?" Lilly asked me, drawing closer. She slapped a twenty down on the bar and grabbed her vodka tonic.

"I don't know what to think, Lilly." I massaged my temple, dumbfounded.

"It's couples night." She shrugged. "They wouldn't have let me in if I turned up by myself."

My throat started to close up, and I grabbed my water and chugged it until I'd swallowed every last drop.

The first time I put myself out there, and this is what happens?

I felt used and small. Downright foolish. It wasn't that she had brought me to a sex club. (The naked couple next to me and the people behind the curtain looked like they were having a hell of a lot of fun.) It was that she had lied to me. She had been rude to all those women back at the dinner, and to make matters worse, I had gone along with it. I had egged her on. Is that who I was?

Was a woman like Lilly the only kind of person I deserved to be friends with?

I knew it would be hard making new friends as an adult. But I didn't know it would be like this.

9

"Is it a hangover, sweetie? Or heartbreak?"

Becket was teasing me. He had also never called me "sweetie" before. I rolled over on my pillow, pressing my cell into my other ear, and refused to acknowledge either comment.

"It's tough out there—"

I groaned, cutting him off. Everything hurt. Even the sound of his voice.

"You've got to be careful of those players, you know. They'll say anything to get you into . . . a sex cl—" He burst into a fit of giggles, unable to finish his sentence. I couldn't help but laugh, too, but the vibrations made my temple throb even harder.

"You're killing me, Becket."

"Aw, hon. You sound awful. Should I come over?"

I shook my head into the pillow.

I hated that a few (or more) sips of cosmos could render me hungover, that I was hungover in the first place. Had I really turned to alcohol because I was *sad*? That felt even more pathetic than hearing the Spice Girls gossip about me in the restroom.

I imagined telling Natasha about Cosmos and Conversations later that morning at brunch, role-playing what she would say, how I would respond.

Are you sure you didn't subconsciously want to let loose, sis? she might ask. I didn't think it was true, but maybe it was. And suddenly I was angry at imaginary Natasha for asking.

"I should go get ready," I said quietly. I could hear Becket breathing into the phone. "I'm meeting Natasha in an hour."

"That'll be nice." He paused. "What about afterward?"

I knew what Becket was angling at. He wanted to know what else I had planned for my Saturday, when I'd be free to see him again, even though he'd stayed over only two nights earlier.

I had nothing planned. After brunch with Natasha, and a pedicure if she was up for it, I'd be free as a bird. I'd be free to bury myself in my work, my career, like I did most weekends.

Free to go to a *sex club*, if I desired. Ha!

"I might go shopping," I said finally. "I left my gloves in the Lyft last night."

He didn't answer, and I gritted my teeth. I hated how hard this was for me. Why did I have to spell it out for him? Why couldn't he just understand? I liked dating him, but I wasn't going to spend every free moment with my boyfriend. Just because I didn't have any other plans. That was how it started. And I would never, ever do it again.

"I'll call you when I'm done?" I said it more like a question to myself, to both of us.

I could hear him smile from the other end of the line, his muscles unclenching just as mine stiffened even more.

"Sounds good. See you later, sweetie."

Sweetie. Hon. Sweetie again. What was next?

I felt more human after I showered and changed into fresh clothes. Outside, the air was still cool and crisp, and I sighed deeply as I skipped down the front stoop of my building. I loved mornings, even when it was drizzling. I loved my neighborhood. And I loved going to brunch at my favorite Australian coffee shop with Natasha, where we'd go nearly every Saturday if she didn't spend the previous night at Mark's. Of course, that was before she got engaged, and every weekend we spent together became all about Pinterest boarding and wedding errands. Before she got married, pregnant, and moved out of my spare bedroom.

I arrived fifteen minutes early, my anxiety rising at the idea of seeing her again. It had been nearly a month, which was probably the longest time we'd ever been apart in our lives. After putting my name down on the list, I went back outside and waited in the sun, swapping out my wire-rim frames for sunglasses.

"Serena, for two?"

I looked over. The host, a new guy I didn't recognize, had stuck his head out the open window, beckoning me.

I raised my hand, rousing myself. God, I was looking forward to some good coffee. "Here."

The host looked at me, confused.

"My sister should be here any minute."

"We can't seat you until you're both here."

Crap. I knew that yet had completely forgotten. I told the host to seat the next two people in line, and I texted Natasha.

ETA?? I'm at the front of the line.

I waited, watched my message go from "delivered" to "read."

And then nothing.

My stomach lurched. She would be coming from Georgetown that morning. Maybe she was on the subway and didn't have service at the moment to respond, but I doubted that she would take public transport. Maybe she was driving? But she wouldn't have looked at her phone then. She was a real stickler about not texting and driving; I'd made sure of that.

When another minute went by and she didn't reply, I texted again.

?

The message went immediately to "read," and a beat later, she responded.

I'm on the bathroom floor. MORNING SICKNESS IS REAL. Maybe next Sat? Soz.

Soz? That was all I fucking got, not even a real sorry?

I was crestfallen. No. I was angry. I glanced at my watch. It was fifteen minutes past when we were supposed to meet, and she'd waited until now to tell me she couldn't make it—and only after I texted *her*. Why was she so inconsiderate?

My nose was running, and I wiped it with my sleeve as I went back into the restaurant. The host greeted me warmly in the cramped foyer, and I told him it was just me. He led me to an open stool at the end of the coffee bar next to the kitchen, and I put in my order immediately: drip coffee, milk and two sugars, and an eggs Benny.

Natasha always had the same.

I didn't want to text her back, but I did. Of course I did. I told her I hoped she felt better, that I loved her, and to let me know when she was free. After, I deleted our entire message history and promised myself I wouldn't reach out unless she texted me first. Unless *she* made an effort.

The restaurant was packed, my breakfast was slow to arrive, and I found myself hunching farther and farther down in my seat, feeling exactly how I'd felt sitting there on the toilet with my feet tucked behind me, eavesdropping on the Spice Girls.

Pathetic.

I craned my neck around toward the kitchen. A waiter expertly balancing four plates on his hands gave me a small shrug that said my order would still be a while. I'd caught up on all my morning news, and I hadn't even thought to bring a book. Reluctantly, I connected to the Wi-Fi and then opened the App Store on my phone. Facebook was always the very first suggestion, as if Apple couldn't understand why I hadn't downloaded it.

Maybe I should just download it, I considered. Maybe I was still living in the twentieth century, resisting the ways people made and maintained social connections. I used Facebook and other social media all the time for my career, but it was always from a consumer and business angle, never a personal one.

Could I join a group, like the one Becket had in Ireland, and meet new people—hopefully, *nice* people who didn't con me into going to a sex club? (I suppose, with Facebook, I could check out their profiles beforehand as a semblance of a vetting process.) Maybe I could even reconnect with acquaintances from high school and university I'd completely lost touch with. If I wanted things to change, didn't I need to change?

I decided to find out.

My coffee arrived, and I sipped it, waiting for Facebook to download. After, I opened the app, and it prompted me to enter some information, so I offered the bare minimum—my first name and last initial, phone number, high school and university graduating classes. Immediately, the page jumped forward, and I was inundated with profiles, suggested friends. I scrolled through the list, careful not to click "Add Friend" on any of them. Natasha, Mark, the girls from high school, friends and acquaintances that had flitted in and out of my life.

Jesse was there, too. I'd been expecting him. In his profile picture, he was standing alone, a bright blue sky as his backdrop. He had gray hairs now, and there were faint wrinkles around his eyes and lips. My heart lurched. He was as handsome as ever. If anything, age had made him only more attractive.

It had been more than a month since I'd caught a glimpse of him jogging. The red tuque. The neon green athletic jacket. Had that blur really been him? I hadn't run after him. There was no point in finding out the truth, because it wouldn't change a thing. And clicking on his profile right now, snooping on a life that I'd turned down, wouldn't change anything, either.

I could feel myself wavering as I set my phone down on the ledge, telling myself to stop. But I couldn't. I clicked.

Jesse Dhillon.

There was no information in his profile about where he lived or currently worked; still, I scrolled down, unable to control myself. Finally, another picture appeared.

It was dated four years earlier, and the location was tagged to a suburb forty minutes northeast of DC. My breath caught as I zoomed in. He was there, two small children on his lap, the arms of a beautiful Indian woman draped around his neck: Anadi. They were on a crowded backyard deck, sitting among other couples and families, everyone smiling except Jesse, who was looking at something off camera. His was mouth was half open, mid-sentence. I wondered what he was saying. I wondered who he was speaking to off camera.

I glanced down at the photo caption, tears falling from my cheeks.

BBQ time with the gang!

It had been twelve years since I let myself cry over him. Twelve years since I'd felt so exposed.

My chest ached, and I felt myself falling, right there, even with my feet planted firmly on the floor. Without eating, I left a twenty-dollar bill next to my plate and then left.

It had started raining. Not the kind of rain meant for magical nights and first kisses, but really pissing down. I trudged toward home, soaked, my thoughts swirling. I thought about calling Natasha and then kicked myself, forgetting the promise I'd made only thirty minutes earlier to keep my distance. But I wanted her to say the words that I desperately needed to hear right now.

Serena, you ended it with him.

Serena, that wasn't the life you wanted.

Suddenly furious with Natasha, at Jesse, at everyone, I walked faster and inadvertently missed my turnoff. When I finally realized how far I'd gone, I was at the farmers market, and my stomach growled as I caught a whiff of something baking. I stopped. I still hadn't eaten breakfast.

Despite the rain, which was starting to die down, the stalls were open, and dozens of people were milling about. Hesitantly, I walked toward it. It was my favorite market in the city, and I tried to go every weekend and shop locally as much as possible. Even though I lived and breathed a corporate consumer world during the week, I often found myself here on Saturdays, buying my fruits and vegetables from organic farmers who lived in the region. Kale. Beetroot. Baskets of blackberries and strawberries. Leeks. There was a baker who made excellent croissants and savory tarts, and a stall that sold dirty chai—my favorite—which was coffee and Indian tea brewed expertly together.

I pulled a crumpled tote bag from the bottom of my purse and picked up a bag of peaches and a chocolate croissant, stuffing the latter in my face in record time. I thought that maybe my emotions were running high because I was hungry, but I still felt crummy afterward, so I made my way to Dirty Chai. It was run by a guy named Nikesh, who was the only Indian guy I'd ever met with a man bun. I'd grown to know him a bit after years of patronizing his stall. He was younger than me, and my affection for him had grown to be quite sisterly.

"Serena!" he called out as I approached.

I smiled at him as I walked up toward his stall, hoping there was no evidence of embarrassing tears on my face. "Nikesh. Good to see you."

"Medium, no foam?"

"You know it." I took in my surroundings as he ground the coffee. Besides dirty chai, he also served regular chai and coffee, sometimes a specialty drink of the day with kombucha, cinnamon, or mint. My stomach growled again.

"Anything to eat back there?"

He smiled as he screwed the portafilter into the machine. "Funny you mention that. I took a baking course about a month ago. And pretty soon Dirty Chai will be serving dirty *muffins*."

"Yowza."

"I'm thinking cardamom, fennel seeds, walnuts . . ."

"Honey?"

"Hadn't thought of that," he said, nodding. "I like it."

"Your wife must get to do all the taste testing, huh?"

"You bet. Although she's—"

"—standing right here," a voice finished. I turned to the side.

Ainsley was standing right next to me.

Nikesh's wife—whom I'd heard about for years—was my colleague *Ainsley*?

"Oh my god, hi!" I exclaimed. "So you're Nikesh's wife? What a coinci—"

"Are you hitting on my *husband*?"

I froze.

"Uh, no, I'm just buying some—"

"Dirty chai. *Right*. That's what they all say." She turned to

Nikesh, her voice getting shrill. "Nicky, how could you do this to me?"

"He wasn't doing anything. I'm so sorry, Ainsley. I wasn't—"

"One minute ago you were trying to break us up, and now you're trying to save us?" she snapped back at me.

I pressed my lips together, my eyes drifting from Ainsley and then back to Nikesh. He seemed nonplussed, his face deadpan as he finished making my drink and pushed it across the counter ledge. I breathed out, shaking my head.

"You're fucking with me."

Ainsley grinned. "I had you. I had her, Nicky, didn't I?"

"Ainsley fancies herself an actor. A failed actor," Nikesh said flatly, although I could tell he was trying not to smile. "So I take it you two know each other?"

"We're coworkers." Ainsley leaned against the counter. "Serena's the one who's too busy to have a drink with me."

"I'm not too busy—"

"Too much of a big shot to have a drink with my wife, huh?" Nikesh said dryly. "Maybe I won't give you any muffins."

I laughed, rolling my eyes at both of them. Ainsley winked at me, and I found myself lightened, somehow. Jesse, Anadi, and the whole "gang" were still on my mind, but at that moment, my concerns didn't feel so terrible.

"Hey, I forgot," Ainsley said. "I left my kid on the playground. Will you come get him with me?"

My eyes bulged. "You *forgot*?"

"All right, fine. I left him with one of the other parents."

I tried to pay for my drink, but Nikesh just smiled and waved away my cash. I thanked him and then followed Ainsley into the park behind the market. I rarely came back here. It was typically littered with children and dogs, but it wasn't too busy today.

There were a few kids climbing on the jungle gym, pulling themselves up the ropes and ladders and down the slides and poles. I spotted Ainsley's son immediately. He looked just like Nikesh, with his dark hair and skin. But he had Ainsley's eyes.

"How old is your son—it's MacKenzie, right?"

Ainsley nodded. "Two.

"He's adorable." I smiled, watching him play. "And I love his name."

"It's my mother's maiden name. I said to Nikesh, 'Sure. The kid can have your last name. But then the first name needs to be Scottish.' "

"Sounds fair to me."

"Tell that to my father-in-law."

We reached the edge of the playground, and Ainsley smiled at one of the adults nearby as she squatted down next to MacKenzie. "How's my little McNugget, huh? Cold?"

He didn't answer, fixated on a rock between his feet. His cheeks were so pudgy I had the almost irresistible urge to reach out and pinch them.

"Do you want to say hi to your Auntie Serena?"

"Hi, MacKenzie." I smiled at him, trying to remember the last time I'd interacted with a child. A friend's baby shower, likely, the summer before. I'd held the child for a mere second before she started screaming, and one of the grandmothers came to her rescue.

"Hi," MacKenzie said. He looked at me shyly, moving his lips around like he was sucking on candy. "Play?"

"Play," Ainsley repeated, and we both sat down next to him. "He's really into rocks these days."

"Cheaper than an iPad."

"No kidding."

Suddenly, MacKenzie stood up on his wobbly little feet and

then sat down right next to me, so close that I could feel the warmth of his back against my calf. I held my breath as he babbled about something incoherently to himself, to the rock. Inexplicably, that picture of Jesse on the patio slipped back into my mind.

I'd heard that he'd married her, but our mutual acquaintances hadn't told me that they'd had children or that he still lived in the area. Neither of these things were surprising, and deep down, I must have known them to be true. So why was the news suddenly shaking me up so much?

"So," I said to Ainsley, determined not to think about Jesse. "How come I've never seen you around before? I've been coming to Dirty Chai for years."

"Nikesh is the primary caregiver while I'm at work, so I stay home with Mac on the weekends while he works the markets."

MacKenzie bashed two rocks together, a weird, well-timed spitting noise escaping his lips as his toys collided. I laughed out loud, surprised by how entertained I was watching a child play. It was kind of like Netflix. But at least when you got tired, you could switch off your screen.

"But the business is growing, so now we're going to come in and help sometimes. Right, buddy?" she asked the baby. He giggled in response.

"I don't know how you guys do it," I said, unsure if I was speaking out of turn. I didn't really know her that well.

"What do you mean?"

"You're both either working or parenting all the time, right?" After she shrugged, I continued. "So, when do you ever get time for yourself?"

"I often don't. It's really fu—" she stopped, spotting MacKenzie. "Flipping hard. It's really *flipping* hard sometimes."

"I don't think my sister has figured that out yet. Right now, I imagine all she's thinking about are the cute little onesies she'll get to buy."

"You should tell her about all the vomit and poop that gets all over those cute little onesies." Ainsley paused, reaching for a rock MacKenzie had cast aside. "Yes, it's hard, sure. There are lots of compromises. More than you can ever imagine. But I do think most of us know that going in. And you've just got to adapt, because it's worth it."

I didn't respond, so she added, "For me, at least. For me and Nikesh it's worth it."

I was tempted to tell her about Jesse, about my thoughts on marriage and children, but wasn't sure how to segue naturally, without offending her. In the past, if I was forthcoming with my views too quickly, sometimes people assumed I was being judgmental of their own more conventional choices. Or worse. Kidding myself.

"It sounds like you two have it all figured it out," I said finally.

"We both compromise, and both put in the effort. Equally. We're in it together." She sighed. "So yeah. *I* think so."

I looked over at Ainsley, reading between the lines. "But your father-in-law doesn't?"

"How could you tell?"

I found another rock and handed it to MacKenzie. "I don't know. I suppose the way you mentioned him a moment ago."

"Well, it's no secret that he's a hard man to impress."

I didn't need to know Nikesh's father or the details of the situation to know what was hard for Ainsley. She had married into an Indian family, and all the cultural expectations and burdens were now fully on her, too. Whatever she was doing to impress him, it wasn't enough, and it never would be, but I didn't want to be the one to tell her that.

"Cold," MacKenzie said.

"You're cold?" Without thinking, I leaned over and picked him up, placing him in my lap, and wrapped my arms around him. "That better?"

He looked up at me, smiling, and I found myself smiling back.

"Auntie Serena," I heard Ainsley say.

My stomach knotted as I thought of Natasha and the child she was carrying.

"When's your sister due?" Ainsley asked.

I smiled, wondering how Ainsley had read my mind. "Oh, not for a while. She hasn't passed the three-month mark yet, but she told me because . . ." I trailed off.

Because she's my best friend. Because we're close.

That's what I wanted to say. But I didn't know if that was true anymore.

"Are you excited?" Ainsley asked.

I shrugged, and then realizing that wasn't an appropriate social response, I exclaimed, "Super excited!"

Ainsley laughed, and I turned to her irritably.

"*What?*"

"You're not excited! Look at you. She's your younger sister, right?" Her stare was unnerving. "You don't think she's ready to have a baby."

I grimaced, wondering how Ainsley had figured it out—or at least part of the truth—so quickly.

"Natasha's only twenty-eight." I twisted my hands. "Sure, it's a bit young, but it's their decision, right?"

"Right."

"And so what if they only *just* got married, if they live with Mark's parents—"

"His *parents*?"

"—they're financially secure. They'll have help. They're . . . prepared."

"Parenting is not something you can prepare for," Ainsley said, after a moment had passed. "To be honest, I didn't know how to be a mom until he fell out of my vagina."

I laughed, shaking my head. "You're so . . ."

"Vulgar?"

"No. Truthful. I've never heard anyone speak about motherhood like . . ." I didn't finish the sentence. Growing up, I saw so many women who, like my own mom, were mothers. And it's what they were expected to be. Women who put their families in front of everything, themselves, even their own personalities. They transformed into someone different from who they were before motherhood.

Not all women were like that. I knew this rationally, but sometimes it was hard not to jump straight to the judgment, or assume that a woman like Ainsley—happily married and in domestic bliss with a toddler—would be totally unrelatable to me. I bit my tongue and wished I'd accepted her invitation for a drink at the Fox when we first met. I'd been totally wrong about her.

"Just so you know," I said, bumping her knee with mine, "I wasn't flirting with Nikesh before."

"Oh, I know." She waved me off. "I'm sorry about teasing you. But seriously, do you know how many people I catch flirting with him? Sweet Nikesh, with his big, dreamy Bambi eyes? His *man* bun?"

"I like the man bun. He pulls it off."

"Everyone likes his man bun."

"Do you?" I asked.

"I like strangling him with it."

I burst out laughing, my dirty chai nearly spewing from my

nose, and then one thing led to another. We started talking about her and Nikesh's (kinky) sex life, *my* sex life, and then, well, *Jesse*.

I hadn't meant to tell her, but it came up like word vomit. I told her about brunch. Natasha's morning sickness. Downloading Facebook. Jesse and his picture-perfect marriage and family.

It felt good to talk out loud about how upset I felt, although I wished it didn't. I would rather have breezed past it, the way I had anytime nostalgia unexpectedly bit me in the ass over the past twelve years, but today it felt nearly impossible.

"I don't even think about him anymore," I said to her, sipping on the dredges of my drink. "It was a lifetime ago, and *I* was the one who didn't want to get married." I shook my head. "I'm sorry. This is all so embarrassing."

"Nothing about this is embarrassing, Serena. It's *human*." MacKenzie had started whimpering, so she took him from me.

"Jesse was a big part of your life, and you *literally* haven't even seen a photo of him since. *Plus*, you saw him jogging recently, and that got the juices flowing. Anyone would have reacted the way you did. You've never had to picture his life without you."

Was that the truth? I supposed it was easier to pretend that Jesse existed only in my memory. I wondered if, after today, I'd still be able to pretend.

A shiver ran down my spine as the rain started up again. Ainsley and I stood up, MacKenzie in her arms, and we started walking back toward the covered area of the market.

"I'm five years older than Nikesh. And I was divorced. Did you know that?"

I shook my head. She hadn't brought it up before.

"I love Nikesh to bits, and I don't give a crap about my ex anymore, but I don't want to stumble across a picture of his not-so-virgin-Mary's birth announcement, do I?"

I opened the door to the market, and we blustered through, the wind pushing us in from behind.

I smiled. Ainsley was . . . awesome. She was down-to-earth. Fun. Clearly kind and empathetic, considering she had spent the bulk of her Saturday morning outside in the drizzle listening to her colleague drone on about her ex-boyfriend. And from the little I'd learned so far, I could tell her life was full to the brim. On top of her family life. On top of her thriving career.

What did people see when they looked at Serena Singh? A busy, career-driven woman, sure, but what else?

We made our way back to the Dirty Chai stand, and then I said my goodbyes and headed home. There was a stack of paperwork on my end table that needed doing, but there was more than that, too. If I wanted to widen my social circle, if I wanted to live *my* life to the fullest, I had a lot more work cut out for me.

Spring

10

I spotted Mark's black BMW as it pulled up to the curb. The city was full of black BMWs, but I always recognized his by the giant #StillWithHer bumper sticker Natasha had slapped on the rear windshield.

I took a deep breath and, walking up to the car, prepared myself to see Natasha. I hadn't reached out to her after she'd blown me off for brunch, just like I promised myself, but that was more than a month ago. It was now April. The only reason we were seeing each other now was because Mom had guilted me into coming home for a family dinner, and Mark offered me a ride.

"Hey, guys," I said, keeping my voice cool as I dropped into the backseat. "How was the Bahamas?"

"It's just me," I heard Mark say.

My stomach dropped as I looked up. The passenger seat was empty.

"Natasha is already out there. She took the day off." Mark craned his neck around and gave me one of his big, dorky smiles. "Come sit up here."

I nodded and walked up to the front seat.

Talk about anticlimactic.

The roads were congested, and I helped Mark navigate through the thick of the traffic. When I was younger, DC felt like a different universe, even though it was only across a bridge. We never came in as a family, so until I started commuting to George Washington during my first year of university, I'd only ever been on school trips to Capitol Hill or one of the Smithsonian museums. So many of my college friends who didn't grow up in the area had been drawn to the city by politics, the hustle and bustle they'd grown up watching on CNN or *The West Wing*, and were confused why I'd studied and then stayed in the city only to go into advertising.

I couldn't imagine leaving.

That's what I always said, which was only partly the truth. Really, I couldn't imagine leaving behind Mom and Natasha.

After we were clear of downtown, I worked up the courage to broach the subject.

"How is she?"

Mark grabbed his sunglasses from the top of the dashboard, keeping his eyes fixated on the road. "Good. Morning sickness comes and goes."

"And how are you?"

"Oh, fine. Busy with work." He leaned over. "You get it."

That was about the extent of our conversation, and we ended up turning on a podcast on rent control. Mark and I never seemed to have a lot to talk about when Natasha wasn't around, but I liked him, and I knew he liked me. We were very similar, in a way, a practical balance to Natasha's whimsies.

As we merged onto the highway, I zoned out, thinking about work and then about Ainsley. That Saturday morning we spent together at the farmers market felt like eons ago, but it had only been a few weeks.

It was nice having someone at work to talk to, really *talk* to, because after I'd overheard Ginger's comments about me in the bathroom, I'd stopped making an effort to be friendly with her altogether. (She wanted a cold, civil work relationship with her boss? That's what she was getting back.) The day before, I'd even eaten my lunch with Ainsley in the break room, instead of at my desk, and had really enjoyed myself. She was fun. She was *funny*. And I could really be myself around her. Yet, at the end of the day, she was a "work friend." Someone to make what could be long, occasionally cruel days a little bit lighter.

I'd been close with my old work friends, but after turning down my invite to go see that Tiffany Haddish movie, none of them had reached out to make other plans, and I wasn't going to do it only to get shut down again. So, two months after switching jobs, it was like that friendship circle had never existed.

I glanced sideways at Mark as he drove. His eyes were pointed steadfastly ahead, but nonetheless, I angled my phone away from him as I opened the "Social" folder on my home screen. On Ainsley's recommendation, I'd deleted Facebook, as I didn't trust myself to avoid Jesse's profile. But I had downloaded Bumble.

Becket knew, of course. I was only using the app for the "BFF" setting, the first step in remarkably transforming me into an engaging social butterfly. (Ha.) A bright red notification popped up, alerting me to a new message. My heart surged. I hadn't worked up the courage yet to contact any of the women I'd matched with, and I quickly clicked through.

> Hi, Serena! How are you!? I see you also work in advertising. We should totally meet up for coffee!???—Aisha

I smiled, reading over the message. *Aisha*. I knew a lot of people in the industry, and I couldn't place her. I tried to zoom in on the picture, but it was a bit out of focus. I squinted. She looked like she might have been younger than me. Maybe that's why I didn't know her. Regardless, I replied.

Hi Aisha—Great to meet you. What agency are you with? I'm surprised we haven't run into each other before. Coffee sounds great.

Finally, Mark and I arrived. My family had lived in the same three-bedroom bungalow in a very South Asian suburb in Fairfax County since my first year of high school. After years of driving a taxi and moving us from one apartment to another, incredibly, Dad had landed a job as an operations manager at Dulles Airport and a high enough credit score to secure the longest mortgage banks had to offer. Mom had always stayed home to take care of us, but to help keep the fridge stocked and bills paid, she'd cleaned neighbors' houses while we were at school. I knew my parents had struggled, that they still struggled, but we never discussed it.

We never discussed anything.

We left our shoes in the front hall and followed Natasha's laughter, which was floating in from the sitting room. I held my breath. She was sitting on the couch next to Dad, showing him something on her phone. He stood up when he saw us, pressing his hands together in front of his chest in greeting to me and then Mark.

"*Sat Sri Akaal*," Dad said, quietly.

"*Sat Sri Akaal*, Uncle," Mark replied, as I mumbled my hello to him, then quickly turned to Natasha.

"Hey, Tash . . ." I wondered if she'd stand up to hug me. "How've you been?"

"Good." She beamed. "You?"

"Good." I nodded, trying to think of a way to signal that there was much more I wanted to say to her. Things we wouldn't talk about in front of Dad.

"Do—"

"Hey. Come see what cake Dad likes." She tapped the cushion next to her, and even though it wasn't clear which one of us she was speaking to, Mark sat down. The knot in my stomach tightened.

Was that it? After this much time apart, was that all she had to say to me?

"I like it," Mark said, looking at the phone. "Great choice, Uncle."

"*Really?* Even that ugly chocolate frosting?" Natasha laughed, punching them both on the arms. "Both the men in my life have terrible taste, huh?"

I watched all three of them laughing, their shoulders bumping against one another. Dad caught me staring, and as soon as our eyes met, he looked away.

"What's the cake for?" I asked.

"The gender reveal," she answered. I could hear her voice shake ever so slightly. Was she nervous, too?

Without looking up, she asked, "Want to see?"

"Sure," I said, swallowing hard. "Just let me get Mom."

I turned the corner into the galley kitchen, the worn-out carpet giving way to a harsh yellow linoleum that looked unclean no matter how many times Mom scrubbed it. The room was small. If I stood at its very center, I could nearly touch the walls on either side, the refrigerator door, the window overlooking our neighbor's den. Still, this is where Mom seemed to spend most of her time, where—without fail—she'd be whenever I came home.

She had her back to me, facing the stove. Lately, she had started wearing more western clothes outside the house—slacks and loose blouses Natasha and I helped pick out for her at Target or JC Penney—but at home she was always in a traditional *salwar kameez*. Today, she was wearing a cotton pale paisley top. The billowing pant bottoms were a soft cream, and so was the *dupatta*, which was draped elegantly around her head and shoulders. There were turmeric stains all over it.

I wished she'd understand that I'd spend more time with her if she deigned to come into the city. It's not that I didn't want to see *her*; I just hated going home. I hated seeing her stuck in this kitchen.

Growing up, she always ate last, making sure everyone else had hot *roti* throughout their meal, hovering over us, insisting we eat more while I begged her to come sit down at the table. Finally, when the rest of us were nearly done, she'd shovel down her cold food before bolting off to start on the dishes, the laundry, some endless task or another. And when she wasn't at home, she was at *gurdwara* cooking for worshippers in the community kitchen, taking the occasional break to attend one of their friend's dinner parties or functions. I knew it wasn't fair, but I often found myself comparing her to women like Deborah or Ainsley. Back when we were still together, even Jesse's mother.

Gently, I set my hands on Mom's shoulders as she hovered over the stove, so as not to startle her. She leaned back into me, and I caught a whiff of the *tarka* she was frying, the rich smells mixed with her honey-sweet scent.

"Have you offered Mark a drink?" she asked me.

We didn't keep alcohol in the house, except for one or two bottles of beer they kept at the back of the fridge for their son-in-law, which he never drank.

"Yes," I lied. "Why don't you go sit down? I can fin—"

"It's not finished, *beti*."

I watched her pick up the saucepan and expertly sweep all of the *tarka* into the lentils simmering on the back burner. She mixed it together and then turned off the heat.

"Now are you done?"

"I still need to make rice."

"Let me."

"*Nah*, you will burn."

"*Mom.*" I turned her around forcibly. "Please? I promise not to burn it. Natasha is talking about having a gender reveal. You told me you wanted to host the baby shower, didn't you? A gender reveal is kind of the same thing, so now would be a good time to ask her."

"What is *Junn-dar* reveal?"

I rolled my eyes, reaching for the rice jar above the fridge. "Ask Natasha."

Finally, Mom went into the other room, and as I rinsed the rice, I listened to Natasha attempt to explain the logic behind a gender reveal party. I tried not to cringe, focusing on the task at hand.

"It sounds fun, *beti*," I heard Mom say later. She spoke in English whenever Mark was around. "Where will be the location?"

"Our place," Natasha said.

There was a long pause as I set the pot of rice onto the stove, turned the heat to low.

"*Your* place?" Mom asked. I could hear the hesitation in her voice even from the other room, and I willed her to continue. For once, to say what she actually thought. I walked over to the doorway, and Mom looked up. I caught her eye and nodded for her to continue.

"I would like to host the party," Mom said, looking at the ground. "I would like to have the party for my baby girl."

"Are you kidding? *Here?*"

I balked. "Natasha!"

"*What*, Serena?"

She glared at me, and I didn't drop her gaze.

"Babe," Mark said, "let's consider our options—"

"What's to even consider? This place wouldn't fit half my friends, let alone Mom's friends, *your* mom's friends. And besides . . ."

She trailed off, and I thanked god she didn't finish her sentence. Why did she have to act embarrassed about where we came from, and in front of our parents, no less?

"It smells great in there, Auntie," Mark said, breaking the silence. "Is there anything I can help with?"

"Thank you for offering, *beta*. Everything is complete. Serena is just making rice, and then we can eat."

"There's no *roti*?" interjected Natasha.

"I thought tonight we'd have rice for a change . . ."

"*Oh*." Natasha pouted, and for the first time, I didn't think it was cute. I wanted to slap her.

Natasha the princess. Natasha the baby of the family. Natasha, our little golden girl.

I rubbed my eyes as it dawned on me. Natasha was selfish. Plain and simple, she was a spoiled brat.

Maybe she always had been. And I was done making excuses for her.

"Sit down," I told Mom when, predictably, she stood up to go make her daughter fresh *roti*. "Rice is fine."

"*Beti*, your sister wa—"

"It won't kill anyone to have rice tonight." I fixated my gaze on Natasha. "Will it?"

"Why are you being like that?" Natasha whined.

"Like what?" I spat.

A considerate daughter? Appreciative of the fact that Mom had spent her whole day—no, her whole life—slaving away in that goddamn kitchen?

"Honestly, Natasha," I started, ready to confront her. "You're being—"

"Serena," Mom barked, as she disappeared into kitchen. "*Bus.*"

Which meant *enough*.

But it was never enough. A woman's work or worth—it would never be enough.

The tension in the room sizzled, and I titled my head so I could see Dad in my peripheral vision. He was on the far end of the couch, tapping his knees, a habit of his for as long as I could remember. He hadn't said a word since I got home, or during Natasha's tantrum, and I wondered if it had ever occurred to him that another kind of husband would have spoken up for his wife. A different kind of man would have defended her time and her heart.

Did those men exist? I wanted to believe it was possible, and there were moments when I came close. But then I'd come home. And I'd remember why I didn't.

SANDEEP

"See how fast I am?" Sandeep asked, rolling out the atta. "The *roti* will only take five minutes."

"That's not the point," Serena answered dryly.

Sandeep knew that wasn't the point, and she knew very well that she'd spoiled her younger daughter, but right now she needed to keep the peace. Serena's tone—judgmental, angry—was typically reserved for Sandeep. Today was the first time she'd seen it wielded against Natasha.

Were her two girls fighting? Sandeep had a feeling that their tiff had nothing to do with *roti*. Sandeep wanted to ask about their troubles, but anytime she'd pried in the past, no matter the subject, Serena shut down. Sandeep would never make that mistake again.

"Natasha is pregnant, *beti*. And she wants *roti*," Sandeep said instead. "Be thoughtful."

Serena didn't respond, and Sandeep bit her tongue. That had come out wrong. Of the two daughters, Serena was the most thoughtful. Without a doubt, if Serena had decided to have children, she would have allowed—no, *requested*—that her own mother host her baby shower. It was the thoughtful thing to do.

If anything, Serena was too kind. She let the world rest its weight on her shoulders for her to carry around. A husband would help with the load, the burden of it all, but Serena would hear nothing of it, so Sandeep had stopped trying. Serena wanted her mother in her life, but not her opinions. She didn't trust her mother to have the right opinions.

And Sandeep couldn't really blame her.

"Can I help?" Serena asked, and Sandeep snuck a glance. Her eyes were red, and she'd flipped her phone over and slid it to the other side of the counter.

Sandeep slapped the *roti* onto the *tawa* and then reached out her palm and rested it on Serena's cheek. The pain in her heart was on her face, too. "*Nah*. You rest. You work so hard."

"How long do you leave it on each side?" Serena asked.

"Until it's done. You check it like this." With quick movements, Sandeep slid the *roti* edge off the cast-iron pan. It was heating through, so she flipped it over on the other side. "See?"

Serena nodded, leaning her weight into the kitchen counter. Sandeep saw her reach for her phone and then, without warning, pull her hand away. Serena was forever glued to that phone, and not because there was a man demanding her attention.

Deborah Kim. Was that her name?

Sandeep had looked up the name of Serena's new boss before she arrived, just to be sure she wouldn't get it wrong if she came up in conversation. From what Veer found out on the Internet, she was an important woman, which meant Serena was an important woman. Sandeep flipped over the *roti* one more time and then, pinching the corner, moved it to the gas burner.

"This is the final stage," Sandeep said, glancing at her daughter. "It puffs up on the open fire."

Serena nodded. Surely, she knew this already; she'd watched Sandeep cook hundreds of times. But Sandeep was scared to ask her daughter about this Deborah Kim, about her high-powered career, so she returned to a familiar subject.

Because, what if Sandeep were to ask the wrong question?

What if the question made Sandeep sound . . . stupid?

It was easy to feel inferior around two bright girls fully versed in American, in the way of life this country demanded. Her daughters were constantly correcting Sandeep, pointing out when she made missteps or missed social cues, like when she tried to bargain with the saleswoman at Target.

The cardigan was on the clearance rack without a price tag. How was Sandeep to know the price was *still* fixed?

Sandeep knew her daughters meant well, but it didn't make their criticisms any easier to handle. Often, she felt like she was in the backseat on a long, winding car journey entirely unclear of the destination. Veer steering. The two girls in the passenger seat. Serena, sullen and staring out the window, while Natasha laughed in her singsong way and gave directions.

With the first *roti* complete, she buttered it, folded it twice across, and then handed it to Serena.

"Sure?"

"You must be so hungry." Sandeep smiled. "And I'm making more. *Jao*."

Immediately, Serena tore the *roti* into chunks, eating quickly as she dunked each morsel in the *saag* simmering on the back burner. "Mom. It's *so* good." She paused, chewing. "I miss your cooking."

And I miss you, Serena.

"Do you think . . . you could teach me how to make *roti*?"

Again, Sandeep wondered if this question had anything to do with *roti*. But what else could it be about? Was Serena simply asking so they could have something to talk about, common ground to share?

"*Roti?*" Sandeep shook her head, returning to the task at hand. "It takes a very long time to learn, and the ones they sell at the supermarket are nearly just as good. Do you know, Serena, that even the white grocery stores have *roti* now?"

Serena laughed. "In the city, too."

"*Saag*, on the other hand . . ." Sandeep glanced at the pot full of spinach, cauliflower, broccoli, onion, garlic, and spices worked and blended just the right way. She had made Serena laugh, and now she was feeling confident. "*Saag* I could teach you."

"Yeah?" Serena leaned over, smelling it. "I don't have a pressure cooker."

"No bother. There's another way."

"What about *daal*? Chicken curry, even?"

"*Even* chicken curry."

They returned to the *roti*. Sandeep made space at the counter, handed Serena a rolling pin, and tried not to laugh too hard when her daughter's "round" *roti* came out with two ears and a chin.

This was her happy place. With her family. In this cozy galley kitchen that reminded her of her *buaji's* flat back in Ludhiana. When she closed her eyes, Sandeep could almost smell the sweet orange tree, its branches knocking against the window. The pungent tang of *dhai* curdling beneath a cheesecloth.

Serena hated this kitchen. So if she was in here, at least it meant she loved Sandeep.

12

Aisha. Advertising wiz. Arlington, VA.

I swiped through her profile on Bumble BFF one final time as I walked the last block, forcing myself not to feel nervous or overexcited.

This wasn't going to be an awkward blind friend date. This was simply a prework coffee with another woman in the industry. And, if it so happened that she and I hit it off and became best friends, and had so much fun together and so many common interests that I never even *thought* about that selfish Natasha anymore, so be it. Right?

Right.

I was pleased that Aisha hadn't wasted time with idle chitchat and had cut straight to the chase to ask me out for coffee. So only two days after matching, I found myself walking into the coffee shop in the ground floor of my office building, which Aisha had coincidentally suggested for our meeting.

I paused briefly as I gripped the handle of the front door. That morning, I'd put in a little bit more effort than I usually did, dressing in my favorite boldly patterned skirt and a crisp white collared shirt, buttoned up to my throat. Eyeliner, lip gloss, and a good tinted moisturizer was my usual makeup routine, but today I'd even curled my lashes and worn contacts to mix it up.

I was cool. I was *fun.* Who wouldn't want to be friends with me, right?

Right.

Inside the coffee shop, I cast my eyes around, looking for the somewhat blurry image of Aisha I had in my head. There was the familiar (cute) barista behind the counter, an elderly couple near the front bay window reading the newspaper, and a teenage girl bent over a stack of paper. Studying for an exam by the looks of it.

I worked my way farther into the shop, my eyes skirting the tables, when I heard a voice behind me.

"Serena?"

I turned, startled. I couldn't place the voice.

"Serena Singh?"

I set my hand on my hip. The voice was definitely coming from the front, but from where?

"Over here!"

I followed a flash of color and movement off to the side. The teenage girl was vigorously waving at me with one hand and stuffing a pile of papers into a knapsack with her other.

I took a step forward, eyeing her. "Aisha?"

"Yes!" She nearly tripped moving toward me, extending a hand toward me.

Hold on a moment. *This* was the Aisha I'd been texting with, the "advertising wiz" from Bumble? It couldn't be. She looked so . . . *young*. Like, *real* young. Baby-Sitters Club young. Hannah Montana young. So young that I doubted she would have even understood any of those pop culture references.

"It's so great to meet you," she said, shaking my hand.

She had a firm grip, which I hadn't expected, and I kicked

myself for passing judgment. How many times had clients and even colleagues made comments because they I thought I was younger than I was? Company executives who asked me for coffee because they assumed I was the assistant, not the creative lead on the project about to knock their socks off.

"Nice to meet you, too." I smiled.

The cute barista brought over my coffee just how I liked it, drip coffee with milk and two sugars. Aisha already had her chai, so we sat down, and I idly commented on the weather, the convenient choice of café she'd selected.

She didn't say much. Was she nervous? Even though I didn't want to be, so was I. I'd never gone for coffee with a woman I'd met on the Internet in the hopes of becoming *friends*. I played with the corner of my napkin, ripping at its edges until I forced myself to push it away and look her in the eye.

"I've never done this before," I said, after neither of us had spoken for a while.

She blushed. "Me neither."

It felt, oddly, like a first date. A platonic first date, mind you, and definitely not the most awkward one I'd been on. My first-ever Tinder date was at a restaurant not too far from where we were sitting now. He had been very handsome, pleasant, even sweet, but it would have helped if he spoke at least a few words of English or Punjabi. (In retrospect, his messages had seemed oddly formal, and I should have been able to tell he crafted them on Google Translate.)

"So, you're in advertising, too?" I asked.

She beamed, nodding.

I waited for her to continue, but she didn't. When we were messaging, she never had replied to my message asking where she worked, and I half wondered if she was keeping her cards close to her chest because I was her competition.

"Are you on the media buying side, or creative?" I asked, thinking of a more general question.

"Uh . . ." She paused, spooning sugar into her chai. "Both."

"Both?"

"Uh-huh."

Both? I wasn't aware that there were any agencies left these days that did both.

"So you work at the Deborah Kim Boutique Agency, huh?" She must have seen me hesitate, because then she said, "I mean, you said this café was near your job. Isn't the Boutique Agency in this building?"

I nodded, weirded out by her choice of wording. Nobody in the business would use the full name of the agency like that.

"Tell me *everything*. What's your job like?"

"My job?"

"Yeah, like, you're the creative director. Which character are you from *Mad Men*, do you think? Everyone wants to be Don Draper."

I was so taken aback I didn't even know what to say. Of course everyone wanted to be Don Draper; that wasn't what was weirding me out. It was that, suddenly, she wasn't quiet at all; she couldn't shut up.

"Peggy? *Joan?* I can't decide which one I like better. They are just so, like, feminist, but each in their own ways." She paused briefly, coming up for air. "Do you have an assistant? What's that like?"

"Aisha . . ." I started, the wheels starting to turn in my head. Creakily at first, and then more quickly as my face heated up.

"When I arrived," I said, clearing my throat, "you called me Serena *Singh* . . ." I thought back to the Bumble app, to what it did and didn't say in my profile. "How did you know my last name?"

"I . . . I . . ." she stammered, a bead of sweat rolling down her forehead.

"*You* . . ." I said, prompting her to finish her sentence, but she wouldn't. And then the full realization finally came to me. She had cyber-stalked me. She had looked me up on the Internet and found out my name, what I did for a living, even that I worked right above this very coffee shop. I wanted to laugh. Although I had never looked up a potential date online before meeting him, Natasha used to. I hadn't realized the same vetting process applied when it came to "dating" for friendship.

I took a sip of my coffee to stall, and I snuck a glance at Aisha over my cup. Her too-big blazer was like a Halloween costume on her, and it wasn't just me being ageist, thinking that she was rather youthful. She was straight up young.

"Aisha," I said softly, wondering if that was even her name. "You don't work in advertising, do you . . . ?"

She shook her head bashfully.

"How old are you?"

A single tear fell, pathetically, down her left cheek. "Almost eighteen."

"A*lmost* eighteen," I repeated, sighing. "That's OK. Don't cry." I smiled. "Did you lie about your age to get on the app?" She shrugged, wiping her face with her sleeve, and I continued.

"Did you lie about being in advertising to . . . have some common ground with me?" I shook my head. "You know. I get it. It's hard making friends. But friends don't need to have the same jobs, or even interests—"

"I don't want to be friends."

I stopped speaking, rather taken aback. Suddenly, the sob story of a girl was sitting up much straighter, her confidence transforming her into a whole other woman.

"I want to work for you."

"Huh?"

"I came in two weeks ago to apply for an internship in person. Nobody—not you, not *anyone*—is replying to my e-mails. Nobody takes a college freshman seriously." She tucked her hair behind her ears. "Anyway, I was getting turned away by reception when you came out into the lobby to talk on your phone. You were talking to somebody about Bumble BFF and . . ." she trailed off. She didn't need to finish her sentence.

She hadn't only stalked me, but she'd downloaded the app, found me, and then befriended me, all to get a *job*? I swallowed hard, my ears burning. I felt humiliated.

I'd been conned.

I'd been . . . *catfished.*

"I'm sorry," I heard Aisha say. "But I didn't know what else to do. I'm desperate. I know what I want . . . I want to work in advertising. For *you*, Serena. I saw that article about you online. You were one of the thirty-five under thirty-five up-and-comers in DC two years ago. You were the only woman of color on that list. Do you know that?"

Of course I knew that. My old boss Iain had been equal parts jealous and pleased that my interview (and skin color) had painted his workplace to be capable, *diverse.*

"I have no connections in the industry," Aisha continued, pleading. "And agency placements are few and far between, and they *always* go to college seniors . . . Please? Could you please hire me?"

"Look," I said, unable to hide the irritation in my voice. "I didn't have a single connection in the industry when I started, and I didn't stalk somebody to get my first job."

"I'm sorry," she repeated.

"I know you are."

"I needed an angle to get my foot in the door, you know?"

"Well, there are angles that don't involve manipulating and lying to your prospective employer."

"You're right. I'll go . . ."

I sighed, watching Aisha pack her things. She looked like a sad puppy, and even though she'd literally catfished me, I kind of wanted to throw her a bone.

What if I'd had a mentor when I was her age, a woman like Deborah Kim to look up to? Even just to talk to.

"Wait . . ." I said, as Aisha moved to stand up. She batted her eyelashes at me.

Was I really going to do this?

Advertising could be a demanding, sexist, cutthroat industry, and it was capable of chewing up and spitting out any young woman, no matter how sweet and smart and seemingly capable.

I hated that I'd been duped, but I would also hate to see that happen to Aisha.

"You can sit down," I said, a little stiffly.

Her eyes brightened as she fell back into her seat. "So you'll give me an internship?"

I laughed. Aisha had guts. Maybe this industry wouldn't eat her alive.

"No," I said, glancing at my watch. "But, I have forty-five minutes, so I'd be happy to chat."

"That'd be great." She blushed. "If you have any advice, anything at all, about how to get started . . ."

"Well, my first piece of advice is don't stalk your prospective employers."

Laughing, Aisha grabbed a pen and notebook from her bag. "I'll write that one down . . ."

It's your team, Serena. You run the show how you see fit."

"I know," I said, even though it still felt odd to think that way.

"And Deborah will back whatever decision you make. She's very good about that."

I nodded as Tracy continued giving me advice, and I slid the coffee cup between my hands on the table. The break room door creaked open, and I looked up, startled, as I thought all of our other colleagues had left for the day. Ainsley stood in the doorway.

She looked between me and Tracy, who had immediately stopped speaking when she appeared. "What are we talking about?"

"None of your beeswax, Ainsley," Tracy said playfully.

"Gossiping, are we?"

Tracy didn't answer, eyeing me as she stood up. "Anyway, I should get going. *Think* about what I said, Serena."

I thanked her, and after she left the kitchen, Ainsley sat down in the now empty chair. "A human resources thing?"

I nodded, unsure about how much to reveal. I trusted Ainsley, and she, too, managed her own department, but I didn't want to be unprofessional by gossiping about one of our coworkers.

One of our *horrible* coworkers.

Ginger Spice was driving me up the fucking wall. The minute I'd stopped making an effort with her, she'd become even more rude and disrespectful, which put a nail in the coffin on any lingering feelings of my wanting to have a collegial relationship. I really wanted to tell her off, but the only problem was that she was very good at her job. She had great potential, learned quickly, always followed her briefs, and was even starting to develop a certain creative flair to her work, like a signature.

The extent of her toxicity really hit home the day before when she was out sick. Without their ringleader, the other team members were actually super friendly with me, and it made me realize I needed to do something about the situation.

I gulped. I needed to be a *bawse*.

"It's one of my team members," I said to Ainsley, quietly. "I'm having some trouble connecting."

I was having trouble *not throttling* one of my team members was more like it.

"Understood." Ainsley nodded. "Did Tracy tell you to document everything?"

I nodded. I'd gone to Tracy for some HR advice on how to have an open and honest discussion with Ginger about our work situation (AKA *hell*), and indeed she had recommended that I start writing everything down, and then use those notes to write Ginger a warning letter and put her on probation.

Luckily, I'd been taking diligent notes on all of the Spice Girls—the good and the bad—but putting someone on probation felt so formal. So *severe*. And I wasn't sure that I could do that to a bright young woman with so much potential. Could I?

"Last time I fired someone," I heard Ainsley say, "I gave him *three* warnings. He still didn't get his act together, so . . ."

I turned to her. "You had to *fire* someone?"

"I've had to fire four people over the years."

"Four. *Wow*," I said, rather horrified. I loved my new responsibilities as a manager, but I'd never had to be the "bad guy" before. I couldn't even manage a conflict with my own flesh and blood, let alone someone I had to have a professional relationship with.

It had been nearly a week since I'd seen Natasha, who had spent the rest of our family dinner scarfing down *rotis* and ignoring me. Punishing me. And I hadn't heard from her at all except for a very surprising e-mail I'd initially mistook as spam. An Evite to her gender reveal party.

She'd set the date. And she hadn't even bothered to give me or our mother a heads-up.

I used to call Mom every day because I felt guilty, and then I'd feel even worse after finally getting on the phone and realizing there wasn't anything I wanted to say. Every single call, every single time we saw each other, I told myself, *Serena, make more of an effort.*

Serena, be a better daughter!

Why was it that, now, only after Natasha was being a total ass to her, I was finally motivated to make a change?

Maybe Mom needed me in a way she didn't before. Or maybe I was just telling myself that to make myself feel better.

I'd called Mom immediately after the Evite went out, which had practically shocked her into silence. I suggested that Mom speak up to Natasha, but she'd only sighed and told me that it was her decision. My stomach had sunk, because her refusal to interfere meant Natasha was breaking her heart. And even though it felt mildly pleasing not to be the daughter in the doghouse, it didn't feel all that great, because Natasha was breaking my heart, too.

"What are you up to this evening?" I heard Ainsley ask. She had stood up and was putting away the coffee cups drying on the dish rack. I grabbed a tea towel and joined her, my heart racing.

She was about to ask me out on a *friend date*. I could tell, and I was actually really excited about it. After my catfishing incident, I had decided to take a breather from Bumble BFF. If my experience meeting Aisha had taught me anything, it was that meeting one-on-one was a *lot* of pressure. I should have spent more time on the app getting to know her, asking her questions and getting a feel for possible chemistry, before up and agreeing to meet her in person. With a bit of time and effort, I could have figured out that she was a little con artist a lot earlier.

But the thing was, I didn't have a lot of time, and I didn't want to be on my phone texting any more than I needed to. So instead, I'd gone back to the drawing board, researching some of the websites Becket had shown me. I decided that *activity*-based groups were my next route of attack. I'd signed up for a women-only book club on one website, and a group Tuscan cooking class through another, but those weren't for a while yet.

I'd come in early and worked hard all day, and I had enough leftovers in my fridge, so I didn't need to cook. Tonight, I was absolutely free.

"No plans," I answered, wiping down a mug. "You?"

Ainsley smiled, cocking her head to the side. "Me neither."

"So maybe we should finally have that drink," I said, feeling bold.

"Do you have time, Ms. Busy and Important Creative Director?"

"Ha, very funny. But just as a heads-up, I don't really drink alcohol."

"How about tea? There's a cute café on Fourteenth called Kismet—"

"Kismet," I said, at the exact same time. I *loved* that café.

My stomach somersaulted as we both returned to our cubes to

grab our coats and purses. Ainsley and I were already work friends, but this was officially our first "date."

Oh, baby.

Conversation came so naturally between us, and as we walked over to the café, I couldn't help but feel like I'd known her for years. Were we capable of going the distance? Becoming true friends and transcending our work friendship built on convenience, common ground, and office space?

It hadn't taken me long to figure out that I'd misjudged Ainsley. Even though she was married and had a family, she continued to march to the beat of her own drum and make space in her life for other things. Other people.

I wondered . . . No. I shook my head, pushing out the fantasy that she and I might be perfect for each other. I was getting way ahead of myself. I had a tendency to do that.

Kismet was unusually packed for a weekday evening, but Ainsley managed to find a free table in the back while I ordered us London Fogs at the front counter. I brought them over, and just as I set them down, I felt my phone buzz in my back pocket. It was Becket, asking me if I wanted to come over. I texted to say that I was out with Ainsley and would be a few hours, and suggested that I come over the following night.

"Was that the boyfriend?" Ainsley asked as I sat down.

I nodded. "Yeah. Becket."

"Solid name. So what's he like?" She put her elbow on the table, leaning forward. Apparently, we were jumping straight into the personal questions portion of the date. "All you've said is he's a photographer and cute and fun and . . . nice. So except for the photographer part, he could basically be a golden retriever."

I laughed. "I don't know. What else is there to say?"

"Does he make you happy?"

I nodded, slowly. "Things are great. We have a lot of fun together. But it's still early, you know."

"How long have you been dating?"

"I met him at my sister's wedding. Wow. So it's been more than two months already."

Over London Fogs, I gave Ainsley a synopsis of Becket and our relationship so far, how he was a very dutiful boyfriend and how I was the one taking things at a slower pace, keeping our lives and a lot of our time separate.

"Do you want to get married?" she asked me afterward, bluntly. "Have a family and all that expensive jazz? Feel free to ignore the question. It's a personal one."

"It's fine," I said. "And no. I don't want all that 'jazz.' I don't want to marry or have my own children."

Ainsley smiled. I was surprised by the lack of judgment on her face. It was nice.

"That must have been a fun conversation with your parents."

I snorted. "It was like going to Disneyland."

"Have you told Becket, though?" I shook my head, and she continued. "Because maybe it's something you should talk about before you—"

"It's early still," I said briskly. "There's no need yet." I looked around the café. It was filling up even more now, and I could see one of the baristas setting up a podium. I wondered if a live band was about to play.

"So what about you?" I said, turning back to Ainsley. That was definitely enough about me. It was her turn for the grilling. "Did you always know you wanted to get married?"

"I knew I wanted to get married *once*, but not twice." She chuckled. "But life happened, and here we are."

"Nikesh seems great, though."

"He is. He really is." She laughed. "It's so funny that he knew you before I did. He'd actually mentioned you. He would talk about an Indian woman who came almost every Saturday with short, *short* hair and a tattoo on her neck."

I laughed. "Not a lot of us out there."

"He admired you. He called you brave."

Brave.

Only for a woman, an Indian woman in particular, would just being herself be considered *brave.* Ainsley looked like she was about to say something else, but realizing she'd switched back to me as the subject of conversation, I cut her off.

"So tell me more about your in-laws," I said. "I gather that they aren't exactly supportive of your marriage?"

"Ha!" She stretched her arms up and back and then brought them down quickly. "Unsupportive is the same thing as actively trying to destroy it, right?"

"No way . . ."

"Feels like it." Ainsley sipped her drink. "Actually, my mother-in-law is fine. She's *wonderful,* but she's fed up with her husband and now spends half the year in India."

My eyes widened.

"I know, right? Good for *her.* They're still together, technically, but she's off *Eat Pray Love*–ing her best life, meaning my father-in-law has *no* life, so when he's not working, he's over at our house telling Nikesh to 'be a man,' not a nanny, that he should make his wife stay home and be a 'real mother.'"

I scoffed, enraged on her behalf. Not all Indian men were the sexist stereotypes they were often portrayed to be, but some of them *certainly* were.

"And to him," Ainsley continued, "a real mother shouldn't be the breadwinner. She should be home raising her son. Can you believe it?" She shook her head. "And he never says that stuff to my face, but I know that's what he's saying to Nikesh."

"They speak in Punjabi together?"

"Yeah, but even if I don't understand all the words, I just *know* what he's saying. Is that crazy?"

I shook my head. "More than half of communication is through body language."

"And all his comments to me about how easy it is for 'computer people' to go freelance and work remotely—I just know he wants me to quit. Stay home." She rolled her eyes. "Roll round *rotis*."

I smiled, although it was a sad smile. Rolling round *rotis* was traditionally considered the measure of a woman's domestic skills, her abilities, her worth, and it was surprising to hear Ainsley use the phrase. To fall victim to all this *shit* I'd taken pains to avoid. It didn't matter how hard we tried to be the perfect woman or daughter or daughter-in-law; it would never be good enough. Our *rotis* would never be round enough, and I was very tempted to tell her she shouldn't even bother to try.

"It doesn't matter what he wants, Ainsley," I said softly. "He wants you to quit your job? Fuck that. What do *you* want?"

"I . . ." She caught my eye, and all the milk and honey in my stomach seemed to sour. My question was meant to be rhetorical, but she'd taken it otherwise, and I was worried now about the response.

"Wait, are you thinking about quitting?" I shook my head. "Sorry, I shouldn't have asked that—"

"No," she said quickly. "It's fine. I don't want to go freelance, but . . ."

"But you're thinking about it."

"I would be lying to say I hadn't thought about it, *but* I have been with Deborah since the beginning. So sometimes I do wonder what the next step should be. *When* it should be."

I nodded, unsure of what to say. Although I understood where she was coming from, I was suddenly saddened by the prospect that Ainsley might quit. As a friend—well, work friend—I was happy for her. But on a personal level, it freaking sucked. We were just starting to really click. If she changed jobs, except for the occasional run-in at the farmers market, I'd never see her again.

Shit. I *had* been getting my hopes up. And I kicked myself for it.

"I'm sorry you have to deal with all that cultural baggage," I said finally. "It's not fair, especially because you're not even Indian yourself."

"We both knew it would be hard when we got married. And Nikesh *is* worth it, but sometimes I wonder . . ." She sighed. "If it would be easier to just listen to my father-in-law and do what he wanted."

"It wouldn't make anything easier, and on top of that you'd be unhappy." I sipped my drink, wiping the foam from my top lip. "That's what I hear, at least. I wouldn't know. I never obeyed my parents. My sister did, though. I guess that's why she's the favorite."

"I'm sure that's not true."

I didn't answer, realizing the conversation had veered back in my direction.

"Random question," I said, thinking about the Evite in my inbox. "Did you have a gender reveal party for MacKenzie?"

Ainsley looked at me strangely. "Nope. Why? Oh, is your sister having one or something?"

"Yeah, and I'm definitely a believer that women should do

whatever makes them happy, but I find the whole thing a bit strange."

"Preach," Ainsley said, raising her voice. The café was getting louder. "Are you close with your sister?"

We used to be close. I basically planned her wedding for her, and now I've been demoted to the ranks of an Evited guest.

I was about to open my mouth to reply, without knowing quite how to answer the question, when I was saved by a loud screech coming from a speaker somewhere behind me. We all winced, turning. One of the baristas was standing behind the podium, a microphone in his hand, his cheeks burning red.

"Sorry about that," he said, his voice booming from the microphone. "I'm Tom. And thank you for coming to our bimonthly Poetry Night at Kismet." He grinned at the room, pulling his baseball cap farther back onto his head. "We're going to start in five minutes. Sign-up sheet is by the register. Cheers!"

I turned back, smiling. "Poetry night? Wow. I didn't know they did that here."

"Me neither . . ." Ainsley said nonchalantly. "I'll get us another round. Same thing?"

I smiled. Ainsley wasn't using the event as an excuse to rush home to her family but wanted to keep hanging out.

"Sure, thanks. But do you want to go somewhere quieter?"

Ainsley shook her head, disappearing into the crowd, and I took a minute to check in with myself. We'd been at the café for more than an hour, but it felt like no time had passed at all—it felt exactly how it *should* feel with a really good friend.

How it *had* felt so many times before. Here I was again. Getting ahead of myself.

There was a lineup at the front counters, and Ainsley didn't return with the London Fogs until the poetry night had already started. She slid my drink toward me on the table as the third poet of the evening took the stage. He looked to be in his early twenties, and his forehead was shiny, his voice shaking. I felt bad for him yet was impressed by his courage. To me, the poem he read sounded like a bunch of pretty words strung together, but everyone seemed to think it was great. At least they applauded at the end.

"Do you want to get out of here?" I whispered to Ainsley, after the clapping died down.

"Hmm?" she asked, vaguely.

"I feel awkward. We can't really talk with this going on, no?"

"Maybe in a minute?" She didn't meet my eye as she rifled around in her purse.

"OK . . ." I leaned back in my chair, and just then, the strangest thing happened.

The barista announced my name.

I didn't quite believe it at first. It was as if I were watching myself, the whole scene, on television. The back of my neck heated up, and I could feel the blood rushing in my head. A beat later, I felt someone shaking my arm.

"Serena Singh?" I heard the barista call out again. "Is there a Serena *Singh* in the building?"

"Serena," Ainsley said. I looked over at her, and she had a shit-eating grin on her face, and I realized what she'd done.

Oh dear god.

"Over here!" Ainsley yelled, standing up and pulling me with her. Everyone in the vicinity turned to look.

"What are you doing?" I whispered harshly.

"*Serena*, come on!" Ainsley said loudly so everyone could hear. "Someone's being a bit shy over here . . ."

"We're all friends here, Serena," the barista said, as I tried to squirm away from Ainsley's grip. "We're here to support one another."

"Thanks." I cleared my throat, giving him a quick glance. "But, actually, tonight I'm *not*—"

"I think our friend Serena needs some encouragement, hey guys?" Ainsley yelled, clapping her hands together. "Let's give it up for *Serena* Singh!"

Shaking, I looked around the café. Everyone was looking at me. Clapping *for* me. I threw dagger eyes at Ainsley, but she just smiled, cheered harder. A moment passed, and then another, and panic rose in my chest. Should I just leave? Up and go?

"You can do it!" I heard someone say from behind me and then another to my left, their voices earnest, *encouraging*. I couldn't leave, and I was *definitely* going to murder Ainsley. Slowly, one foot after the other, I dragged myself toward the podium. The barista handed me the microphone as I reached him and then gave me a big pat on the back, like he was my scout leader. Taking a deep breath, I turned to face the crowd.

"Hi, guys . . ."

"Serena!" A holler from the crowd. I knew exactly where it came from.

"I'm a little nervous." I coughed, swallowed the bile. "Give me a minute."

Did I even know a poem? I'd taken a few English lit classes in university, but that was nearly fifteen years ago. I couldn't even remember who I'd studied, let alone the poems.

But maybe I could read some random poem from the Internet and pass it off as my own. Someone like Rupi Kaur but less well-known. I pulled out my phone from my back pocket and clicked through to Google, but I didn't have any bars. *Shit.* There was no reception in the back of the café.

"Come on, girl. You got this!"

Ainsley again. Seriously, remind me to murder her.

I was about to put my phone away, open my mouth, and just *see* what came out, when I spotted my notes app in the corner of the screen.

I clicked on it. I was a religious notetaker, immediately jotting down whatever thoughts or words or ideas popped into my head, in case it was useful for one work campaign or another. Without thinking, I clicked randomly on a file and just started . . . reading.

"Morning," I said, my lips trembling. I barely recognized my voice. Why was I so nervous? I could speak in a boardroom. Surely, I could speak here.

"*Morning*," I repeated, giving my voice authority. "Afternoon. Knight in shining armor."

I paused, gathering my nerves.

"Lipstick," I said. "Licking, sticking, *picking* one out."

I chanced a look up, feeling ridiculous, but then realized the café was completely silent. So silent, I literally could have heard a pin drop.

They were staring at me. They were *listening* to me, and for whatever reason, it gave me a boost of confidence. Ainsley wanted a show. I was going to *give* her a show.

"Pharmaceuticals," I said vigorously, reading again from my phone. I must have been thinking about the Stuart pitch when I wrote that word, a company that was looking to branch into a drinkable daily vitamin. "Don't pop the pills or they'll pop *you*."

"Pop!" I said.

"POP!" I screamed.

"Why not drink it?"

I paused, for effect, staring into a random person's eyes.

"Just drink it, girl. *Drink*, drink it up!"

"Sweet, salty apples. Maybe oranges. But *not* bananas." I laughed, throwing my hair back. "Because that shit is ba-na-*nas*!"

I kept going. I kept reading from my phone in various intonations. There was no rhyme or reason to my notes—they were just words, ideas, stupid notes that I'd needed to jot down to remind me of something, trigger a memory, an idea. I couldn't even remember why I had written some of this down.

"Lavender. Lust. Lily of the valley." I licked my lips and shook my head like I had just heard the most terrible of news. And then I whispered, ever so gently, "Is the end."

Graciously, dramatically, I curtsied, and the applause sounded. I looked up at the crowd and saw Ainsley shaking her head at me, laughing.

"What the fuck was that?" I saw her mouth at me, and I shrugged and, ever so discreetly, gave her the middle finger.

"Wow. Just *wow.*" The barista was beside me onstage, adjusting and readjusting his baseball cap. "For a first-timer, that was *so* brave."

I coughed, trying not to laugh. "Thank you," I deadpanned. "Thank you so much. What a crowd."

"We all have so much to learn from you." He crossed his arms, shaking his head at me. "*Please*, tell us about your piece."

"It's a meditation on consumerism," I said without missing a beat.

He nodded vigorously. "I could feel it. I think we all could. Consumer *culture*. It's killing our planet!"

Out loud, I told him I agreed, although in my head, I was wondering if it would break his heart if he knew my industry fed into the planet-killing culture.

"What's your process? Where do you find your inspiration?" He patted his chest with four fingers. "Here?"

I sighed. "If you really want to know, my inspiration comes from a very dear friend of mine. *Ainsley* Woods."

I heard a tiny yelp coming from the crowd.

"You're in for a treat tonight, folks," I said, finding my *dear* friend in the audience and looking her squarely in the eye. "Because *she* is performing next."

14

"Too dressy?" I came out of the closet, twirling my black skirt. "Does this say I like books and therefore you should be friends with me?"

"It's saying . . ." Becket paused, scrutinizing my outfit. "I'm smoking hot. Let me be your hot friend."

I rolled my eyes and went back in the closet, unzipping my black skirt. "It's too dressy."

"So what happened next?" Becket said from my bedroom, going back to our earlier conversation in which I'd been recapping that bloody poetry night. "Did Ainsley go up there?"

"I would have killed her if she didn't." I picked up my pair of high-waisted jeans from the floor, pulling them on. "Yeah, she came up and started performing the lyrics to a Taylor Swift song."

"Which one?"

"'You Need to Calm Down.'"

"Why?"

I laughed. "No, that's the name of the song. It came out a few years ago."

"Oh. Well, didn't anyone notice?"

"Nope! Apparently, people who go to poetry night don't listen to Taylor Swift."

"Except you and Ainsley."

I smiled, zipping up my jeans. "OK, what about this outfit?"

"It says . . . I'm a hipster. I'm super hot and . . ."

"Becket," I whined, sitting next to him on the bed. "Stop it."

"Stop telling my girlfriend how attractive she is?"

"I'm not trying to look *hot*. I'm trying to look . . . *friendable*."

"You look very friendable." He leaned over, kissing me roughly. "Not to mention fu—"

"Oy . . ." I giggled. "Enough. I have to go."

"No you don't." He grabbed me by the waist, pulling me back horizontal with him on the bed. "You have a new friend now, *Ainsley*. You don't need to go to this book club anymore."

I unwrapped myself from him and rolled over to my side, propping my head up on my elbow. Becket was staring at me like a lot of women might want to be stared at by their boyfriend. I brushed a stray strand of hair out of his eye. He was so nice. *Fun*. And it's not like I wasn't attracted to him. But what would it say about me if I canceled plans for a boyfriend? And sure, Ainsley and I were becoming friends, maybe *real* friends, but who knew how long she was planning to work there and how long this would last. Surely I needed more than *one* friend in my social circle. I couldn't put all my eggs in Ainsley's basket the way I'd done with Natasha.

"Stay," he murmured, biting his lip. "Please?"

"What's the verdict, then?" I asked, ignoring him. "The skirt or jeans?"

"What about . . . a pink thong?"

Half an hour later, I finally managed to get dressed. Becket walked me to the bus stop, and I took the one heading downtown while he hopped on the bus in the opposite direction toward his place.

Unfortunately, reading for pleasure was one of the first things that dropped off in adulthood when work took over my life. I used to *live* at the local library, devouring everything from historical sagas to sci-fi thrillers to the latest hit contemporary title, which the friendly librarians would always save for me. These days, I was lucky if I read a book every few months, and only when I was on a flight or sick or cooped up at my parents' over the holidays.

A book club seemed perfect for me. A social group setting and an encouragement to make time for reading in my day-to-day life? *Yes, please!*

I'd found a club accepting new members that met at a bar close to my office on Dupont Circle. I called Mom on the bus ride into town, and she told me about Natasha's plans for the gender reveal, which she'd only been hearing about secondhand through Dad. To cheer her up, I asked her to walk me through how to cook *aloo gobi*, and then I told her about a campaign I was working on. She didn't have much to say, but she seemed pleased to hear about what I was doing.

Finally, I arrived at my destination. There was a row of TVs behind the bar playing the Capitals game, and I quickly checked the score and then pulled out the book from my purse as I looked for the others. It was a psychological thriller, and it was OK, but I'd predicted the ending by chapter three, and the character motivations were completely off. (Girl, if the power is out and there's a serial killer in your house, *don't* go into the basement. Call the police!)

There was a cluster of women in a booth toward the back, copies of the book and glasses of wine scattered across the table. I smiled, and as I approached them, I didn't feel that nervous. I guess putting yourself out there was something you could get used to.

"I'm Serena," I said when I was right behind them. "Sorry I'm a little late."

They greeted me in a chorus of hellos and welcomes, and all the chairs were taken, so there was a slight commotion as I had to ask a few people at neighboring tables to borrow theirs, but finally, I found one.

"So what have I missed," I asked, dragging my chair into an opening. "Who else didn't like the book?"

"*Excuse* me?" I heard someone say. I froze, looking around. All the women, about ten of them, were looking at me, furiously, for some reason.

But then, I noticed the woman at the head of the table. Her blond bob and warm smile, although she wasn't exactly smiling now. I recognized her.

Her picture was on the back flap of the book.

Fuck.

"Are you kidding me?" The woman to my left scoffed at me. "How *dare* you?"

"I didn't . . . I didn't know," I stammered, my eyes flicking toward the author. I gave her my sweetest look. "I'm *so* sorry. I had no idea you would be here."

"It was on the website!" someone spat. "That was the whole point of tonight; it was to *meet* the author."

"Oh . . ." I was sweating profusely through my blouse. Had it really said that? It *could* have. I'd signed up in a rush, and I hadn't exactly read the listing in detail.

"It's not that I didn't *like* it, I just thought that the heroine, Josephine . . . Well, she was kind of all over the place, right? She—"

"Serena," a woman said, cutting me off. "I think you should leave."

I swallowed hard, my cheeks heating up. I thought I should leave, too. There was no saving *this*.

I dragged the chair back to its rightful table and tucked the book back into my bag. What an idiot! I'd walked into this bar literally two minutes earlier, and already it was over. Embarrassed, I apologized again two to twenty more times and then walked back through the bar. Before leaving, I paused again to check the score. The Capitals were down one, but there was still a period left.

I was about to leave, brushing the hair out of my eyes, when I saw something. *Someone* sitting just in front of me. And he took my breath away.

"Jesse?"

My heart froze, and time stood still. A beat, and then another, and then he craned his neck slowly toward me.

"Serena?"

In an instant, I noticed everything that was different about him—the wrinkles, the graying hair, his broader frame, his style of clothes—and everything that was exactly the same. I could still trace the shape of his nose in my sleep, draw every speck of amber and chocolate brown in his eyes. Except for that glimpse of him jogging on the street, those two pictures on Facebook, I hadn't seen him in twelve years.

I hadn't let myself.

"Hi . . ." My voice cracked, and it broke the spell. Remembering my manners, I smiled at him and the man sitting next to him. Jesse stood up and offered me a short, curt hug and then gestured to the other guy.

"Danny," Jesse said, pointing at me. "This is Serena."

"Hi, Danny."

"Serena, great to meet you." He shook my hand, smiling as he held my gaze. Jesse didn't bother explaining who I was, and Danny didn't ask. I half wondered if Danny knew.

"Wow," Jesse said, leaning back against the table. "It's been forever. How are you?"

"Fine. *Great.*" I nodded. "You?"

"Fine." He laughed. "Great . . ."

"Sorry, guys," Danny interrupted, gesturing to his phone. "My Uber is here. I have to run." He gave Jesse a look I couldn't read. "You good, man?" Danny asked, and Jesse nodded.

"Yeah. I'm going to finish my beer. You go."

After Danny left, I took his empty chair, and it felt good to get the weight off my feet. Take a deep breath and relax into something. I didn't realize I was shaking until Jesse offered to get me a drink, and as I declined, I nearly knocked his beer out of his hand.

"Smooth, Serena." I shook my head. "Sorry about that."

"Don't worry. I'm pretty shaken up to see you, too."

I appreciated that he admitted it out loud. It *was* weird. It was almost too much, being here with him. I ran into ex-boyfriends or flings from time to time—at the movie theater, restaurants, even the grocery store. But Jesse wasn't just an ex-boyfriend.

He was the only man I'd ever loved. The only one I'd ever, fleetingly, considered marrying.

"Are you here to watch the game?" Jesse asked.

"No, for a book club, actually."

"Oh. Is it over?"

I shrugged. "You could say that."

"Wow, you look *exactly* the same," he said suddenly. He lifted his hand, reaching toward the tattoo on my neck. "I like it." He dropped his hand. "It suits you."

"I've had it for nearly a decade."

"I know."

"You know?"

"Yeah. Natasha friended me on Facebook a few years ago. I've seen pictures of you together online. How's your family doing?"

As I gave him a brief recap on the past twelve years, all I could think about was the new knowledge that Natasha and Jesse were Facebook friends. She'd never told me, and I didn't know whether to feel gratitude for the secrecy, or betrayal.

"It sounds like you finally got your dream job," Jesse said after I told him about my new role. I hadn't excluded any of the details because I knew he'd be proud of me.

"I did. I really did."

"Congratulations."

"Thanks," I beamed. "I'm lucky—"

"No, don't start that. Don't downplay it. You're not *lucky*." He looked at me, hard. "You deserved it."

I didn't say anything to that and, instead, took a sip of the glass of water next to Jesse's pint of beer.

"That's not mine."

I spewed the water out, half choking.

Laughing, he shook out his hand, which had been caught in the splash zone. "I'm *kidding*. It's mine. Help yourself."

I rolled my eyes, a weird knot twisting in my stomach. I grabbed an unused napkin and wiped my mouth and then the table.

"I knew about your new job already," he said, after. "I'll come clean. I Googled you a few months ago. It had been a while since I looked you up . . ."

I nodded. A few months ago, *why*? I wasn't really sure what he wanted me to say to that.

"Have you ever looked me up online?" he continued.

He held my gaze, and I knew that he'd be able to tell if I lied. "OK, fine. I looked you up once."

"Only once?"

I nodded.

BBQ time with the gang!

"And?"

"And . . . I'm very happy you're happy, Jesse." My throat constricted as I thought of Anadi, of his two children. "I think we both are where we wanted to be."

He smiled at me sadly, lifting his pint glass to his lips. "No, I'm not."

My heart surged, terrified he'd say something nostalgic or just plain stupid.

"I mean, who *wants* to get divorced?"

Divorced? Jesse was *divorced*?

"I'm so . . . sorry." I reached for him, regretting it the moment my palm touched his shoulder. I wasn't sure if Jesse was trembling or I was. "I had no idea."

He shrugged, and I took the opportunity to lift my hand back into my lap.

"We've been separated for over two years."

Two *years*?

"But we finalized the divorce only a few months ago. That's when I moved downtown. I have an apartment around the corner."

I nodded. So that's why I'd seen him around jogging on Dupont Circle. He lived really close to my office.

Jesse ordered another beer and told me everything, even though I didn't ask him to or necessarily think it was a good idea. He told me how his relationship with Anadi was forward-looking, always defined by a milestone.

A romantic engagement. A *pakka* four-day Punjabi wedding. A trip to Europe.

Children.

"And then?" Jesse asked rhetorically, both palms gripping his glass. "And then there was nothing left to look forward to."

"That can't be true . . ." I paused. "The kids—"

"Not that, Serena. There was nothing left to look forward to between us, between me and Anadi." He swallowed hard. "There was nothing left."

I glanced away, concentrating on the television above us. Four white men in suits were on a panel, presumably commenting on the game that had now ended. The Capitals had won in the end. I watched them, blinking, unsure if I needed to give Jesse a moment to compose himself. Give *myself* a moment.

"Sorry."

I turned back to him. He was sitting up straighter, a sheepish smile on his face.

"Why?"

"I'm still in that phase where I can't help but bring up the divorce and then won't shut up about it. My therapist says it'll pass." He drained his beer. "And apparently, I'm also in a phase where I can't help but bring up my therapist."

"Well, I'm glad you have somebody to talk to."

"Have you ever seen a therapist?"

I shook my head. "What's it like?"

He laughed, knocking his knee against mine. "It's like having a really good, wise friend who lets you talk about yourself the whole time. Kind of like what you're doing now . . ."

"Except this is free."

"Sorry . . ."

"I'm kidding." I looked him in the eye and smiled at him in a way that let him know I really was joking. I had had my turn to share when we first sat down and had told him as much about my family as I was ever going to. And, really, after what felt like hours sitting together, I still didn't know so much about him. There was still so much ground to cover. Where did he work? Had he lived in the DC area this whole time and we'd just never run in to each other?

What had his life looked like since we last saw each other? I could conjure up a few stereotypes I harbored about domestic bliss, but I still couldn't really picture it. I wasn't sure I wanted to.

"I'm starting over, Serena," I heard him say. "I'm thirty-*seven* years old, and I'm starting over."

"Why do you make it sound like such a bad thing?"

He looked at me, and he looked so sad, so pathetic, I was tempted to hug him against my better judgment.

"Jesse, like you said, you're *only* thirty-seven. You're young. Your kids are young. And you're healthy—" I paused, seeing the look on his face. "You're jogging, aren't you? So you're healthy."

"How did you know I started jogging?"

"Do you own an obnoxiously neon green jacket?" He smiled, and I continued. "I saw you. At the crosswalk by the Metro station."

"It's true. I jog now. Not that you can tell." He cheerfully slapped his belly, which was just the slightest bit rounder than it used to be. But then again, so was mine.

Jesse opened his mouth as if to say something but then closed it.

"What is it?" I asked.

He stretched his hands across the bar counter, tapping his fingers as if on a keyboard. "We should be friends."

"Friends?"

"Do you live around here, too? We could go jogging together. I don't know."

Friends. Jogging. Really?

"No, I'm in Columbia Heights." I shook my head, a knot forming in my stomach. "But my office is just around the corner from here . . ."

"Well, maybe you can show it to me sometime." He glanced up at the TV, blinking. "We could go for lunch."

Lunch. Friends went for lunch. But did exes?

"I don't know . . ."

"We were going to stay friends, don't you remember?"

"Yeah, but two minutes after we broke up, I heard you got together with Anadi—"

"So what? She wouldn't have cared if we stayed friends."

"Jesse, you know she would have."

He didn't respond for a moment. The talking heads disappeared from the screen, and a commercial flashed on. A dark gray sports car, driving down a flat, open road. How typical. The SUV commercial I'd worked on (no open roads to be seen) had won an award.

"Oh, come on," I heard him say as the car drove into the sunset. "What's the harm? It's been *twelve* years."

He was right. It had been twelve years. What felt like a lifetime. Jesse and I were different people, had led different lives, gone down two diametrically opposed paths that now happened to converge. He was divorced, melancholic, and to be honest, a bit of a mess.

And me?

I had my shit together, mostly. A good job. A nice boyfriend.

What I didn't have enough of was . . . *friends.*

"Friends," I said, reaching my hand toward him. Jesse shook it, his large, warm hand enveloping mine.

"Friends."

15

SANDEEP

Twelve years earlier

"Veer," Sandeep whined. "The neighbors can see."

"So let them watch."

"You are being very improper—"

His arms slid down from her waist. "Don't you like it when I'm being this way?"

Sandeep giggled and then playfully shoved him away. She turned around. Veer had pretended to fall over against the mailbox, and the back of his hand was draped across his forehead.

"You are such a drama queen, my dear husband." She kissed him very quickly in case the nosy couple across the street really was watching and then fished her keys from her purse.

"Go take a shower. The kids will be here soon."

Veer went straight to the bathroom, while Sandeep unpacked their picnic basket at the entranceway. Sitting on a blanket outdoors in the sweltering heat wasn't usually their friends' idea of fun, but Sandeep had been dying to try out the American tradition and organized the whole thing.

They brought blankets, hats, paper fans, and cardboard boxes full of potato chips, pretzels, and cold cans of Coke and 7 Up. Sandeep had attempted to organize the potluck with American staples like macaroni and cheese and potato salad, but none of her friends knew how to make such things. Instead, they brought containers full of *daal*, *saag*, other *subjis*, and *roti*.

There was enough shade in the park nearby, and they'd played Bhabhi—Sandeep's favorite card game—while the men held a cricket match. Veer being Veer was selected as pitcher, and he was a sweaty, *sexy* mess by the time they retired to the shade. Placing his bat in the hall closet, Sandeep blushed, remembering the first time she'd watched him play, back when he was just the handsome captain of the local college team. It was several years before she realized their two families were acquainted, and his parents brought him around the house to propose her hand for marriage. All the girls from school were jealous. Even Sandeep's own cousins.

She heard the shower come on and toyed with the idea of joining him. Natasha was with a friend from school for the whole weekend—her parents had a beach house a few hours away—and they weren't used to the luxury of alone time. But it was already past four p.m., and Serena and Jesse would be arriving any minute.

She'd cooked that morning and the evening before in preparation. All of Jesse's favorites and plenty of leftovers to send home with him. Sandeep lifted up the heavy cardboard box of empty containers from the picnic and balanced it on her hip as she slowly inched her way into the kitchen. She was about to set it down or go interrupt Veer to come help her, but then she heard the laughter.

She pushed through and made it to the edge of the kitchen

counter, setting the box down lightly. There was no one there. Was she going mad? A few seconds later, she heard it again.

It was coming through the open window above the sink. She tiptoed over and sighed in relief when she saw Serena and Jesse side by side on the outdoor love seat, which sat flush against the house wall. The top of their heads were touching, and they were hunched over something. She leaned over the sink to see what it was. It was just Serena's laptop.

"That's really good," Jesse said suddenly, sitting back. He kissed her on the forehead, and instinctively, Sandeep stood upright quickly so he wouldn't see her in his peripheral vision. "Hilarious. They're going to love it."

"You think?"

"How could they not?"

"Iain never picks my stuff. And if he does, he takes the idea and then assigns it to one of the guys."

"I know, sweetie." Jesse kissed her again, this time on the *mouth*. "You need to get out of there. You've been there two years already. Maybe it's time to look for a new job."

"I don't know." Serena shrugged, lolling her head onto Jesse's shoulder. "I like the clients, though. The work is interesting. If I stick it out just a bit longer . . ."

"Why don't we look for jobs together," Jesse said. "In New York."

Sandeep's heart started beating wildly through her *salwar*, and she crept farther away from the window.

New York?

She shouldn't be listening to this. This was their private business. Rationally, she knew she needed to walk away, but as a mother, she could not.

"I don't want to move back to Philadelphia. My parents don't expect it, either," Jesse continued. "I'd be happy here, or we could try out a new city together. We could find a studio in Brooklyn—"

"Right," Serena interrupted. "Let's move to New York and live *together.* I'm sure my parents will love that."

"Well, there's something I could ask you, Serena. A question we could talk about to make them more comfortable with it . . ."

Sandeep gasped, pressing her warm hands against her face. Jesse was going to propose.

Finally.

She'd assumed he would after they both finished university two years earlier. But then weeks passed. Months. Serena started work at the advertising agency. Jesse began a master's program in a subject Sandeep could never remember the name of.

Serena moved out.

Sandeep had tried to forbid it, but Serena had the money saved and the will to see it through, so there was nothing they could do but watch. It didn't even matter that Jesse lived in student accommodations and Serena in another house with roommates—she instantly became "the talk of the town." An unmarried woman with a boyfriend, and she didn't live under her parents' roof?

It would never happen back home, but evidently, it was happening here.

Even in the two years since Serena left home, other Punjabi girls in the community followed suit. To her family's dismay, one girl moved all the way to Los Angeles to pursue acting, of all things, and another just across the state line to her boyfriend's.

It was the way of the world now, and she'd grown comforted by the fact that this day would come and Jesse would eventually propose. He was a nice boy, and Sandeep herself couldn't have made a more perfect match for her daughter. Jesse's family was Sikh, yes, but they were also educated and raised in America.

They would treat Serena with love and respect and not like a dishrag, the way some of her friends were treated by their in-laws.

"So what do you think?" she heard Jesse ask. "Would you want me to ask your parents for permission?"

"No—look, Jesse, we can't get married just to make my parents happy."

"That's not what I'm saying." He repositioned on the love seat, facing her. "Yes, we're only twenty-four . . . but we're going to get married anyway, right? We might as well do it now."

Serena didn't answer, and Sandeep again felt like she should walk away. But she didn't. She started to imagine what the wedding might look like.

"We don't have to move to New York. We can stay in DC," Jesse said. "Hell, we can move anywhere. Even Canada if you want. But my master's program is nearly over, and I need to start applying for jobs, Serena. You never want to talk about this, but we have to start making plans soon."

"Jesse . . ."

"We don't have to have a big wedding." He laid his hand on her knee, squeezing. "And I promise to pull my weight. I can plan the whole thing with our mothers if you want."

Sandeep smiled, watching them. Her fantasy was becoming real. What had she done to deserve such a son-in-law?

"Jesse," Serena said quietly. "You're not listening. You never listen to me—"

"I do, sweetie. I know you. And I know this stuff freaks you out, but I'll—"

"It's not the wedding that freaks me out, Jesse. It's the *marriage*."

"What—what you do mean?"

Serena sighed, resting her head in her hand. "I don't think I *want* to get married."

Sandeep's heart dropped into her chest.

"What are you *talking* about?" Jesse asked. "That's crazy. Of course—"

"No, I don't. And I do try and talk about this with you. You just never want to hear it." Serena paused, folding her legs up onto the love seat. "Do you know there are no women over the age of thirty at my agency? No mothers. No women that aren't at the bottom of the totem pole like me?"

Sandeep pressed her hand against her chest, trying to understand what was happening, to make sense of the words she shouldn't have been hearing.

"I know I complain about Iain and those guys, but Jesse, I love what I do. One day, I want to be the *best* . . . Hell, I want to be Iain's boss. And I want more for myself than—"

"Than what, Serena? Than *me*?"

"You don't understand."

"I'm trying to, babe. Look—"

Sandeep knocked over the box with her elbow. Hard. On purpose. Everything crashed to the ground, and she quickly hunched to the ground to gather it all up.

"Mom, are you OK?"

Sandeep glanced up, coyly. Jesse and Serena were peering through the kitchen window, concerned looks on their faces.

"Oh, Serena?" Her heart was still racing, but she kept her voice even. "Jesse? I didn't realize you were home."

16

Through my earbuds, I played the soundtrack to *Wonder Woman* and tried to channel my inner Amazon. To anyone observing me, I was going over some sample graphics Posh Spice had prepared for our client's organic laundry detergent campaign, but in my head, I was a Punjabi Gal Gadot and kicking some serious ass.

Promptly, at eleven forty-five a.m., I stood up and grabbed The File from my locked bottom drawer, which contained all my notes on Ginger Spice. One last time, I pictured myself in a slightly more modest version of Wonder Woman's outfit, hands on hips, elbows powerfully jutting, and then tapped Ginger Spice on the shoulder.

"Vic?" I said, after she pulled out her own earbuds. "Do you have a minute?"

I didn't make small talk as we walked to the boardroom. Holding the door open for her, I waited for her to sit down, and then I gently closed the door behind me and took the chair directly opposite her.

Today, her red hair was braided beautifully down her neck, her makeup and clothes flawless, impeccable. Not only was she an excellent copywriter, she also looked the part. She had the confidence to *act* the part, and I knew exactly why Deborah had hired her.

"What's up?" Vic said icily.

Hell, I would have hired her, too. And even though I was her boss, the idea of *confronting* her was making me sweat through my blouse.

"Are you happy working here?" I asked. It took me everything to keep my voice steady, and she looked surprised by the question.

"Are you?" I asked again.

"Yeah. *Yeah*, why?"

"Because most of the time you act like you don't want to be here."

"Of course I want to be here."

"And you certainly don't act like you want to report to me," I added, even though I felt like saying, *And I know you wished you'd gotten my job and didn't* have *to report to me.*

Vic didn't answer, and coolly, I held her gaze. I was about to reach for The File but at the last second decided against it. I didn't need it.

"Do you have concerns about my performance?" she asked, sarcasm dripping from her voice. "Because last I checked, I was doing a really good job. Like, you haven't given me any negative feedback, and Deborah *loved* my pitch on . . ."

I let her finish talking, and then I said what *I* came in here to say. Folding my fingers together on the boardroom table, the way powerful women bosses do on TV, I went on to diplomatically outline my concerns about her behavior. That as smart and capable of a copywriter as she was, she was not meeting the requirements of being a "team player," something Deborah and I both valued as part of our friendly, female-led workplace.

"So you're telling me off because you think I have *attitude*," she said flatly, after I was finished.

"I'm putting you on probation because you have a *negative* attitude."

Her face went as beet red as her hair.

"Tracy will be handing you a letter this afternoon, where we've stated our concerns in writing and outlined actionable steps that need to be taken." I paused. "You'll note that the letter is signed by myself, Tracy, *and* Deborah."

Vic's mouth gaped at my mentioning of Deborah's name. Her eyes narrowed. I could tell that she wanted to scream at me, kick up a fuss, call me a bad word. I wondered if this was the first time she'd been put in her place, and while I felt bad, it also gave me a guilty thrill.

"If you have any questions, let me know." I stood up abruptly, but I didn't break eye contact. "We can set up a meeting."

My heart raced as I walked out the door and back to my desk, my chin held high. I'd informally supervised people before, but I'd been lucky enough to have enthusiastic, *nice* reports; men and women who didn't hate my guts. This whole situation of having to be a tough *bawse* was entirely new to me, and I hoped to god I'd done the right thing.

I rounded the corner, and as I passed Ainsley's pod, she waved me over, pulling down her headphones as I walked up.

"How did it go?" she whispered, giving me a look.

"As well as it could have."

"Did she . . ."

"Stab my eyes out? Luckily, no, but I might sleep with one eye open tonight."

Ainsley smiled, sinking back into her chair. "Well, you'll have to give me the full debrief later because Becket is here."

"Becket?" I narrowed my eyes at her. "Can't be. I just saw him last night . . ."

"Well, there's a very handsome gentleman talking Tracy's ear off, ready to take you to lunch." Ainsley crossed her legs. "Also, you never told me Becket's of Indian heritage. Sorry, when you said he was *Asian*, I thought you meant—"

"He's not . . . *Oh.*" I shook my head. "That's not Becket. That's *Jesse*. He must be early for our lunch."

"Jesse?" Ainsley paused, and my heart sank as I remembered that Ainsley knew all about Jesse; that day at the farmers market, she'd seen me at my worst over him.

"Facebook Jesse?"

I leaned over, speaking softly, "I ran into him last week. We decided to be friends . . ."

"Oh . . ." Ainsley sounded surprised, and even a bit judgy. "How does Jesse's wife feel about that? And Becket?"

"Jesse's divorced."

"I see."

"And I didn't tell Becket." I stood up straight, suddenly wanting the conversation to be over. "I don't need to. It's nothing romantic with Jesse . . ."

"Oh. OK."

I bit my lip, looking at her, and neither of us broke eye contact.

"Anyway," Ainsley said dryly, pulling her headphones back on. "He's in the kitchen."

"Thanks . . ." I trailed off as I didn't think she was listening, and I didn't really know what else to say.

I tried to shake off my conversation with Ainsley as I grabbed Jesse and we left for lunch. Why was I so irritated? What gave her the right to think she could make assumptions about my relationships with Becket and Jesse?

Jesse was in a much better mood than when I'd run into him

at the sports bar. He was *super* chatty and even seemed to have a spring in his step, and I let him take the lead in the conversation as we walked to lunch. He told me about his job in data analytics for the *Washington Post*, where he'd worked for the past five years, and then the minor renovations he was planning for his new apartment downtown.

"I want the kitchen tile to say . . . 'Respectable Bachelor.'" He stopped walking, pointed to the sidewalk as if we were standing in his kitchen. "But I also want it to say, 'Super Dad.' You know what I mean, right?"

"Of course," I deadpanned. "Although I hear that tile is very expensive."

"I've basically been living at Home Depot—hey, you should come with me sometime. What do you think of plaid curtains?"

"*Plaid?* Like lumberjack plaid?"

"Yeah, why?"

I made a face at him as we arrived at the local diner where we were planning to eat. "No plaid?" I shook my head, and he shrugged in such a goofy, warmhearted way that I couldn't help but laugh.

As Jesse held the door open for someone exiting the diner, I snuck a look at him. It was the first time I'd seen him dressed up for work. He was wearing shiny brown shoes, dress pants, and a collared powder-blue shirt that fit snuggly over his broad shoulders. The top button was undone. One more and I would have been able to see the beginnings of the thick black hair that covered his chest. When I first saw it years earlier, I'd been so surprised, and a little freaked out, that it had hurt his feelings. Within hours, I'd loved it.

The host sat us at a corner booth by the window. I'd been here before, but only ever for a coffee and muffin when I was running late for work and had forgotten to eat that morning. It was a 1950s diner, very old Hollywood, and in our texts, Jesse had sworn by their all-day breakfasts, something he ate often, especially when first moving back into the city.

The waiter arrived, and Jesse ordered the house special. Without even asking what was in it, I ordered the same. I was still feeling off about my conversation with Ainsley and couldn't really be bothered to look at a menu.

"Oh," Jesse added. "And one chocolate milkshake, please. Serena, want to share?"

I grimaced. "Share?"

"Yeah."

"No, I'm good—"

"But you love chocolate milkshakes!"

"Yeah, you're right . . ." I turned to the waiter. "I'll have a chocolate milkshake as well."

After he left, I gave Jesse a hard look.

"What?" he asked.

"What do you mean, *what*?" I shook my head at him. "We can't share a milkshake, Jesse."

"Why not? They're big here."

"But sharing milkshakes, sharing food—that's all very relationship-y," I said decidedly. "So I think we need to set some ground rules. For the sake of our friendship."

He raised his eyebrows at me, his left ever so slightly higher than the right one. "Is that so?"

"I can't come to Home Depot with you. We can't share food . . ." I shook my head. "We can't do anything that could be perceived as relationship-y . . . or blur boundaries, cause confusion—"

"But I have *confusion* about what curtains to buy . . ."

"Jesse," I said in a stern tone. "I'm being serious."

"Me *too*."

The food arrived. The milkshakes were, indeed, very large. As we ate, we talked about work, mostly—a topic I deemed to be safe, something friends discussed. I told him more about my new role, some of the campaigns I'd been working on, and that I'd given my first official warning as a boss.

"This is nice, isn't it?" He stuffed a potato wedge into his mouth, chewing. "Us being friends and all."

"It is nice," I admitted. "And it's nice to see you happy. I have to say, last week you looked—"

"Terrible. I know. I was having a bad day."

I nodded. "I guess those happen sometimes."

"Right before I ran into you, Anadi switched weekends on me, *again*, after I'd already planned to take the kids—"

"Jesse." It was my turn to cut him off. "No. You can't talk to me about your divorce anymore. OK? It's too weird."

"Is it?"

I nodded. "It needs to be a rule."

"Fair enough." He sighed. "I guess I have my therapist for that."

"That you do."

"Well, are there any other rules I should know about?"

I nodded, thinking them up on the spot. "I think we should restrict our 'meetings' to daytime." I gestured to the window. "Daylight hours."

"Meetings," he chuckled. "Sure. And how about we can't drink alcohol during our *meetings*. You don't drink really anyway, right?"

"Right."

"So that'll be easy."

"And I don't think we should go over to each other's houses."

"Wouldn't be able to keep your hands off me, eh, Singh?"

I hit him lightly on the shoulder. "And no flirting!"

"Then no hitting. Hitting could be considered flirting."

I grinned. The way Jesse was looking at me, I couldn't help it.

The waiter walked by to check on us, and I took a moment to compose myself. Jesse's presence still affected me. A smile, a joke, even a look could lift me out of a fog, a terrible mood, and make me feel like myself again. But couldn't a friend make you feel that way, too? It didn't have to be confusing if you didn't want it to be.

"Anything else?" Jesse asked me after the waiter had left.

"I don't think we should talk about dating or our relationships."

"That'll be easy because I'm not in a relationship." He leaned down toward his milkshake, the bright red-and-white straw falling between his lips. "You?"

"Sort of." I hesitated, imagining Becket wouldn't like that response. "Yes, I'm in a relationship."

"Oh?" Jesse sucked on the straw, looking up at me. "Spill the *tea*, girl!"

I rolled my eyes at him. "What did I just say?"

"Just the basics, and I'll leave you alone." He shrugged. "Name, age, height, occupation, girth—"

"*Jesse!*" My face burned red as I glanced around us to make sure no had heard. When I looked back, Jesse was giggling like a little kid, his eyes lit up as he sipped his milkshake. I laughed, shaking my head at him.

"You're incorrigible."

"I nearly failed English class, don't you remember? I have no idea what that word means." He pushed his glass away. "OK, fine. I'm sorry. I'll stop. Just tell me his name."

"Becket." I shrugged. "We've been dating since February. He's nice."

"Nice."

"Yeah." I nodded. "He's really nice. And that's all you're getting out of me."

"Right. Moving on, then." Jesse sat back in the red leather seat. "So what can we talk about?"

"The weather," I said dryly. "Current events. Sports. Bollywood movies. Family—"

"How *is* your family?"

"Good. Natasha's pregnant." I nodded. "Mom and Dad are the same as they have always been."

"Well, pass on my congratulations!" He paused, spearing a fried tomato with his fork. "You and your dad," he added. "You still don't really talk?"

"What's there to talk about?"

Jesse bit into the tomato. "The weather. Currents events. Sports. Bollywood movies . . ."

"Ha ha . . ."

"Your new job. *His* job—"

"Jesse." I crossed my arms. "I earned more at the age of twenty-five than he did for ten years driving taxis. Do you think he really wants to hear about my job?"

"Have you ever asked him that?"

"Can you stop?" I pleaded, practically whined. "Family is not off-limits, but I think this"—I gestured to his chest and then back to mine—"pretending we still know each other *is*."

"Don't we still know each other, though?"

I didn't answer, shoveling in a big forkful of baked beans, and when I looked up, Jesse was still looking at me.

"I think we should play an icebreaker."

I narrowed my eyes. "A what now?"

"An icebreaker," he repeated. "To get to know each other again."

Jesse was teasing me. He thought the ground rules I'd set were ridiculous. I straightened my shoulders.

"I'd love to," I said, calling his bluff. "What's the game?"

Grinning, Jesse pulled out a pad of paper and two pens from his messenger bag. "I don't know what it's called, but my daughter told me about this game she played with her big buddy at school—"

"What's a big buddy?"

"Younger students get matched with older students to like—I don't know—become buddies?" Jesse started folding and ripping the paper into smaller squares. "Anyway, each of us has to answer ten questions, and after, we have to guess what the other person wrote down."

Jesse found a random list of icebreaker questions online, and after we each wrote our own answers down, he started reading out the questions.

The early ones were pretty silly, like, "What is the least terrible Subway sandwich?" This led to a heated debate between ourselves, the waiter, and the table next to us about Jesse's answer, the Classic Tuna, which everyone else agreed was actually the *last* thing on the menu we'd order. Jesse defended his answer with spirit, making our side of the restaurant laugh, and impressively, kind of making me crave a Subway Classic Tuna. I loved seeing him so fired up, the way he could get in college, whether it was pushing back against something the professor had said about the Chicago school of economics, or trying to convince a lifelong Capitals fan at some party that they should really be cheering for Jesse's hometown Philadelphia Flyers. So many of my friends had mellowed with age, growing more complacent and caring less about what used to light the fire in their belly.

Although he was only talking about a Subway sandwich, I could tell that it hadn't happened to Jesse. If anything, his joie de vivre had only intensified.

Finally, we moved on, and gradually the questions became more personal. We incorrectly guessed approximately how many people the other had kissed (eek) and then both had to figure out what was in the other person's bag. I was completely off. (Who knew that Jesse had been accidentally carrying around his son's miniature Mr. Potato Head? Certainly not Jesse.) He, on the other hand, was right on the money about what I had in my purse. (Although, let's be real, it's quite predictable that a thirtysomething-year-old woman would keep a wallet, keys, smartphone, tampon, and spare lipstick with her at all times.)

"Final question," Jesse said as we got to the bottom of the list. I tapped my foot, hoping the game would wrap up quickly now. I'd been away from the office for well over an hour and needed to get back to work.

"What's the most important thing to me in the world?"

"That's easy," I said. "Your children."

Jesse nodded, clicking his tongue. "Nice one."

"And what did you guess for me?"

"I have two possible answers—"

"You're only allowed one."

Jesse paused, making a show of studying my face as he drummed his fingers against his cheek. I slid my rose-gold frames down the bridge of my nose, challenging him. His eyes rolled over my forehead, the bridge of my nose. A flush of heat ran through my body as his eyes landed on my mouth, and I resisted the urge to bite down on my bottom lip. Suddenly, I felt short of breath. Panicked. Exhilarated. And just when the moment became too much, thank god, Jesse spoke.

"Family," he said, leaning back into his seat. "You wrote down 'family.'"

"I . . ." I stammered, finding my bearings. "That's your guess?"

"Well, your career is a close second for sure, and you'd probably not admit it out loud, but yeah. I guessed that family is the most important thing to you." He shrugged. "Was I right?"

I cocked my head to the side, glancing down at my paper. Indeed, in large block lettering, I'd written down FAMILY. When Jesse had read out the question moments earlier, I hadn't hesitated.

None of my friends, coworkers, not even Natasha would have intuited my answer, but as complicated as we were, I would drop everything for my family. Even though I didn't act like it half the time, they were my real *priority*, and I suddenly felt queasy thinking about how no one else in the entire world but Jesse still knew that.

"Yeah," I answered breezily, sitting up in the booth. "You were right. Anyway . . ." I trailed off and, desperate for somewhere else to look, started searching for the waiter. It was time to get the check and return to work.

"What is it?" I heard Jesse say.

I caught a glimpse of our waiter. He was busy with a nearby table, and I flicked my eyes back to Jesse. "What's what?"

Jesse didn't prompt me again, but from the look on his face, I could tell he wouldn't let me brush this aside, either.

"Nothing," I said forcefully. Jesse raised his left eyebrow at me. It made him look like a cartoon version of himself, and I laughed.

"It's not nothing. What was your on your mind just then?"

I sighed, stalling for time. "I suppose . . . I feel guilty. Not suppose. I feel extremely guilty."

"For?"

"I don't necessarily act like my family is important to me," I said, avoiding his gaze. "Except for Natasha, I've never made them a priority. I don't go home very much. And I barely ever talk to my aunts and uncles and cousins. I should. But I never do."

"We could all do better," Jesse said. "You're being hard on yourself."

I smiled at his generosity. Yes, I could do better, but I'm pretty sure Jesse was already trying his best. If he was still the same guy

I knew back in college, he was a wonderful family man. He'd spend hours every weekend on the phone with his parents, his siblings, and even kept in regular contact with distant family members, like his third cousin through marriage, Pinky, who emigrated to Denmark and whom he'd only met twice.

"Well," I said. "I have been making more of an effort with Mom lately. It's not easy. But I'm trying."

Jesse nodded, and I could tell he was about to ask me something else.

"I'm so full," I blurted. Jesse's gaze was getting a bit too intense, and I needed to change the subject. "Good call on coming here for lunch, but these portions are *way* too big."

Jesse leaned over and looked into my aluminum milkshake glass, and then dramatically into his own. "Funny how we're both full yet happen to have half a milkshake left. It's almost as if we could have shared."

Without missing a beat, I picked up my milkshake and started chugging. Within five seconds, my stomach hurt and my throat and mouth burned with the cold, but I didn't stop and kept swallowing, even when the first touches of a brain freeze set in.

Pushing past it, I took one last gulp, downing the last of it. Then I slammed the glass back on the table, and a beat later, a sharp pain gouged the sides of my head.

"Ow . . ." I sat back in the seat, pressing at my temples as the pain sharpened. "*Fuck*. Brain freeze."

"Was it worth it?"

My head felt like a block of ice, blindingly cold, and I shook my head as I watched Jesse laugh his ass off at me. "Totally."

"Talk about an *ice*breaker."

I giggled, which made my head throb even harder. "Talk about a *dad* joke."

17

My stomach felt unsettled as I walked up the steps to the Hartshornes' town house. I wasn't sure if it was because I was nervous or if it was the giant milkshake still digesting in my belly. I opened the door, which Natasha had left unlocked. As hurt as I was by her recent behavior, when she'd texted me that afternoon and told me that Mark was on call, and invited me over for dinner, I'd dropped everything to come. I'd been waiting for her to reach out to me. And besides, she was still my sister, and I wanted her to make it right between us.

"Serena?" I heard her voice ring out. "I'm in the kitchen!"

I took my shoes off. The hardwood floor was cold against my bare feet, and I was distracted momentarily by the Hartshornes' family cat, a whitish-gray tabby they called Reagan. (If it was a political reference, I didn't get it, especially because the whole family were registered Democrats.) A long corridor led to the open-plan kitchen at the back of house, which faced a dramatically landscaped yard.

Natasha was at the kitchen counter, chopping garlic. I'd never been over here with just the two of us, and for a moment I tried to imagine her life. Not just because of the family she married into, and all the bells and whistles that went along with their lifestyle, but because of her *life* as a married woman. As an expectant mother. She was wearing clothes I didn't recognize, quite a bit looser than what she typically wore, and if I hadn't known to look at her slightly thicker belly, I wouldn't have been able to tell she was pregnant.

What had it been like for her all this time? The experience of literally *growing* a baby, a life that was irrevocably attached to her own. She looked happy, but when I closed my eyes and tried to imagine myself in her place, all I felt was trapped.

"What are you doing over there?" she asked, her eyes not leaving the chopping board. "Come chop. We're making quesadillas."

My heart lurched. Besides Mom's cooking, that was my favorite meal. Maybe this was the olive branch I'd been waiting for.

I walked over to her and hugged her from behind, wrapping my arms around her shoulders. I didn't want her to see the mist in my eyes. After, I washed my hands and then joined her at the countertop.

"How are you? It feels like it's been forever."

I chopped through the onion, hard. The knife was extremely sharp, and it went through much easier than I'd anticipated. "It has been forever."

"I tell you what, I'm glad the first trimester is over. I can finally keep food down."

"Oh yeah?" I paused, waiting for the apology, for blowing me off at brunch, our spat in front of our parents. For the Evite. Anything, really.

"How's the new job?"

I hesitated, not yet wanting to switch conversation topics.

"Is that ginger one still being a bitch?"

I smiled, pleased that Natasha had remembered something about my life, and then filled her in on my warning shot at Ginger Spice that morning. It felt so good to talk to her, but at the same time, it was strange to be giving her an "update" the way you might an acquaintance, a relative you hadn't seen in a while. When we lived together, Natasha and I knew every single detail of each other's lives.

"Anyway," I continued, "things were a bit weird this afternoon after I got back from lunch . . ." I looked up, unsure of whether I was ready to tell Natasha I was back in touch with Jesse, but then I realized she'd stopped listening. She was taking a photograph of an arrangement of baby tomatoes and coriander on a wooden chopping board.

"*Anyway,*" I said again, watching her. She moved the chopping board to a different part of the counter, next to a vase of wildflowers, and then cleaned the knife she'd been using on the edge of a tea towel.

"Could you take a picture of me?" Without looking up, she handed me her phone. "Use portrait mode, yeah?"

The familiar knot in my stomach returned as I watched Natasha arrange her props, herself, her hair flowing down her back just so. She placed her left hand on her hip and her right on the slight curve of her belly. I was so shocked, I didn't even say anything; I just went along with it.

She made me take about a dozen pictures and then grabbed her phone back and sat herself up on a high-top stool. I finished chopping the garlic she'd abandoned, and from where I was standing a few feet away, I could see her screen. She was on Instagram, switching and testing filters. She didn't say anything, so I moved on to the tomatoes. Finally, minutes later, she looked up.

"Can you proofread my post?"

Had my mother and I not taught her how to say "please" and "thank you"? I shrugged, and I knew I looked annoyed, but she didn't seem to notice and simply slapped her phone into my hand and then hopped off the stool.

Sighing, I looked at the screen. She looked radiant in the filter she'd chosen, and I could tell she'd adjusted the saturation, because the tomatoes definitely weren't *that* green, yellow, and red in real life. I glanced down to the caption.

Me and #bean cooking up a storm! #bean #fiesta #pregnancy journey

My breath caught in my chest. She'd tagged Whole Foods, Everlane, and Williams Sonoma and had set the location to Georgetown. She'd even mentioned her unborn baby.

But she hadn't mentioned *me*.

"Smells good, girls!"

Natasha's phone nearly flew out of my hand. I looked up, startled, and standing there like a goddess in a white, flowing kimono, as if she'd just appeared out of thin air, was Mrs. Hartshorne.

Ugh.

"Mrs. H!" Natasha said. "How was yoga?"

"Brill, as usual. Serena, you're here! How *are* you, darling?"

Oh good lord. I wasn't prepared for this. I wiped my hands on a tea towel as she fanned her way toward me and, from across the counter, double kissed my cheeks.

"Great, thank you. What a surprise . . ." I tried to catch Natasha's eye, but she was thumbing her way through a cookbook. What was her mother-in-law doing here? I thought the Hartshornes traveled most of the time and stayed in town only a few nights here and there, coming and going from their family home in Bethesda. Wasn't that the whole reason Natasha and Mark had agreed to live here in the first place?

"I didn't realize you were in town . . ." I stammered. "Nice to see—"

"Of course we're here! We've been back a month now. Traveling *really* takes it out of you. First Hong Kong for business, and then I had to practically *force* Mr. H to take a week off with me in Ceylon—sorry, *no*, Sri Lanka . . ."

The Hartshornes had been living with Mark and Natasha for a whole month? Correction. Mark and Natasha had been living with the Hartshornes. If I wasn't so upset with Natasha, I'd definitely have teased her.

"*Then* to London," Mrs. Hartshorne said, continuing her monologue. "Brussels for a few weeks—more business, of course, although I had a chance to catch up with friends from boarding school. What *drama*, I tell you. Then Paris. It was supposed to be a full month there, but we didn't last five days."

I eyed Natasha, but her eyes were down on her phone.

"Of course, spring can be dreadful anywhere, *even* Paris. We thought we'd might as well be at home . . . Especially now that there's a bun in the oven!"

I continued chopping, and Mrs. H continued talking. And talking. After a monologue about how well she spoke French, even though Parisians claimed not to understand her, her words seemed to trail off.

Had Mrs. H finally stopped talking? I glanced up to confirm my suspicion, and indeed, she had.

"Paris," I said finally. I was struggling to form words; maybe I could have borrowed some from Mrs. Hartshorne. "I'd love to go."

She scrunched her nose, reaching for a bottle of Perrier. *Here we go again.*

"Weather. *Shit.* People. *Shit.* Even the service at the Hôtel de Crillon was *shit.*" She unscrewed the bottle and daintily took a sip from it. "I told Mr. H, I'm leaving. Stay if you must, but I'm leaving."

"Mark and I stayed at the Hôtel de Crillon when we went last fall," Natasha said, nodding. "They denied us a late checkout. Can you *imagine*?"

Can I *imagine*? I barely recognized the tone in Natasha's voice.

"We went to that restaurant you recommended, though," Natasha continued. "I tried the coq au vin—"

"No, *no*. You should have had the lamb. Their coq au vin is entirely ordinary. Trust the French to ruin French cuisine," she said, cutting Natasha off. "Girls, that is a *lot* of garlic. What are you making?"

"Quesadillas," Natasha said.

"*Quesadillas?* They have quite a bit of dairy, I *dare* say." Mrs. Hartshorne tapped her cheeks with the pads of her fingers. "Dairy makes us puffy, girls. Haven't you heard?"

I wondered if it had crossed her mind that the puffiness was from all the Botox.

Mrs. Hartshorne axed the quesadillas and overtook the kitchen. She instructed me to leave the dishes we'd already dirtied for their housekeeper, Pam, and started afresh on vegan tofu, broccoli, and brown rice bowls, which ended up tasting as bland as our conversation during meal prep.

It was a warm spring night, so we took our bowls out to the terrace, and I picked at the food while Mrs. Hartshorne and Natasha started talking about a charity gala they were both attending that weekend, and what they were wearing and who was going to be there. I tried to think of something to say, but I didn't know how to contribute.

My phone buzzed in my back pocket, and I was grateful for the interlude. I thought it would be Becket, maybe even Jesse. Surprisingly, it was Ainsley.

What are you up to this evening?

I hesitated, wondering how to respond. I hadn't really talked to her since she called me out for having lunch with Jesse. Both of us were in meetings most of the afternoon, and when we had crossed paths in the office, it had been downright awkward.

I'm having dinner with my sister and her mother-in-law. You?

My text wasn't exactly friendly, but it was the truth, and polite. A minute later, Ainsley replied.

I'm making a mess. If I'm not in tomorrow, alert the authorities. DEATH BY LASAGNA!

I smiled.

Death by lasagna?

She replied a beat later.

I thought I was making 4 servings . . . ended up with 4 trays! I don't know how to read a #$%&* recipe. As you can tell Nikesh usually cooks.

I laughed out loud but then stopped when I remembered Natasha and Mrs. Hartshorne were sitting next to me. They had moved on from the fundraiser.

"It's quite . . . common, isn't it?" Mrs. H asked.

"It is." Natasha nodded. "But the other ideas I've seen online are just so . . . *tacky*."

"Shame. You wouldn't want to be ordinary, now would you? But I suppose there's something to be said for tradition . . ."

Natasha brought a spoonful of rice to her lips. "I *suppose* we'll just have to make do."

"What are we talking about?" I asked, feigning interest.

"The gender reveal party," Natasha said. "We've settled on a cake for the reveal, but if you think of a more original way to do it, let me know."

I didn't respond. She wouldn't talk about the party with her own mother, but Natasha was including Mrs. Hartshorne?

"I picked up this fabulous little cake book in New York." Mrs. Hartshorne raised her eyebrow and practically shimmied out of her chair. "You know me and my *books.*" She slid open the patio door. "I'm so glad we're doing this together, girls. I'm *happy* to help. I know you girls grew up . . . differently."

My mouth gaped open as I watched her disappear inside.

Differently?

I looked over at Natasha. She was playing with a piece of broccoli in her bowl and looked up when she caught me staring.

"What?"

"Did she really just say that to you?"

"What are you talking about?"

I guffawed. "She said we grew up 'differently.' What the hell does that mean?"

"Don't be so sensitive." Natasha rolled her eyes, stretching her arms up and back over her head. "You know exactly what she means. Mom and Dad didn't exactly prepare us for the real world. I'm learning a lot from Mrs. H."

Like how to eat dairy-free food and attend fancy parties? How to speak like a pretentious jerk?

"I know you helped me out a lot with the wedding, but she did, too. She made it *beautiful*, elegant. It was exactly what I wanted." Natasha scowled. "Mom and Dad's idea of a wedding would have been, I don't know, streamers and confetti in the basement of the *gurdwara*, with an old guy beating a *dhol.*"

I looked down at my hands, shaking. "Why couldn't you just

let Mom host your gender reveal party?" I didn't mean for my voice to sound angry, but it did. I *was* angry.

"I already told you—"

"She's excited for you. She wants to feel involved, and you didn't even have the decency to tell her the date before sending out the Evite?" I took another deep breath, trying not to raise my voice. "If you're not going to let her host it, at least let *her* help pick out the cake." I lowered my voice, glancing behind me. "The wedding was all about what the Hartshornes wanted—"

"Of course it was. They paid for it!"

"That's not the point—"

"This is really rich coming from *you*, Serena." Natasha glared at me, leaning forward on the table. "Suddenly, you care about what Mom and Dad think? You're never even there! I go home to visit all the time—"

"To visit or to put your feet up so Mom can serve you *roti*?" I snapped.

"Serena," Natasha said, her words biting, "I go home to spend *time* with them. Something you would know nothing about—"

"Everything all right, girls?"

We both turned to look. Mrs. Hartshorne was back. I swallowed hard, the bile rising in my throat as I watched her display her fucking cake book on the table.

I hated her, and in that moment, I hated Natasha, too. She was a selfish brat. Had she always been, and had I just enabled her? I thought back to every sweet moment between us, every thoughtful gesture. Like how she'd noticed me flirting with Becket at the reception and invited him to the after-party. Had she really cared, or did she just not want to have to worry about her big, single sister putting a damper on her wedding night?

She'd wanted me involved in her wedding, sure. But I didn't

give the toast. She'd only asked me for help with all the unglamorous organization tasks nobody else wanted, to MC the wedding because she knew I could fend off the Uncle Singhs from the microphone. And she'd moved into my spare room and lived there for years, but was it to actually live with *me*? Or had she just wanted cheap rent, an escape from our parents, and later, a crash pad on the nights she didn't stay over at Mark's?

Even tonight. She'd wanted to make quesadillas. Did she even know they were my favorite? I pressed my hand over my mouth, hard, when it occurred to me that she didn't.

Quesadillas were Natasha's favorite, too.

Mrs. Hartshorne droned on and on about the pros and cons of the traditional layer cake, the naked cake, fruit-based cakes, and as I sat there, all the guilt, sadness, and confusion I'd felt about my relationship with Natasha just sort of faded away.

Natasha and I were never really best friends. And even if we were, I realized that I didn't *want* to be anymore.

And maybe my friendships with other women *hadn't* faded because they chose marriage and motherhood. Although it was likely a factor, it couldn't have been the only reason. It took two people to let a friendship go. And even though Natasha would always be my sister, I was ready to move on from this one, too.

I pulled out my phone and was suddenly desperate to be away from Mrs. Hartshorne's castle of dairy-free cakes and tofu bowls, hungry for something more substantial.

Four whole trays of lasagna, huh? Do you have enough to feed a friendly neighbor?

My heart raced as I watched the message go from sent to delivered to read.

Oh god yes! You're not a vegetarian, are you? I will pay you to come over and help me eat this.

"Unfortunately, duty calls," I lied. "I have to run back to the office."

"What a shame . . ." Mrs. Hartshorne lifted her hand from the cake book, which she'd been flipping through, and pressed her hand against her chest. She looked about as heartbroken as she did the previous summer when, during a family dinner, she'd found out her aunt had died. "You work *so* hard, Serena."

"Well, I love my job."

"Good for you."

Good that I loved my job, or that I was one of those ordinary people who actually needed one?

"Anyway, thank you for dinner. It was very . . . tasty." I smiled at Mrs. Hartshorne and then Natasha, but she wouldn't look me in the eye. "I had a nice time."

"Always lovely to have you, dear. Come anytime. Don't I say that, Natasha? Invite your sister. Make her bring her boyfriend—"

"She never brings home her boyfriends."

I stood up, forcing out a smile as I cleared the bowls. I was heartbroken, but it was just a fact now. The pain was gone. I think I'd already grieved.

"Leave the dishes," I heard Natasha say. "Pam will get them."

I stared at her, blinking.

"Pam," Natasha repeated, reaching for her phone. "The *housekeeper*?"

Ainsley's town house was warm and cozy. Friendly. MacKenzie was already in bed, and Ainsley said Nikesh was out in the garage working on his "brew." She said it sarcastically but with so much love and affection I could tell she was proud of him. I felt slightly awkward for having invited myself over. At the same time, being over here felt totally natural.

"I'm sorry," I said suddenly. We had taken our plates of lasagna to the couch, and I set mine down on the coffee table. "It got pretty weird at work today."

"It was my fault. I overstepped. Your relationships are your business."

"But maybe you're right." I shrugged. "Maybe I should tell Becket I've been spending time with Jesse."

She shrugged. "Did you feel guilty when you saw him today?"

Was our lunch of fried eggs and milkshakes only today? It felt like ages ago.

I shook my head. "Nothing's going on between us. But the optics are bad whether I say something or not."

"Optics. Ha!" She laughed. "You're such an adman."

"Oh, *whatever.* But you get it, right? Not telling Becket about Jesse makes it seem like I'm hiding something. But if I told him? It would just give rise to suspicion."

"Well, I suppose if I was in Becket's position, I'd want to know. And if you're having a talk, you might as well make clear you're not planning to have a fam—damn it! Sorry. I'm overstepping again."

"You're not. You're being a good friend. And I guess . . . *friends* sometimes say things you don't want to hear." I laughed, lifting my feet up onto the couch. "Anyway, let's change the subject. We're both failing the Bechdel test right now."

"Fuck the Bechdel test." Ainsley rolled her eyes. "Sometimes, two women just need to sit and chat about dudes, and it doesn't make us any less feminist, now does it?"

She smiled at me as she wiped a bit of tomato sauce from her cheek. We'd only known each other for a few months, but suddenly I couldn't imagine a time when she wasn't in my life. When I wouldn't want her to be in my life.

"Ainsley," I said, shyly. "I really like you."

"Aw, shucks, girl. I'm married."

"Shut *up*." I laughed.

"Sorry."

"You know what I mean," I said. "I really like being friends with you, and I want to be . . ."

"Friendlier?"

"*Yeah.* I want to be like . . . Joey and Chandler on *Friends.*"

Ainsley nodded. "Oprah Winfrey and gal pal Gayle?"

"Kate Winslet and Leo."

"I didn't know they were friends," she said.

"They are. Since the *Titanic* went down."

Ainsley grinned, shoveling another bite of lasagna into her mouth. "So we're taking this to the next level, huh? Should we go get our nails done together?"

"Girl," I said, flipping my hair. "Let's go to Vegas!"

"Girl," she repeated. "I want to meet your *parents.*"

"Wow," I said, laughing, kicking her with my feet. "Now you're getting ahead of yourself."

We went on like that for a while, and after the giggles had passed, I thanked her for letting me come over and told her all about my evening with Natasha and Mrs. Hartshorne. Quickly, I found myself telling Ainsley a lot of things. About my deteriorating relationship with my so-called best friend. My quest to find new friends, regain the social circle I'd had when I was younger. The book club disaster.

The sex club, too.

"I totally get it," she said later, after she was done laughing at me. "It's harder to make friends as an adult. When I go back home, I see my group of girlfriends, and it's like nothing has changed, even though *everything* has changed. We're thirty years older."

I nodded, understanding exactly what she meant. On the rare occasion I saw my school friends, we had a great time together. It was fun and wonderful; it's just that those occasions didn't happen very often.

"So when you have to start over," Ainsley continued, "like I did when moving here, like you're doing now in this stage of life, it's *hard.* Because it's hard to create a friendship from scratch, without history. It's a lot of effort, and especially when you're a grown-up with responsibilities who still wants to sleep seven hours a night, it's hard to make time for that effort."

Ainsley had articulated everything so clearly. I'd been searching out all these ways to meet new, like-minded people, but I couldn't just expect a new friend to appear out of nowhere. It took work. It took effort. And whether it was motherhood, marriage, a demanding career, or something else entirely, there were a lot of other demands on our time.

"It is a lot of effort," I said, after a moment had passed. "But I reckon you're worth it."

"Girl," Ainsley said, stuffing a pillow behind her head. "You *know* I'm worth it."

The house was silent except for the white noise coming from the baby monitor by Ainsley's feet and the occasional clang from the garage outside. We continued eating our lasagna, and its warmth spread from my stomach and into the rest of my body.

"Hey, Serena . . ." Ainsley said, a few minutes later.

"Yeah?"

"Can we circle back to the fact that your sister nicknamed her fetus *Bean*?"

Want to play Settlers of Catan?" I asked, unfolding myself from his arms. I twisted my upper body, turning back to face him on the couch. Becket's eyes were half closed.

"Don't you need at least three people for that one?"

I paused. "Scrabble, then?"

He laughed, and with his eyes still closed, he lifted his arms up, flailing them around like a zombie until they found my waist, and he pulled me back down flat on the couch.

I sighed, looking at our dishes on the coffee table, the dirty pots and pans in the sink, my work laptop on the counter, my running shoes in the foyer. There were a million productive things I could be doing right now on a Friday night—ones that I was used to doing on a Friday night. Meal prepping while finally watching the new Netflix show everyone was talking about. Exercising. Catching up on a week's worth of news, having only had time to cast an eye over the headlines during the week.

It was early May now, and we'd just sailed past the three-month mark. (Although, thankfully, neither of us wanted to make a big deal about it.) We were getting comfortable—*I* was getting comfortable—and this was usually the point in the relationship when guys walked away. Because they were players and got bored or felt emasculated. Sometimes, they grew tired of my busy schedule, feeling that I didn't make enough space in my life for them. One time, to quote, he got "sick of feeling like the chick in the relationship." (Boy, was *he* a winner.)

But Becket wasn't walking away or complaining or asking anything of me other than what I had to offer. And right now that was two or so evenings a week, a phone call and a few texts throughout the day, and no more. I hadn't seen him since the previous weekend—we'd both had a busy few days—and earlier that evening, he'd shown up with a smile on his face and a canvas bag full of udon, fresh shrimp, and bok choy. Things were going well. They were exactly how I wanted them to be, and I definitely didn't want anything to change.

I knew Ainsley thought I should have "the talk" with Becket, clarify what I wanted my future to look like so we could decide if that picture matched his own. But why ruin a good thing? Becket seemed equally intent on enjoying the present and worrying about the rest—well—in the *future.*

My phone buzzed, and I leaped for it. It was Ainsley, and I smiled at the fact that we were thinking about each other at the exact same time.

What's your opinion on Amy Poehler?

I giggled. That was random.

WHY?? Please tell me she's not canceled. I loved Parks and Rec!!

I set my phone back down and slid my bum to the other side of the couch, tucking my legs underneath Becket. "You sure you don't want to *do* something tonight? Should we go see that new Marvel movie?"

"No." Becket shook his head, his black hair flopping around like a shaggy dog. "I'm perfect here." He paused. "Who was that, by the way?"

"Ainsley."

"It seems like you two are really hitting it off?" He opened his eyes, winking. "Sounds like you have a new *buddy*."

"I do." I grinned. "She's the best."

"Well, I'm glad you found her. After all those crazy friend dates you went on, who knew that your perfect match was sitting fifteen feet away from you the whole time."

"Uh-huh . . ."

"And all anyone really needs in life is one good friend, right?"

I didn't answer as I stood up from the couch and cleared the dishes. I put them in the sink and then turned around. Becket was looking at me, the back of his head in his palms, his elbows jutting out wide. Once again, I started hearing Ainsley's voice. There was something else she thought I should clarify with Becket. And about that, at least, she was probably right.

"I made another new friend, recently," I said to Becket, wiping my hands with a tea towel. "Jesse."

"The catfish?"

I rolled my eyes.

"The woman from the *sex club*?"

I laughed, shaking my head. "Not Jessie, as in Jessica. *Jesse.* As in Jasmeet. I met him during my third year of university." I paused. "We dated for a while."

"Huh." In one swift movement, Becket sat straight up on the couch. "What's a *while*?"

"Four years."

"Uh-huh."

"I haven't seen him since I was twenty-four. So basically a lifetime ago." I paused a few feet in front of him on the couch. "I ran into him a few weeks ago after book club. He was at the same bar."

Still, Becket didn't respond. I couldn't tell if he was jealous or not. I'd never seen him express an emotion other than variegated shades of happiness.

"You have nothing to worry about, OK?" I sat down next to him and squeezed his hand, as if my touching him could prove it. "Becket. Can you say something?"

He looked at me, as if he wanted me to keep talking. To say something that would reassure him in better, more articulate words that it was Becket who I cared for, not Jesse. Becket who I wanted to spend my Friday nights with. I tucked a stray piece of hair away from his forehead, letting my fingers drag down his cheek, the stubbled contour of his jawline. Something deep inside me ached, and without thinking, I kissed him. Hard and raw and deep, and we were both breathless by the time he pulled away.

"OK, OK." Becket laughed, wiping his lips with the back of his hand. "I believe you. I have nothing to worry about."

I smiled, kissing him again. "Good."

"Can you humor me, though, Serena?" Becket set his hand on my knee closest to him, pulling at it. "Can you tell me when you see him? I don't want to feel like you're sneaking around."

"I'll tell you. I promise." I paused. "Is there anything else you want to know?"

I tensed up, waiting for the questions I wasn't sure I could answer truthfully.

"How many times have you seen him, since the bar?" Becket asked, after a moment had passed. I could tell that he wanted to ask more but that he wouldn't. I breathed out a tiny sigh of relief.

"Just once. We went for lunch earlier this week."

"Lunch." Becket nodded, and I could tell by the tone of his voice and the pressure of his body that this fact had brightened his mood. "Lunch is . . . *good*. I love lunch."

I knew what he meant by that comment. Lunch meant meeting during daylight hours; implicitly, it meant boundaries.

I thought about telling Becket of the rules I'd set for Jesse and our friendship to ensure those boundaries were kept, but something told me Becket would perceive them as a further cause to worry, rather than reassure him.

19

The month of May flew by. I packed away my tights, sweaters, and wool skirts at the top of my closet, trading them for the summer dresses and breathable cotton garments I'd need soon, as DC's sticky, hot summer crept in. The weather was perfect when I woke up in the morning, and on the days Ainsley didn't work from home, we'd bus or walk to work together, one of Nikesh's cold brews in hand as we chatted about anything. Everything. Sometimes, it seemed, absolutely nothing. But it wasn't just Ainsley I was becoming close to; it was her whole family.

Nikesh and MacKenzie were a huge part of her life, and I loved that they were part of our friendship, too. I'd see them at the farmers market on Saturday mornings, sometimes with Becket, who got along with Nikesh famously. I even made Indian food for everyone one night, while Becket babyproofed all the sharp edges of my apartment with Bubble Wrap. Mom was so proud that I was cooking. I took pictures of every dish and texted them to her.

It was tense at home, more so than usual. And for the first time in my life, it wasn't because of me. It wasn't Serena refusing to go to *gurdwara* or bringing home a guy at the age of twenty or getting a neck tattoo for all the aunties to see. Moving out before she was married. Saying out loud that she didn't ever want to get married.

It was Natasha.

Mom would never say a bad word behind someone's back, let alone her favorite daughter, but every single day when I called Mom, I could tell she was upset with her. Even I was upset with Natasha. The pain of losing Natasha's friendship had started to subside, but I still couldn't believe the way she was treating our mother. Excluding her from her life and her pregnancy, acting like she was ashamed of where she came from. According to Mom, Natasha wouldn't even let her bring a dish to the gender reveal party. (Just let the woman make you samosas, you brat! Everyone likes them.)

The day of the party finally arrived on a sunny, balmy Sunday in early June, and somehow, I'd managed to convince Ainsley to come along with MacKenzie. Becket and I walked over to their house at the appointed time and found her strapping MacKenzie into the car seat in the back of her truck. She was more dressed up than usual. She rarely dealt with clients or had external meetings in her role, so her wardrobe was a roster of jeans and trendy T-shirts. I don't think I'd ever seen her with makeup on or in a dress, and the emerald-green material contrasted well with her bright red hair and made her eyes pop. We walked up the driveway, and I let out a long whistle.

Ainsley leaned her head out of the car, grinning.

"Looking good, Woods!"

"I waxed my armpits for this, Singh. It better be a good party!" Ainsley walked down to meet us, giving Becket a warm embrace. "Nikesh is inside. I warn you, he might make you taste test his new brew." Ainsley lowered her voice. "Cumin. Seriously, I almost threw up."

Becket laughed. "I've lived off generic brand instant coffee for fifteen years. I can drink anything."

I kissed him goodbye, and we watched him walk into the house to hang out with Nikesh. From what I heard about their plans, they were going to drink beer and watch "the game," and even though I had no idea what sport would be on, I half wished Ainsley and I could stay home and join them.

"Is he upset?"

I turned to Ainsley. She was looking at me, her arms slightly crossed. "Becket? No. Why would he be?"

"He didn't want you to invite him to Natasha's party?"

I shook my head. I had been a little worried Becket was expecting an invitation, but luckily, he'd brought up the subject first and suggested he stay behind. That bringing over the new boyfriend would take away the attention from Natasha and Mark. This worked out perfectly because, to be honest, the possibility of inviting Becket—introducing him to my family—hadn't even crossed my mind.

"That's so thoughtful," Ainsley said when I told her what Becket had said. "Or . . ."

"Or?"

"He's putting the brake on." Ainsley paused. "Does that bother you?"

"Bother me?" I rolled my eyes. "It *thrills* me. It means Becket and I are on the exact same page."

We showed up right on time, but dozens of guests had already arrived. The main floor of the Hartshornes' town house had been transformed by an absurd number of fairy lights hanging from the ceiling. It looked beautiful. Instagrammable. But it didn't look anything like the Natasha I used to know.

I caught sight of her and Mark on the love seat across the

room, posing for pictures with their friends, a two-tiered cake just in front of them. She was wearing a flowing off-white dress, and she was showing even more than the last time I'd seen her. I choked up just looking at her.

"Are you sure it's OK for MacKenzie and I to be here?" I heard Ainsley say, and I turned to her quickly, thankful for the interruption. She looked anxious, which was odd to me, because the way she commanded herself in the office with her team, I'd never seen her anything less than confident before.

"Of course it is," I said. "It's BYOB. Bring your own baby?"

Ainsley followed me to the kitchen, where we set out the bottle of prosecco and a bottle of nonalcoholic sparkling apple cider we'd picked up from the farmers market the previous morning.

"What *do* we have here, girls?"

A shiver ran down my spine, and I took a moment to plaster a huge grin on my face before I turned around to face her.

"Mrs. Hartshorne. *So* nice to see you."

"You didn't need to bring anything—*we* specifically said in the invite *not* to bring anything."

"Oh, it was no bother—"

"Let's put these away, shall we?" She stiffly grabbed the bottles and then craned her neck around. "Pam? *Pam?*"

A young woman appeared as if out of thin air, and Mrs. Hartshorne practically threw the bottles at her and then wiped her hands together, as if they were covered in dust. "On the dining table, Pam? With the rest of the *guest* wine?"

She smiled at me crisply. I suppose I was a *guest*.

"And who is *this*?" Mrs. H said, looking over.

"I'm Ainsley. And this wee one is MacKenzie."

"MacKenzie. *Hello.*" Mrs. Hartshorne beamed. "What a lovely name. How old?"

"He's two—"

"A lovely age." She nodded, cutting Ainsley off. She leaned against the counter, tossing back her head, dramatically. "I'm just so *thrilled* I'll be a grandmum soon. First time, you know! I thought Bethany would be the first; she's a few years older. But . . ." She trailed off, and I understood why. Natasha had told me all about Mark's sister. These days, Bethany and her husband were a bit too preoccupied with party drugs to be thinking about having their own gender reveal party.

"Anyhoo!" Mrs. Hartshorne said brightly, just as I was about to come up with a reason to excuse ourselves. "I can't tell you how long I've been looking forward to this afternoon, and I can't quite *believe* that it's here. That I'll know in"—she glanced at her gold Fitbit—"twenty-two minutes whether I'll finally have a little granddaughter!" She paused, coming up for air. Sometimes I wondered if she had gills and didn't really have to breathe like us humans at all.

"I know I'm not supposed to have a preference. But I do. Is that terribly *naughty*?"

I opened my mouth to reply, but she continued.

"I shouldn't say it out loud. I wouldn't want to *jinx* it." She looked up suddenly, as if remembering she had an audience. "Annalise, did you have a preference?"

Ainsley gave me a look as she gently shifted MacKenzie, who had fallen asleep in her arms. "It's Ainsley. And no, I didn't. My husband and I only hoped that our baby would be healthy."

"Well, of course you did." Mrs. Hartshorne sounded annoyed, as if she'd been told off. "Still, it's hard to believe that you didn't even have a *slight* preference. At your gender reveal, didn't you—"

"We didn't have a gender reveal," Ainsley said, cutting her off.

So *that* was how you got Mrs. H to shut up. You needed to interrupt her.

"I mean," Ainsley continued, "at the end of the day, isn't gender just a social construct?"

I coughed, choking down a laugh as I covered my mouth with my palm.

"And even if MacKenzie was born the male sex, and it's his *assigned* gender right now, that doesn't necessarily mean that's truly his gender, if he even has one, does it?" She paused. "And the same goes with your future grandchild."

Mrs. Hartshorne looked horrified. I was literally dying, and I had no idea how Ainsley was keeping a straight face.

"So this whole social directive that parents—particularly mothers—have to have a *party* to celebrate something society still doesn't really understand is . . . really quite toxic." Ainsley smiled brightly. "Don't you think?"

"I . . . I . . ."

I'd never seen Mrs. Hartshorne at a loss for words. She looked utterly bamboozled. I felt like hugging Ainsley. It was glorious.

"Well, then," Mrs. Hartshorne said finally, as she pretended to wave at someone across the room. "Host duty calls. Refreshments are *that* way, girls."

"Girls?" Ainsley said, after she'd stalked off. "Last time I checked, I wasn't a girl. *Girls* don't have cellulite, and they're not pre-premenopausal."

"Pre-*pre*menopausal?"

"It's a thing. Google it."

I rolled my eyes. "I'm sure it is. Anyway, thank you for telling her off like that. I've never had the courage."

"I'm sure you would have if she wasn't your sister's mother-in-law." Ainsley winked. "Lucky for me, after this party, I'm never going to see her again in my life."

Ainsley and I made our way to the "refreshments" table and

helped ourselves to glasses of ginseng and coconut water. (The theme of the party seemed to be *snob*.) While pouring our glasses, I caught sight of a woman I once knew well. Very well. Jasmine looked exactly the same, but her hair was shorter and now a trendy gray-brown, rather than the bottle blond she used to rock. She had a toddler in one arm and was dragging a young, crying child with her other hand.

Our eyes met. She let go of the child and waved at me, smiling brightly, but then noticed that the crying child was now dry of tears and was darting toward the dessert table. I could hear her whisper a curse word, the one I'd heard her say countless times under her breath in class, at the gym, or to describe her now wife, yearly, when she forgot their anniversary.

I waved back, smiling, but I don't think she saw me. She was running after the escaped child.

"Who's that?" Ainsley asked, looking after her. "Do you want me to tell her off, too?"

I shook my head. "No. She's lovely, actually. Her name is Jasmine. We went to business school together."

"Have I heard about Jasmine before?"

I shook my head. "No, but I was . . . her bridesmaid."

Ainsley's jaw dropped.

"I helped plan her four-day bachelorette in Atlantic City."

"Atlantic City?"

"We stayed at one of Trump's hotels. Mind you, this was way before he ran for president."

"Still!"

"She wanted to have a *Jersey Shore*–themed night out," I said flatly. "We used to watch it religiously. Obviously, I dressed as Snooki."

"Jesus Christ." Ainsley laughed. "I can't *imagine* the pictures. No wonder you're not on Facebook."

I smiled, remembering the good old days. Jasmine was a few years younger than me, and because I'd included Natasha in every part of my life, she'd become friends with her, too. I should have known that she might be here.

I made a note to go seek her out later and reconnect. When had we grown apart? The details were blurry, and it pained me to realize that, whatever the reason, I'd been at fault, too.

More guests were arriving by the minute. The invite had stated that the grand reveal would be at three p.m. *sharp*, and now we were only seventeen minutes away. I scanned the room for Mom and Dad but couldn't find them. I hoped they'd arrive soon; the Hartshornes ran a tight ship, and I wasn't sure they'd delay the reveal.

There was a joke the younger generations liked to tell about the "aunties and uncles" who always showed up late, sometimes hours late, that they still ran on "Indian Standard Time." I mentioned this to Ainsley, which made her laugh so hard that it woke up MacKenzie, and she had to go into the other room to change him.

Ainsley declined my offer to help, so I waved to the few people I knew there and mingled with Natasha and Mark's friends, even some of the Hartshornes' friends. They were all very nice, down-to-earth people, and I felt bad for having felt so judgmental about the party, about this world. Working in advertising, I had to think of target demographics, commonalities, but the truth was people were all different. Just because Mrs. Hartshorne was a stone-cold WASP (I could sell her anything if I tried) didn't mean all of her friends were.

There were children everywhere: well-behaved ones dutifully sitting or standing by their parents; rambunctious children, on a mission to seek out any possible household object that could present danger; sleeping children all over the place, a few—to Mrs. Hartshorne's visible annoyance—even on the floor.

"He's so tired today," Ainsley said, coming up to me just as I was excusing myself from a conversation with one of Mark's frat bros. "He wants to sleep *on* me. Not anywhere else. Serena, my neck is killing me. Would you try holding him for a bit?"

She instructed me to sit down in an armchair, gently placed MacKenzie in my arms, and then tucked a cushion behind my back. I leaned into it, as MacKenzie nestled into me, wrapped his chubby little legs and arms around my body. His eyes closed immediately, and his weight felt good on me, like I was cold and in desperate need of a wool blanket.

"You're a natural."

I didn't answer, my eyes not leaving MacKenzie.

"Oh, hey. I met your parents." I could tell she was grinning by the tone of her voice. "And you wanted to keep our friendship casual . . ."

"Ainsley the comedian," I said, pausing. "So they've arrived. Good. I was worried they'd be late."

"Your mom is very sweet. *So* sweet. And your dad is *hilarious*, oh my god! My father-in-law barely looks me in the eye."

My body stiffened as she spoke.

"They're *so* lovely, Serena. I wish I'd married into your Indian family."

"I doubt it . . ." MacKenzie was dreaming. I could tell. He was gently wriggling in my arms, and his eyelids and lashes were fluttering rapidly. What was he dreaming about? Wherever he was in that moment, I hoped he was safe. I hoped that I could protect him.

"Where are they?" I asked after a while, looking up. Ainsley gestured across the room, and I followed her gaze. Mom and Dad were now wedged awkwardly on the love seat, posing for a photo with Natasha and Mark. You could never tell by the look of pure joy on Mom's face that she was upset with Natasha, even though I knew she felt wronged and hurt for being excluded. You could never tell with Mom.

Dad was also smiling, and for a moment I let myself study his face, the crow's-feet that were now set in. His dark gray hair, still thick on the top of his head, a slightly lighter shade than his beard. He said something, and everyone in his vicinity laughed. A part of me wanted to know what he said, how he felt. Anything.

Suddenly, he looked up. He held my gaze, and I in turn held his. He looked so sad, and I hated him for it. He tilted his chin ever so gently, a movement that would have been imperceptible to anyone else in the room, but I knew what it meant.

Come take a picture with the family.

Come here. Please? Come back to us.

I swallowed hard and looked down, pretending I hadn't noticed the look. Pretending, like I had my whole life, that I hadn't noticed anything.

I couldn't help it as the water welled in my nose, my eyes. A single tear dropped, splashed onto MacKenzie's little earlobe, and I quickly wiped it away.

A moment passed, and out of the corner of my eye, I saw Ainsley crouch down beside me. Had she seen it, too? She leaned in and pulled out a tissue from her bra.

"Do you want to talk about it?" she whispered. I pressed MacKenzie into me, his sweet, warm breath against my chest, and shook my head.

Summer

20

Jesse: You like banh mi, right? Be at our bench in ten.

Our bench? I shook my head, stretching my hands upward as I stood up from my desk. I would have to remind Jesse of the ground rules for our friendship. It was not "our" bench. It just happened to be a wide, two-person seat in front of the National Geographic Museum, where we met once in a while to eat lunch now that the weather had turned warm. He sat on his side of the bench, and I sat on mine.

I invited Ainsley and Tracy to join us as I headed out the door, but both of them declined, as they had remembered to bring their lunch that day. (The fact that it felt perfectly normal to invite others along to our lunches felt like validation that Jesse's and my friendship was nothing other than completely appropriate.) I took the stairs down the few flights, smiling as I pushed open the door, and swapped out my wire frames for my pair of prescription aviators.

I loved early summer, when it was hot but not oppressively so, and there was still a certain energy to the city. A rhythm I could feel while waiting for a walk light. Running up the stairs from a Metro station. Staring out the south-facing window near my desk.

And I felt different, too. I finally felt settled into my job and was gaining confidence with my pitches, my clients, even my coworkers.

Ginger Spice clearly still hated my guts, but since I'd put her on probation, at least she was trying to hide it better. I now spent the day largely enjoying social interactions with my coworkers and felt lighter leaving the office each evening rather than worn-out. I spent evenings and weekends hanging out with Becket, on FaceTime with Mom while she gave me cooking tips, and increasingly, with Ainsley. We had started walking home together after work, too, and often took turns going to each other's houses for dinner. (I always invited along Nikesh and MacKenzie to my apartment, although sometimes Ainsley insisted she needed a night off and wanted to come alone.) And then there were my weekly lunch dates with Jesse, who was turning out to be a really great friend.

My job had become no less demanding, and there were still the same number of hours in a day, but I'd discovered that I did have time for a fuller life. Because it was other people that made life meaningful.

"Hey, buddy," I said cheerfully, as I approached the bench. He was already there, seated, two brown paper packages laid out next to him.

"Chicken or tofu?"

I hesitated and then arbitrarily picked the one closest to me.

"That's the tofu."

"I *love* tofu."

Jesse grinned, reaching for his own sandwich. "You're in a good mood."

"What's not to feel good about? It's summer. *And*," I added, remembering that we were about to have a few days off work, "it's nearly the Fourth of July."

We started eating and, mouths full, updated each other on the past week since we'd last met. My updates largely revolved around Ainsley, work, or my latest attempt at Mom's recipe for *baingan bharta* or *daal* in the kitchen. And most of Jesse's were about his children, Maya and Ajay.

"Hold on a second." Jesse set down his sandwich, fishing his phone from his pocket with just his thumb and pinky—the other fingers being covered in sriracha. With his little finger, he swiped on the screen, and a moment later a smile appeared on his face.

I closed my eyes, a memory appearing that I didn't want to be reminded of.

Jesse smiling, exactly like that, as he flipped open his old Nokia to show me a text.

Serena? Check it out. Your dad just invited me over to watch the Washington game. Can you believe it? I'm in!

"Serena?"

Jesse's voice snapped me back to the present, and I opened my eyes. He was looking at me, holding his phone outward to face me.

"I said, do you want to see?"

I nodded without knowing what I was agreeing to look at. The sun was bright, and I blinked as the screen came into focus.

It was a video of Maya and Ajay, sent by their mother earlier that day. Maya was sitting at a kitchen table with her sunglasses on attempting to beatbox while her little brother banged on bowls with a spatula and a wooden spoon. It made me laugh.

"Funny, right?" Jesse grinned, tucking his phone away. "Maya's got talent. I've shown you the video of her choir concert, haven't I?"

I nodded. He'd shown me twice.

"I think she could be the next Ariana Grande. I think she could be . . . anything she wants."

My breath caught, so I ripped off a huge chunk of my banh

mi with my teeth. The tofu was spicy—Jesse always ordered food extra hot—and it burned my mouth. I chewed fast, and within a few bites it was all gone. I wiped the sauce from the corners of my lips with a napkin, trying to ignore the pulsing in my stomach.

He was a good, loving father. I knew that already, but each time he talked about them, the realization hit me like a shock wave.

I'd kept my head down during school and university, always focusing on the next exam or goal. Until Jesse, boys were just a fun distraction. Until Jesse, I hadn't actually considered what I wanted my future to look like. If that future included children.

It turned out it didn't, and until recently, I didn't even enjoy being near children. They downright annoyed me on planes and in restaurants, and I couldn't handle how coddled some of them seemed to be these days. But lately, I didn't mind them so much. I still didn't want kids of my own—that I was sure about—but the first thing I did whenever going to Ainsley's house was to seek out MacKenzie. Hold him, play with him, volunteer to feed him or even change his diaper. (Gross. But also kind of sweet?) And I was even beginning to feel myself getting attached to Maya and Ajay, just by virtue of Jesse talking about them so much.

I'd told myself I'd lost touch with so many people when they became parents because they were busy. And that's true. But maybe I'd also accepted their excuses and longer and longer gaps between visits because I didn't want to be included in their new life. A life I couldn't imagine.

My stomach hurt, but not from the spice of the banh mi. Natasha was having a boy. Everyone had celebrated when she and Mark had cut into the blue cake. (Including Mrs. Hartshorne, even though I noted her Botoxed mouth momentarily falter into a frown of disappointment.) And as we all cried and cheered and hugged, inside I'd felt a sick, sinking feeling at my very core.

Some would call it biological, my ovaries screaming to me that if I wanted *this*, too, that I'd better hurry up. But I knew myself better. I wanted to know this little boy the same way I was craving to know MacKenzie, or Jesse's children. If the parent *meant* something to me, then the child would, too. But would I get to know my nephew if I didn't mend my relationship with Natasha? I hadn't spoken or heard from Natasha since the gender reveal, and if we could fix it, I wasn't even sure how to go about it.

"Are you going to finish that?" I heard Jesse say. He leaned in so close I could smell his aftershave.

I pushed his face away. "Yes, I am."

"I went jogging this morning. I'm hungry."

"I'm hungry, too."

"But I gave you the bigger one," he whined, pulling on it.

I tugged it back. "Sucks to be you, bro."

I looked up at him just as the sun dipped behind a cluster of trees, and his face became more visible. He hadn't shaved that morning. His stubble was thicker than usual, and I couldn't help but wonder what he'd look like with a full-grown beard, the way a lot of Sikh men wore it. Most clean-shaven Sikh men, like Jesse, grew out their beards for their weddings, for religious reasons, but also because it looked good in photos with a turban, fancy kurta pajama, and kirpan. I quickly scanned Jesse's face, wondering if he had gone full beard for his wedding, too, when I spotted a zit on his cheek.

"What?" he asked me.

I stared at his face just a beat longer. It was massive, and I wondered how I hadn't noticed it earlier. Had I not looked at him directly this entire time?

"Fine," I said. "You can have it." I lifted the remaining half sandwich from the sticky paper it came in, and a second after handing it to Jesse, it was gone. As he chewed, I snuck another glance. The pimple was pink, like a flesh wound, and white at its volcanic tip. I shivered. It was *staring* at me.

"Why you being weird?" he asked.

"I'm not being weird." I leaned my head back until it rested against the bench, and the sunlight beamed down on my face. "Ah. This is heaven."

"Being here with me?"

"Oh, quiet down."

I sat up straight, and in my peripheral vision, again, I saw the zit. It had grown larger. Gargantuan. I leaned slightly away, in awe of it, ready for my escape. It had taken on a new life of its own and was coming for me.

"Serena, seriously," I heard Jesse say. "We need to talk."

"Huh?"

I couldn't stop myself from staring. It was taking up my whole field of vision.

"Serena, you can't do this. We can't be friends if . . ." He trailed off, and I forced myself to look away from the zit and into Jesse's eyes. He looked genuinely stressed, and I had no idea what about.

"We can't be friends if I what, exactly . . . ?"

"If you keep looking like you *want* me!"

"*Excuse me?*"

"You were just looking at me like you're longing for me. All that *Pride and Prejudice* crap." He threw his hands up, exasperated. "We can't, OK? You have a boyfriend. And I'm still in a weird place. We wouldn't be a good idea right now—"

I burst out laughing, cutting him off. I laughed so hard my lungs hurt and tears poured from my eyes.

"What? What is it?" I heard him ask over and over, increasingly annoyed as I tried to control myself. "Jesus, why are you laughing?"

"You think I want you, Jesse?" I shook my head, wiping my eyes. "I don't *want* you!"

"They why do you keep looking at me?"

"I'm not looking at you. I'm looking at him!" I pointed at it and laughed as Jesse touched his face and found it for himself.

"Ouch!" He said, recoiling. "It's huge."

"It has its own gravitation pull."

"Ha ha."

"Remember those turmeric masks I used to put on your face for acne?" I asked.

"I do remember," he said gruffly. "They used to stain my cheeks yellow."

"That's because you're such a *gora*."

Sulking, Jesse grabbed the packaging from our banh mis and started walking toward the recycling bin on the other side of the path. He thought I *wanted* him? The giggles returned as I watched him shoot our refuse like a three-pointer, miss, and then pick it up off the ground.

We wouldn't be a good idea right now.

My skin prickled when I remembered what he'd said, and the laughter subsided. What did Jesse mean by that? Did he mean he thought "we" might be a good idea *eventually*?

"Would you rather I have not told you about it?" I asked him when he returned. I gestured to the zit on his face but kept my gaze neutral. My thoughts, too. Surely, Jesse had misspoken before, and I needed to brush past this.

"I have an important conference call this afternoon. Shit." Jesse sighed. "I guess I'll just keep the camera off."

"Will your zit have its own call-in number?"

"*Serena* Singh," Jesse said, a smile creeping over his lips. "Will you cut it out?"

The office was quiet when I got back. Ainsley was alone at her pod, her noise-canceling headphones plugged in, her hair in a carefree yet stylish knot at the top of her head. Despite my temporary freak-out, I was still in a good mood, so I tiptoed up to her and, when I was just inches away, swiveled her chair hard around toward me.

"Boo!"

"Aghh!" She screamed, her keyboard and mouse flying to the side. I burst out laughing, and when the panic subsided and her face returned to normal, her cheeks glowed beet red.

"Shit, Serena! You really scared me."

I cackled and helped her find the mouse, which had scattered beneath a neighboring desk and luckily hadn't been broken. She was quiet and not jostling me or threatening to retaliate like I would have expected, and for a second I wondered if I had gone too far. But this was Ainsley. We did shit like this to each other all the time. There was no going too far.

"That it?" I asked, as she connected her keyboard. "Sorry if I interrupted your flow . . ."

She smiled weakly. "No. I wasn't even working."

"No?"

She shook her head, and I sat down in the chair next to her, dragging it forward on its wheels to be closer.

"What's up?"

"Look at this," she whispered, gesturing to her screen. Ainsley was logged in to what must have been a personal e-mail account, and there was an e-mail from a Mr. Jason Hernandez, a recruiter. My stomach twisted as I scanned the rest of the e-mail, the phrases popping out at me.

Happy with your current position

Salary, flexibility, challenges

"This is the third e-mail this month." Ainsley sighed, drumming her hands on her thighs. "In tech, these e-mails are common . . . People move around constantly. If you're happy in a position, then it's easy to click, delete, and not think about it again. But . . ."

But. She wasn't happy. She was going to leave, wasn't she?

"I've been here with Deborah since the beginning. Seven years of my career, Serena. It's great. I love it. But I've grown . . . complacent. I could do this job with one hand tied behind my back."

"So you . . ." I cleared my throat as the words caught. "So," I tried again, "you want a new challenge?"

"Well, I don't know. But maybe at this point in my life, if I'm going to make a change, I should be looking for something that isn't just about what's good for me. But what's good for my . . ." She paused. Now she wasn't meeting my eye. "My family."

Family.

I recalled what she'd said to me at the poetry night: her father-in-law was pressuring her to quit, to go freelance. Was that why she was mulling over leaving? To make her in-laws happy instead of herself?

I licked my lips, trying not to pass judgment as I thought about all the times I'd chosen myself over my family. Of course I had. If Mom and Dad had it their way, I would have married Jesse straight out of university, and right now I'd be the mother of three. Cooking *saag* and *makki di roti* in one hand, managing the happiness of everyone else around me with the other. Forget the career goals. My own social life or anything of my own. The ambition, even the panic, that made me want more for myself.

"If Nikesh's business takes off, I really will need to be around more," Ainsley said, breaking the silence. "Can't imagine it will fly with Deborah to work from home full time, eh?"

It sounded like she was trying to convince me, so I smiled.

"Don't listen to me. I'm just having a weird day." She exited out of the browser and then leaned her head into her hand, facing me. "How are you?"

I shrugged. Ainsley was becoming a true friend. Dare I say it, my best friend. If she left the agency, it wouldn't matter that we didn't spend ten hours a day sitting a few feet away from each other. At least, I wanted to believe that was true.

21

My conversation with Ainsley really bummed me out, but I forced myself to block it out and get back to work. I had shit to do. I had a client to win over.

A big part of my job was helping the account and development teams prepare pitches for new business from prospective clients, which tended to be companies trying to go "green" or launch socially ethical brands or campaigns. Deborah's agency had been trying to find a beverages company for its client base since the very start, but she'd never been able to get one on board. (I'm not saying it's because old white men tend to hire young white men who remind them of themselves, although research has shown that's often the case . . .)

Anyway, as luck would have it, I got along famously with the owners of a regional beverages conglomerate based out of Richmond, Virginia, whom I'd worked with for years at my old job. Bottled flat and sparkling waters, nonalcoholic ciders, organic colas, juices, hot chocolate, and coffee. They had the whole nine yards, and to be honest, I'd been instrumental in most of their campaigns.

Several of my clients had followed me to Deborah's agency

without my even having to ask them, but this one was different. It was a big company, and they couldn't move agencies carelessly. I'd kept in touch with Jerry and Patricia, the wholesome, healthy power couple in their early seventies who had started and built up the business from scratch. Without overstepping, I'd made it clear to them that I wanted their business, and a few weeks ago Jerry had reached out to say he'd like to meet. He wanted "my thoughts" on how I would pivot their existing brand of supermarket tonic waters into a "green" luxury brand.

He wanted *just* my thoughts? Yeah, right. He was going to get the full Don Draper Treatment. Or should I say the Serena Singh Treatment.

Creative Director. Badass Brown Girl. Advertising Ass-Kicker.

I worked late that evening, declining Ainsley's invite to walk home with her, and by the next morning, I was as ready as I'd ever be. I'd planned on hitching a ride with one of my colleagues in Accounts and Development, but at the last moment Deborah said she'd like to join in on the meeting and offered me a ride. I swallowed, hard, following her to her Tesla in the parking garage. She'd never come to a pitch with me before, and it made me realize how important this meeting was.

If I could win over Jerry and Patricia's tonic water, a fraction of their portfolio, maybe we could win over their whole business.

Deborah could probably tell I was nervous, so we didn't speak much during the drive, keeping the conversation to things like the weather, her grandchildren, the availability of charging stations for electric cars. The company's local office was across the Potomac in Arlington, and we arrived in good time, a few minutes before our colleagues in Accounts and Development, who had taken a separate car.

We set up presentation materials and the slide deck in the

boardroom, and I took my place at the head of the table, my shoulders pulled back. My game face on. And I was ready when they walked in the room.

"Serena!" Jerry bellowed, pushing through the glass door.

"Jerry," I said, standing up. "It's been too long."

Jerry was a jovial man. Tall, balding, and a bit of a belly, although not quite as big as the last time I saw him. He told me that Patricia was in New York for one of her philanthropic projects that he "couldn't keep track of," and then I introduced him to Deborah and the rest of my team, and he introduced us to his marketing directors, one of whom—Kriti—I'd met several times before.

"Should we get to it?" I asked, after we'd all taken a seat. I grabbed the flicker off the podium and breathed in deep, twice, before turning around to face everyone.

"I—"

"Serena, I'm gonna have to stop you right there."

I closed my mouth, confused, and looked over at Jerry. He was about fifteen feet away from me at the exact opposite end of the boardroom table. His hands were locked together on the table. His prominent forehead was shinier than usual, and even from here I could tell that he was blushing.

Fuck. Had I screwed it up already? They hadn't even heard my pitch yet.

"I really, really like the roughs you've sent through. Exactly what I pictured, *but* . . ."

But? My stomach knotted, and I forced myself not to glance at Deborah for validation.

"—*but* I was talking to Patricia on the phone last night, and apparently there're already a few luxury tonics out there!"

"Yes, yes, there are . . ." I reached for my portfolio. "I sent you a competition brief in last week's—"

"Well, I must have missed it. I thought we were going to be the first ones to market!" Jerry threw his hands up in the air, his signature move. "Kriti, did you know?"

Kriti smiled and nodded. "I did. Serena sent the brief . . ."

"Shucks. How did I miss it?"

I could tell Kriti was trying not to laugh, so I looked straight ahead at Jerry and cleared my throat. This was salvageable. I could still do this.

"Jerry, at the end of the day, it won't matter that you're not the first to market. There's space for another luxury tonic. For *yours*." With my flicker, I switched to the first slide. "We're going to take your existing tonic and rebrand it as the first socially conscious—"

"No," Jerry said, interrupting me. "I'm not going to sink any more money into *tonic*. Who even drinks gin and tonics anymore? Kriti, whose idea was it?"

"Yours, Jerry."

"*Christ*."

Kriti and her colleagues chuckled softly while I tried to keep my lips from trembling. It was over already, and I hadn't even gotten to the meat of my pitch. I closed my folder, thinking of all the teams' good work getting flushed down the drain.

My ego.

I didn't have the courage to look over at Deborah and my colleagues in accounts. We had put a lot of time and effort into this pitch. Surely, they'd be gutted. *I* was gutted.

"Well," I said after a moment, meeting his gaze. "It was great to see you, anyway, Jerry. Should we go grab an early lunch?"

"Now hold your horses," he said, leaning back in his chair. "We're not done here."

I did my best to hold my hopes in check as I sat down in my chair.

"Kriti and I were having a real interesting conversation on the drive up from Richmond this morning," he said, looking over at his colleague. "Weren't we?"

"We were, Jerry."

"About tonic water?" one of their other colleagues asked, and Kriti shook her head.

"This doesn't leave the room," Jerry said, eyeing his team. "We have to finalize the paperwork before we announce the deal, but you're looking at the new owner of The Fifth Ingredient."

There was a hush of excitement from their side of the room, although all of us from DC had no idea what for. A moment later, Kriti explained.

"The Fifth Ingredient is really making waves in the local craft beer scene. They have five products—the sour is my favorite—and the kid who owns it likes the idea of a big check that will fund his lifetime vacation to Bali."

The room laughed, and I joined in, struggling to remain still in my seat.

"We're going to have to redo the labels so it aligns with the rest of our brands, but we'll keep the name," Kriti continued. "It's already known as a premium organic beer without a carbon footprint."

"*Really?*" I asked.

Kriti and Jerry took turns filling in the room on their plans to increase production and set up regional distribution centers.

Finally, they both turned to look at me, smiling. "So, what do you think?"

They told me their projected advertising budget, and my jaw dropped.

"I think it's . . . a great opportunity."

"Well, it's your opportunity if you want it," Kriti said, "We need somebody smart."

"And fast," Jerry added. "Can you get us on track for a Christmas launch? Reckon you better hightail it down to Richmond for a couple weeks and spend some time with product development."

Christmas? This was fucking *huge*, and they needed the work done, like, *yesterday*.

"Patricia and I have been talking about our sustainability goals with the board, and we'd like the whole company to cut all water wastage and have a zero-carbon footprint in the near future," Jerry said, locking eyes with me. "I'm thinking The Fifth Ingredient will be a bit of a trial run."

A *trial run for your company, or a trial run for me?*

"Are you up to it?" he asked.

I hesitated just for a moment. Designing a campaign from scratch and launching a new product that would impress Jerry and Patricia enough to hire me for their whole business, on an impossible deadline, would be the biggest professional challenge of my career.

"Jerry." I narrowed my eyes. "Of course I'm up to it."

"Great work today," Deborah said on the drive back to the office. I smiled. She wasn't overzealous with her praise, so when she said something like that, I knew she meant it.

We were at a red light, and she turned to look at me, pulling her sunglasses slightly down the bridge of her nose. "I hope you didn't feel ambushed."

"By Jerry?"

"No. By me." The light turned green, and Deborah glanced back to the road. The window was open, and the air rushing in was blowing her Diane Keaton gray hair wildly across her face. "I didn't think you needed a babysitter. I probably shouldn't have come."

"Not at all." I shrugged. "This is your company."

"It's all very exciting. It's been a while since I've felt the thrill." She paused. "Letting go of creative control is . . . well, it's harder than I thought it would be."

I didn't know what to say. Her words surprised me, and for a few moments, we sat side by side in silence. I'd been so obsessed with proving myself to her and my team that I hadn't even considered that she was going through a difficult time transitioning away from being the company's creative face, taking a backseat to, well, *me*.

"The Fifth Ingredient is going to be a crash campaign. And it sounds like you're going to need to spend some time in Richmond."

I nodded, unsure what she was getting at.

"Would you like me to take point on a few existing accounts? Just for a while." Deborah glanced at me quickly. "I'm not trying to step on your toes. You'd be doing me a favor, really. I would love to get my feet wet again."

"Sure . . ." I said, even though I wasn't. Did she think I wasn't capable? Did she think I wasn't *ready* to handle what was coming?

Out of nowhere, Deborah swerved out of traffic and pulled into a bus lane. The car in park, she turned to me, sliding off her sunglasses.

"Listen, Serena. I'm not going to think you're a 'pussy' if you accept help. Got it?"

I nodded, uncomfortable with her word choice.

"Does he say that word still, Iain?"

I shrugged. For an adman, my old boss Iain had used a lot of derogatory words in the office.

"What a fucker." She gripped the steering wheel. "Do you

know, when I worked with him in the nineties, he used to call me the 'office geisha.'"

I gasped.

"Notwithstanding the fact that I'm Korean, not Japanese, *yes*, the implication was that our director had brought me on to 'please' the clients."

"I'm so sorry, Deborah. I can't believe it." I shook my head, enraged. "You know what? I *can* believe it."

I closed my eyes, trying to imagine myself in Deborah's shoes. She'd been in the business decades longer than I had and had to put up with way more crap from clients and bosses, sexism and racism. And she'd made it. She'd cracked the glass and made it easier for women like me to break through.

It still hadn't been easy. I wanted to break down and cry thinking about the worst days. Still, I'd never asked for help.

Not at home. Not at work. Not ever.

I'd gritted my teeth and lost sleep to prove to everyone I could make it on my own. That I was *good enough* without them.

"The word 'help' wasn't in my vocabulary when I was your age, either," Deborah said, as if reading my mind. A horn sounded behind us. There was a bus pulling in, the driver gesturing angrily for us to get out of his way.

Could I really do my best at The Fifth Ingredient if I still had all our other clients to attend to? All of our existing and forthcoming creative campaigns to manage?

I couldn't, so a few minutes later I said, "I do need your help."

Deborah nodded without responding. She must have known how hard it was for me to admit.

22

SANDEEP

Serena?" Sandeep peered up from the gardening bed. "What are you doing home? Are you sick?"

"I decided to take the afternoon off." Serena waved from the bottom of the driveway. She was wearing a business suit, much like the one Detective Olivia Benson from *Law & Order* would wear, except Serena had a bright top underneath, the color of saffron. She looked radiant.

"We didn't really have time to talk at Natasha's gender reveal."

Sandeep nodded, brushing the dirt from her leggings as she stood up from the ground. The party was weeks ago now, and all the unpleasantness she'd felt toward her younger daughter for excluding her had evaporated for that day, particularly when it was revealed that Sandeep would be blessed with a grandson.

She'd enjoy doting on a young man, which wasn't to say she hadn't relished having two little girls to raise. In fact, daughters were what she had preferred. She despised that in their village, the birth of boys had been celebrated and the arrival of girls mourned.

As a young child, Sandeep heard stories about how her *papaji* refused to hold her for months, angry about something over which neither she nor her mother had any control. Luckily, attitudes had changed a bit by the time Serena was born. Luckily, her husband, Veer, would never have done such a thing.

"What did you think?" Serena asked. "Of the gender reveal."

"It is an exciting custom," she said in English.

Serena stared at her blankly.

"Truly, *beti*. I had a lovely time at the party. Natasha's new mother is a very welcoming woman."

"*You* are her mother . . ."

Sandeep knew that. She'd misspoken, but perhaps there was some truth to the blunder. After marriage, Sandeep had gone to live with her in-laws. They were a traditional family, and if she and Veer hadn't later moved to America, they would have stayed there and looked after his parents until they had passed. She would have belonged to *them*. Mistakenly, Sandeep had assumed that Natasha's choice to marry a *gora* meant that she wouldn't lose her.

But here in America, you lost your daughters differently.

"I know you're hurt she's excluding you, Mom," Serena said. "Do you want to talk about it?"

The sun was fierce today. Her *dupatta* had fallen off her head, and she pulled it back up for the shade as she looked at their house. The roof needed work, and yes, the windowsills flaked paint like a snow cloud, but it was *their* house. Their property. A family home where all of them, including Ms. Fancy Pants Natasha, belonged.

So, no, Sandeep didn't want to talk about it. She wanted Natasha to respect her elders and humbly understand where she came from.

Leaving Veer's family for America had been devastating, even more so than leaving her parents' home. Sandeep put on a brave face for Veer, for Serena, but the first year, she'd sobbed herself into hysterics every time she had a moment alone. Sandeep was the first of her family to leave Punjab. In the years that followed, her brothers emigrated to the UK, and various cousins found themselves in Hong Kong, Australia, British Columbia. Her grandparents and then her own parents passed away, and the house they'd grown up in had been sold at auction and then bulldozed.

Family kept you grounded, but they'd all been uprooted, scattered, and were now like tumbleweeds blowing recklessly around the globe. Sandeep had done everything in her power to change that, to build anew. She cleaned houses, despite the upturned noses of some her friends, so they could save more quickly, so her daughters would have space to grow up, like they would have had in the village.

And so later on, her daughters would have somewhere to bring their families.

She'd imagined this place would have grown lively in age. Empty bedrooms filled with boisterous grandchildren on sleepovers, running around like chickens. Serena, Natasha, and their husbands enjoying themselves, eating, filling their silent house with laughter.

It had been too big of a dream, and sometimes, like when Natasha refused to let her host the gender reveal, it still crushed her that it didn't come to pass. Her daughters' lives were not extensions of her own—she understood that now—but still, it didn't make the reality any easier. Still, she should have focused less on creating a big, perfect picture and more on the broken people inside of it.

"Have you eaten lunch yet?" she heard Serena ask. "Let's go somewhere."

"I've just made *halwa*." Sandeep beamed. The sweet, dense semolina mixture was Serena's favorite, especially the way Sandeep made it, with raisins and *lots* of cashew nuts. "Come inside and we'll eat together."

"Mom, for once can you not put up a fight?" Serena's voice was measured, firm. "I know you can cook, but we always eat here."

That's because I like having you here, Serena.

"Please? Let me treat you."

Sandeep was parched and sticky from the sun, and she sighed, defeated. "Sure. *Chalo*."

Veer had carpooled with a neighbor to work that day, so they took the car one town over to an Italian restaurant where Sandeep had never been. It felt trendy, a word she often heard Natasha use to describe her social engagements, and she was glad she'd changed out of her house clothes.

"Can I help you decide?" Serena asked, staring at her over the menu. Sandeep smiled stiffly and shook her head. Just then, the waiter approached to take their orders.

"I'll have the pumpkin gnocchi, thanks," Serena replied, handing him the menu. "Mom, are you ready?"

Sandeep nodded even though she wasn't. Panicking, she felt her blouse grow sticky beneath her armpits.

"I will have . . ." She started scanning the long list of pastas with her pointer finger. She got all the way to the bottom and then moved back to the top.

"I think we need more time—"

"*Nah, beti*. I'm ready, sir." She tapped on the first option. The description promised that it would be light: pasta noodles with some sort of tomato sauce.

"Spaghetti marinara?" Serena asked, after the waiter left. "That's so plain, Mom."

Sandeep nodded, fanning herself with the napkin.

"I thought you might want to try something new. They have this four-cheese ravioli that's to die for. You'd love it."

Sandeep did love cheese, paneer in particular, but now that she was over fifty, the way it unsettled her stomach overpowered her weakness for fatty, rich foods.

"Sounds tasty, *beti*."

Serena grinned. "Then I'll go ask the waiter to change your meal—"

"No need to make a fuss—"

"There's no fuss," she said, rushing off. "He hasn't placed the order yet."

Sandeep sipped her water, wondering why she didn't tell Serena that she would have preferred the plainer pasta, that her digestive system wasn't what it used to be.

Was it because Serena seemed so excited to introduce her to something new? Maybe. But if Sandeep was being honest, that was only part of it. She hadn't told Serena the truth because that's what she'd grown used to. If she told her every little thing—a harmless argument with Veer, a bill they hadn't yet managed to pay, a blood pressure reading that was slightly higher than what her doctor felt comfortable with—it would only cause worry.

Serena returned to the table, animated. She slipped off her blazer and, without any prompting on Sandeep's part, told her about her day, the former clients Jerry and Patricia. Sandeep's heart swelled with pride as Serena explained the new business they'd given her and how much it had impressed her new boss.

"Deborah Kim?" Sandeep asked hesitantly, and Serena had grinned.

"You remembered."

Yes. She'd said the right thing.

Serena continued on with her story, the "creative strategy" she already had in mind. As hard as it was on Veer, Sandeep appreciated that Serena was making more of an effort to call her and come visit. To *talk*. As Sandeep continued listening, her ears grew hot, suddenly feeling shameful. Her daughter was trying, and Sandeep had gone and lied about something so silly as wanting that damn cheesy pasta. She *should* have been truthful. But now it was too late.

The food arrived, and Sandeep ate it with relish, deciding that if she was going to be stomach sick regardless, she might as well enjoy herself now. Sandeep did her best to match Serena's energy as they conversed. Partway through their meal, Serena's phone buzzed. It was the first time she'd looked at it.

"Work?" Sandeep asked, suddenly fearful her daughter would rush off to the office.

"No. Sorry, one minute." Her thumbs moved rapidly on the screen, and then a beat later, she set the phone down. "It was just a friend."

"Jenna?" Sandeep tried to remember the names of the other girls who used to perpetually tie up their landline or turn up unannounced wanting to play ball or hopscotch, but she blanked.

"Or your new friend Ainsley? She was so sweet, *hah*? And her son is very cute." Sandeep smiled, remembering the young boy. "Half Indian. Half American. I wonder if Natasha's baby will look like him."

"Maybe," Serena answered. She was holding her fork but wasn't eating, and it sat limply in her hand. Then she sighed and set the utensil down. "And no, I was actually texting . . . Jesse."

Sandeep furrowed her brow, confused, but then the look on Serena's face confirmed her fear.

Jesse? Her ex-boyfriend Jasmeet Dhillon?

"And *no*. We're not together. We ran into each other a while back and decided to be friends." She put her hands up. "So don't start with me—"

"Did I say anything?" Sandeep asked demurely. She was surprised by how even her voice sounded, although this news was causing her to sweat again.

"We're a lot older now, you see, and he's just gotten divorced. We have a lot in common, and he lives in the city . . . and . . ."

And? *And* Serena was acting foolish. *And* this was a very stupid decision for such an intelligent woman.

"And . . . he's a good friend now. That's it."

She wanted to ask Serena if that really was "it," then why was she being so defensive? But she bit her tongue instead.

"Thank you for telling me." Sandeep patted her lips with the cloth napkin and then set it back down on her lap. Truly, she was grateful, although she was more surprised that Serena had shared something so personal.

"I'm glad you have some companionship."

Sandeep had long understood that Washington, DC, was not India and that times had changed and demanded she adapt. She'd come to terms with Serena's decision to "date," to flaunt her modern relationship with Jesse, even though after four years it did not lead to marriage.

It hadn't mattered that everyone had gossiped, that Serena had lost her place as the "good girl" in the community. *No*. All Sandeep had cared about was her daughter's happiness, and breaking up with that sweet boy, Jesse, had done anything but make her happy.

So why was she seeking him out now? Was she punishing herself?

"Natasha must be pleased by the news," Sandeep said, curious if her younger daughter had tried to talk some sense into Serena. "She always adored him."

"I haven't told Natasha."

The waiter arrived, interrupting them to clear their dishes. Sandeep studied her daughter as she handed him the dishes and then asked for the check.

The girls were fighting. They were *still* fighting.

Sandeep's lungs burned as she thought about how close the two sisters used to be. There were so many rifts in their small family already—was this cherished bond between sisters gone, too?

From the day Natasha was born, Serena had mothered and protected her in all the ways Sandeep could not, educated her on the important things Sandeep simply did not know.

But there was no one to do that for Serena. She had had to learn everything the hard way. Vividly, Sandeep could remember Serena translating for her at the school when they first arrived in America, explaining to the teacher that Sandeep was crying because she'd taken the wrong bus to pick her up, again. That new immigrants often felt lost, and not just by directions.

She was only in kindergarten.

"You're a very good girl, Serena." Sandeep reached out her palm and squeezed her daughter's hand. There was so much more to say, but she finished her meal and failed to muster up the courage to say a single word of it.

"Come with me to the cooking class. *Please,*" I begged Ainsley when the end of the week rolled around.

Ainsley shook her head. "My parents are in town for the Fourth of July. Why don't you come over for dinner?"

"I don't want to intrude."

"I've met *your* parents, haven't I?" She paused. "How are they, by the way?"

"Oh, fine." I gestured to the lunch I was eating. After our lunch date, Mom had taught me how to cook *matar paneer,* and I was still eating the leftovers. "My mother is turning me into quite the chef."

"Was your dad home?"

I didn't answer, and Ainsley held my gaze as we sat eating together at the break room table. Ainsley and I had never talked about the fact that I'd cried (quietly) like an idiot after seeing Dad at Natasha's gender reveal party, although she'd tried to ask me about it a few times. She was trying again now.

"Anyway," I said, breaking eye contact, "I guess this means more Tuscan food for me."

"Is that like Italian food? And why not take Becket?"

"I assume it is," I said. "And I can't take Becket. It's not meant to be a 'couples' thing."

"*Oh.* You signed up for this when you were on the *prowl*, didn't you?"

"Ha ha."

"Thought you'd seduce a nice young lady and make her your . . ." Ainsley looked at me with utter disgust. "*Friend?*"

"Are you done?"

"Like you did to me? Sought me out, made me *like* you—"

"All right." I laughed, standing up and clearing my dish. "Back to work, Woods."

She giggled at her own joke for another minute as I washed my dish and set it on the rack to dry. I turned around, studying her for a moment. We both liked to eat earlier than our colleagues and were alone in the break room. Ainsley was typing something out on her phone and shaking her left leg under the table, like she always did, probably to the beat of one of those god-awful funk bands she made me listen to.

I smiled, watching her. And no, I wasn't watching her like a stalker, but the way a person might gaze at someone and think, *Damn, she is cool!*

In four short months, I'd grown closer to her than I ever would have predicted, maybe even than I ever was with Natasha. So what would happen if she quit?

My throat closed up whenever I thought about her leaving, and how everything would inevitably be different. Would she still make time for me? Working together meant our lives slotted in together seamlessly, but that would change if she went freelance. Her hours would revolve around Nikesh's business, MacKenzie, who would get older, more active, more time-consuming.

I swallowed hard, imagining us drifting apart, even if we

didn't want to. Even if we fought it. Overcome with emotion, I opened my mouth to say something. To ask her if she was still toying with the idea of leaving the company. To make my feelings *known*.

But then she spoke first.

"Tuscan food does *not* sound like Italian food, Serena," she said, reading from her phone. "At least the Italian food I'm used to."

I turned away, reaching for the coffeepot so she wouldn't see my face if she looked up. "Oh?"

"There are a lot of beans, apparently."

"The magical fruit," I retorted.

"Some of the dishes sound good, though. Save me some?"

"No way. You've abandoned me, after all . . ." I stopped, betrayed by the tone of my voice.

Ainsley hadn't abandoned me. At least, not yet.

That evening, I found myself on the bus to a bougie kitchen shop on the H Street Corridor, where the cooking class was being held. It was too hot to walk without turning up like a total mess.

I'd been tempted to forgo my deposit and bail, but I fought through the urge. Work that day had been hellish—between handing back projects to Deborah for supervision, diving into the research phase of The Fifth Ingredient campaign, and figuring out staffing issues and team assignments with the increased workload.

I had even sat down with Vic and asked her to work alongside me on the new campaign. She agreed, smiling and saying the right things, although I couldn't tell what she actually thought about the arrangement. We'd have to spend a lot of time together, and maybe she would grow to respect me, even decide that she could learn from me. Maybe there was still hope that the two of us could start our relationship over.

"Over here!" a friendly looking woman called out to me as I arrived at the class. "Are you Serena?"

She pointed at my name tag at her cooking station, right next to one with *Rachel* on it.

"Nice to meet you. I take it we're partners?"

She nodded. "I'm so glad you showed up. I thought I'd get stuck up here alone."

"Sorry. My bus got stuck behind a motorcade."

"No worries." Rachel handed me a recipe card. It had Italian words on it I didn't recognize.

"Is this what we're making tonight?"

"Mm-hmm. *Fettunta*, *panzanella*, *acquacotta* . . ." Rachel lowered her voice. "I was expecting we'd make . . . tortellini or something. I have no idea what any of this is!"

"Me neither." I laughed, turning over the card. "But the recipes all call for a lot of olive oil and salt. So I bet it's going to be really good."

The instructor must have been waiting for me, because she immediately started the class. After an introductory spiel about Tuscan cuisine, the basics to good cooking, and what we'd be preparing that evening, she asked us to set out all of the ingredients and start with the washing and chopping. I peeled and chopped the garlic while Rachel did the herbs and introduced herself. She was a lobbyist and had lived in the DC area since college, although she grew up in South Carolina.

The instructor handed out a glass of white wine to everyone in the class, and I didn't want to be rude, so I accepted, even though when I brought the glass to my lips I only pretended to take a sip. Rachel was very chatty and also in good spirits, and I found myself having a lot more fun than I had expected. This was the kind of experience I'd been looking for when I first started trying to make new friends and regain a social life months earlier. Women enjoying one another's company, supporting one another, getting to know one another—and over Italian food, no less.

The first course turned out well, and we were allowed to have a small taste of our *fettunta*, a *delicious* bread, before moving on to the next course. I diced tomatoes as Rachel worked on the onion and told me about her job. I was grateful that she hadn't asked me too many questions about myself. I had never really understood what lobbyists *did* exactly, but I got distracted during her explanation by the buzzing in my back pocket. It went on and on; someone was calling and not giving up. Finally, it stopped, but Rachel had moved from politics and was now telling me about her roommate's elderly cat, who kept ruining all her clothes. I didn't want to be rude and check my phone, so I left it.

"Can you believe it? She said she wouldn't pay me back for the shoes. I'm so nice, I didn't charge her rent last month because she had to fly home unexpectedly for a family emergency. And I took care of that flipping cat while she was away!"

"That was very generous of you."

"Right? I . . ."

My phone started buzzing again. It was another phone call. I glanced over at Rachel. She had stopped chopping the onion and was wiping the corners of her eyes with her sleeve, so I quickly wiped my hands on a dishrag and reached for my phone. It was Jesse. He never called, only texted, so I replied.

Busy! What's up?

I texted Jesse back in a hurry and then surreptitiously hid my phone on the counter partway beneath an oven mitt.

As Rachel continued talking, I snuck a look at my phone. Jesse had texted back.

Anadi and her parents are taking the kids to Disney World. I wanted to take them to Disney World. It was my idea, Serena. MY idea. And she took it.

"Have you ever had a terrible roommate situation?" I heard Rachel ask.

"Yeah. I have." I nodded, turning back to her, feeling sad for Jesse. "Before I got my own place, I shared a house with five inconsiderate, *messy* people in Adams Morgan."

"Did any of their cats try to eat your shoes?"

I laughed. "Luckily, the landlord forbade pets."

I glanced back at my phone. Jesse had texted again.

I hate to ask. But can we talk?

Talk *now*? I hesitated, unsure of what to reply. I was busy. And not only that, I knew that if I called him, he'd talk about the divorce, and that would be breaking one of our rules. On the other hand, we were friends. And weren't friends there for each other when you needed them most?

"Is that your boyfriend texting?" Rachel asked suddenly. My face flushed red, and I turned to her.

"Can't leave you alone for one night, hey?"

"No, it's just a friend in distress."

She nodded, and suddenly her silence—her lack of chat—was palpable. Lazily, she covered the vegetables we'd chopped and peeled with a balsamic vinegar. Again, my phone buzzed on the table. Jesse was calling.

"Is it an emergency?" Rachel's friendly tone had taken on a different quality. I bit my lip and then quietly gathered my things.

"It is." I nodded. "I'm so sorry. I have to go."

I waited until I was outside to call him back. Jesse spoke for the next ten minutes straight without taking a breath, and even though I was tempted, I didn't interrupt him to remind him that he wasn't allowed to talk to me about the divorce.

"I'm never going to see Maya's face when she sees Princess Jasmine for the first time. That's never going to happen."

I didn't answer, and I didn't think I was supposed to. He just needed to vent and process and wallow. He needed to grieve that he wasn't always going to be around for his children.

I'd heard people say that their kids became a limb to them, even an organ, something they couldn't live without. I would probably never fully understand, but these days, I was getting close. My eyelids fluttered to a close, and the smell of MacKenzie's hair suddenly flooded in. I loved him. And as much as I didn't want any of my own, I knew I would do anything to protect the children in my life.

Except for the gender reveal, I'd barely seen or spoken to Natasha in months. Would I get to know her son the same way as I was getting to know MacKenzie?

And what about Maya and Ajay? Would I . . .

I dug my fingers in the flesh of my thighs as I tried to derail that train of thought. What was I doing, daydreaming about meeting Jesse's children? If getting together with each other's families wasn't already an official ground rule for our friendship, surely it should be.

We wouldn't be a good idea right now.

He'd said it in passing when he thought he'd caught me admiring him, and I hadn't let myself think about those words since. But now, suddenly, irritatingly, the last two words kept playing over and over again in my mind.

Right now. Right now.

What *about* "right now"? We were friends, we made *sense* as friends, and there was no reason for that to ever change. He must have said that without thinking.

Right?

"Sorry. *Sorry*, Serena," Jesse said, gratefully interrupting my thoughts. "Thanks for listening. I know not being the one to take them to Disney World isn't the end of the world."

"Don't be sorry." I had found a bench across and up the block and sat down on it. "If you want to keep talking, I'm here. Although I'm not sure I have any sage advice to impart."

"It's OK. I appreciate you listening." He let out a loud yawn. "So where are you right now?"

I glanced to the side. I could see the cooking class going on through the window. Rachel had joined the station behind us and was chatting to the two women there. A part of me wanted to go back inside, but the other part of me wondered what the point would be.

"I was at a cooking class," I said finally.

"Shit. I'm so sorry—"

"It's over," I lied. "It's fine."

I could hear rustling on the other end of the line. Was he on the couch, on his bed? I wondered what his apartment looked like. I knew he was there right now. He wouldn't allow himself to be so vulnerable in public.

"Have you ever had a terrible roommate?" I asked suddenly, thinking about the story Rachel had been telling me back in the kitchen.

"Sure. Don't you remember Robby?"

I nodded, remembering the pot-smoking ladies' man Jesse had lived with in grad school. "Didn't he sleep with the wife of one of your professors?"

"That's the one."

I sighed. "I wondered what ever happened to Robby."

"According to Facebook, he's quite high up at the World Bank."

"He is *not* . . ."

"And I hear that Cliff is making a play for office—"

My jaw dropped. "Keg-stand *Cliff*? Which office?"

Once I hung up the phone and started walking to the bus stop, I noticed that everyone in the cooking class had started to clear their things. The class was nearly over, and it had been two and a half hours since I'd faked an emergency and left to talk to Jesse. I sighed, suddenly famished and parched and unable to remember most of the details that had made up our hours-long conversation.

We'd talked about our college friends for a while, the Labor Day weekend before senior year we'd spent at Virginia Beach, and from there it spiraled outward. To real life. To the ups and downs of our workdays. To things as insignificant yet all-encompassing as what we ate for breakfast.

From the beginning, I'd known that a friendship with Jesse would involve reliving the past, because it was something we shared. What I didn't realize was that it would mean so much in the present, too.

He'd needed me tonight, and it felt good to be there for him.

So maybe I was happy to listen. Maybe that rule I invented was pretty arbitrary, and he *could* talk about the divorce with me.

But then, what rule would we break next? And then, what would happen after that?

Right now.

I yawned as a dull fatigue set in. Right now we were *friends*, and as I hopped on the bus that would take me back to Columbia Heights, I decided to put myself—and the issue—to bed.

24

Looks like Nikesh's business is taking off," I said, admiring the boxes of Dirty Chai bottles piled up on the porch. The Fourth of July had come and gone, as had Ainsley's parents, and she'd invited Becket and me over for dinner. After only four days apart, I was looking forward to seeing her, even though I'd had a busy weekend in my own right. I'd alternated working on The Fifth Ingredient campaign from my sweltering balcony and air-conditioned living room, and spent a few nights out with Becket checking out new restaurants and food festivals. Jesse and I met up for lunch once, too. (It was so ordinarily friendly it's barely worth mentioning.)

"I hope it does," Becket replied, and it took a moment for me to remember we were talking about Nikesh's hustle. "It's the best coffee I've ever had."

"Dirty chai is tea *and* coffee," I corrected, smiling. "Anyway, Ainsley says he's been talking to a few investors."

"Oh yeah?" Becket replied vaguely.

I tripped on a box as we made our way to the door, and Becket grabbed my hand to steady me.

"Thank you."

He smiled without looking up at me and then reached for the doorbell.

I furrowed my brow, unable to read him. Something seemed off. It was the first time in our relationship—I was proud of myself that I'd started using that word—that he was the one acting distant. It was unnerving.

I reached for his hand and pushed it away from the bell.

"Becket?"

He didn't answer. I reached up and brushed his cheek with my hand, like his face was a canvas. He must have shaved just before coming to pick me up because it felt smooth, as smooth as I'd ever felt it.

"What's wrong?"

He grabbed my hand, holding it in his. I was preparing to have to pry the information out of him, crack all sorts of jokes to cheer him up, but then he actually came out with it. No prompting required.

"Wedding season." He sighed and then let both our hands fall down to our sides. "I'm not as busy this year. There's just too much competition right now."

"Oh."

"It's demoralizing."

I nodded, surprised by how honest he was every time I asked him a question. There was a wicker bench somewhat free of clutter, so I took a seat, and Becket squeezed in next to me.

"I wish I wasn't so reliant on weddings." He met my gaze. "Anyway, ignore me. Nothing like a slow work week to emasculate a man, hey?"

I shrugged, clasping my fingers through his. "Is there anything I can do?"

His face went dark and he nodded. *Oh god.* I was trying to be nice. I hadn't actually asked that question seriously, and my gut wrenched as I prepared myself for whatever "relationship" ask he was about to make.

"I . . ."

Oh good Lord . . .

"I really need . . ."

"Yes, Becket?"

"A blow job."

My heart sank into my stomach.

"You *need* a blow job."

"Yes."

I snorted.

"*What?*" He laughed. "You asked."

I rolled my eyes at him, and the joke made me realize we hadn't been intimate in two weeks, even though he'd slept over several times. Had this just occurred to him as well?

"Anyway, I just need to recalibrate a bit. That's it," Becket continued. His optimism sounded forced. "My parents did warn me against art school. Maybe I should try something new."

"Becket . . . you're so talented. Don't say that."

He was really talented. Natasha's wedding photographs were gorgeous and original, and his other work was even better. He'd shown me his photography and design portfolio early on, and I'd been impressed by his eye for detail, the way he could capture an image and, somehow, make it even more real.

"Hey . . ." I said, a lightbulb going off in my head. "Why don't you . . . work for *me*. Would that be weird?"

He laughed. "Are you being serious?"

"Yeah. I actually have a meeting with Deborah tomorrow. We need to find more freelancers. With The Fifth Ingredient, everybody is swamped."

I told him about the available projects, and as I suspected, Becket had the exact sorts of skills and experience we were looking for. I would have hired him even if he wasn't my boyfriend.

"So, do you want the gig?" I asked. He was smiling, grinning even.

"Let's do it!"

He high-fived me, hard, and it was so unexpected that I couldn't help but laugh.

MacKenzie was still awake, and I spent the first fifteen minutes ignoring everyone except him. I'd only known him for five months, yet I could see him changing already. The Paddington Bear pajama onesie that used to hang on him like a potato sack now looked snug. I imagined myself walking into a department store and buying him a replacement. Paying full price, which I never did, for ridiculously cute pajamas that would only fit him for a few months. I wondered if Natasha and Mark would want something like this for their son. If, on a random weeknight evening, I'd be invited to play with him.

Ainsley and Nikesh let me feed him his bedtime bottle, and then Nikesh pried him out of my hands to put him to bed. Becket went up with him, and I sighed deeply after they went upstairs.

"What's the sigh for?" Ainsley was in the kitchen, directly behind the sofa I was sitting on. "Do you have baby fever or something?"

"Just for your baby. Do you need any help?"

"All done. We'll eat when he's asleep." Ainsley appeared beside me, two glasses of kombucha in hand. (When I first met Ainsley, I thought it was disgusting, but she'd converted me on the trend.) She sat down heavily next to me, setting the glasses in front of us. Through the baby monitor, we could hear MacKenzie crying and the creaks of floorboards as, presumably, Nikesh patted him, walked him back and forth across the room in preparation to lay him in his crib. MacKenzie had napped that afternoon and wouldn't go down easy that evening, so Ainsley decided we had time to do the turmeric mask I'd told her about after relaying Jesse's "zit" story. Jesse and I used to do those masks together all the time. Turmeric's antiseptic properties worked wonders for the skin.

Ainsley and I scrubbed makeup from our faces and then mixed together turmeric, yogurt, and honey in a stainless-steel bowl. We applied it over the kitchen sink, careful not to drop any of it on our clothes or the counter. Turmeric stained like a bitch.

"How long do we have to leave this on for?" Ainsley asked me after we'd sat back down on the couch, old tea towels draped over our shoulders.

"Ten minutes." I glanced at her canary-yellow face. "Well, maybe five for you."

"Why?"

"Because you're a *gori*, and you'll look jaundiced if you leave it on any longer."

"*Gori*," Ainsley repeated. "I thought 'white person' was *gora*?"

"'White man' is *gora*. *Gori* is 'white woman.'"

"Right." She nodded. We could still hear MacKenzie over the baby monitor, although his cries were getting fainter.

"So did you ever end up going to that Trojan cooking class last week?" Ainsley said after a while. "How was it?"

"Tuscan." I laughed. "And it was . . . nice."

"Nice?" She winked at me. "Did you meet anyone? Do you have a new *friend*?"

I blew on my fingernails. "Too many to count."

"You player!"

"I get around."

She giggled, hitting me on the shoulder. "Seriously, though. How was it?"

"Good. We made this bread thing, and I can't remember what else."

"You can't remember? It was four days ago."

I reached for my kombucha on the coffee table, stalling for time. I hadn't told Ainsley about my cooking class because I was worried what she'd think about why I left early. But it's not like I could lie to her, either. Friends didn't lie to each other.

"You're being weird, Serena. I'm just throwing that out there."

"I actually left early." I took a sip, shrugging. "Jesse called. He needed to talk."

Ainsley made a face somewhere between surprised and irritated, but I couldn't really tell because of the face mask.

"About what?"

I told her, and all she did was nod, so I kept talking, although more slowly because the turmeric was starting to dry and crack on my face. I told her about the ground rules I'd made for us, that it was the first time I'd let him speak about the divorce.

"Two and a half hours," Ainsley repeated. "He went on about his divorce for that long? That must have been hard for you to listen to. You're a good friend."

"He only talked about that for ten, maybe fifteen minutes." I shrugged. "The rest of the time, I don't know . . ."

Another wail erupted from upstairs, and Ainsley looked up at the ceiling, like she was ready to fly through it. A moment passed, and MacKenzie's wailing died down.

After, Ainsley was quiet. She was never quiet, so I knew she was holding her tongue about something. The last time she'd passed judgment over my relationship with Jesse, I'd shut her down, but this time, I wanted to know what she was thinking.

Having Jesse in my life again was throwing me off, and though our friendship was nothing more than platonic, of course it was confusing. How could it not be? I needed my friend to be honest with me. And when I told her that, she responded, "What do you think I'm thinking?"

"You're thinking . . . *Good God, Serena. You didn't tell Becket the whole truth, that's* saying *something, isn't it?*" I turned toward her on the couch more fully. "And I'd say back, *Gosh no, Ainsley. We get along well, and sure, he's still a straight-up hottie, but it's* strictly *platonic.*"

"'Good God'? 'Gosh no'? Are we in an old Hollywood movie?"

"Maybe."

She smiled at me, and my whole body relaxed. Her smile was one of the reasons why everybody liked her. At the office, or our waiters or baristas, or strangers sitting next to us on the subway. She smiled in a way that appeared to be for you and only you.

"It's platonic. You're just friends. I believe you. But . . ."

"I knew there'd be a but—"

"*But* I'm not even sure that's relevant. Sure, you could be friends with Jesse. But *should* you be?"

"I'm not following."

"You almost married the guy, Serena. And now you don't believe in marriage. So your relationship with Jesse is still affecting you. And you're bringing all of that with you into your friendship with him and . . . your relationship with Becket."

"I don't know if that's true."

Ainsley shrugged. "It's just an opinion. You can take it or leave it."

I wanted to leave it. Bury what she said underneath the couch and never go there again. She didn't really understand what happened. I'd never told her. But maybe, separately, there was a grain of truth to what she said.

Was Jesse the reason Becket and I had stopped being intimate? I didn't think so. It's not like I was rejecting Becket's advances; we were both not making an effort in that department.

And I *was* being honest with Becket about my friendship with Jesse. I'd even told him I'd spoken to him on the phone for hours, and Becket hadn't even seemed to mind.

Maybe the flash of jealousy I'd first seen on him had dissipated. Or, maybe Becket wasn't all that into me anymore. It's not like I wanted to drive my boyfriend crazy, but jealousy did tend to be a symptom of passion, and on the porch just now, he had high-fived me like a *buddy* . . .

"Hello?"

A voice called out from the front room, interrupting my line of thought. Deep and male. I glanced over at Ainsley, and it looked as if she'd seen a ghost. She stood up, and I followed. A beat later, the silhouette of someone appeared in the doorway.

He was the spitting image of Nikesh, but with more wrinkles and a receding hairline.

"You have company?" he asked without saying hello. His face soured as he gave me the once-over, his eyes lingering on my mask-covered face and then, predictably, the black ink on the side of my neck.

"Hello," I said flatly.

"*Sat Sri Akaal*, Uncle," Ainsley said, and I smiled at her pronunciation. It was getting better. "This is my friend Serena."

"Where is my boy?"

"Nikesh is putting him down."

He set down his briefcase by the stairs and slowly peeled off his jacket. Every movement was precise, intimidating. His eyes were transfixed by something in the kitchen.

"What is this I smell?" he said, placing his hand on the banister. "I do not recognize it."

"We made Greek tonight." Ainsley cleared her throat. "Would you like to try some?" She brushed past me and into the kitchen and seemingly at random opened cupboards and drawers, rearranged the pots, pans, and plates on the stove and counter. "Let me warm some up."

"No," he said sternly. "Thank you."

"Dad, what are you doing here?"

Nikesh was at the top of the stairs, a coddling blanket folded over his arm. He spoke in Punjabi. He sounded completely different, though it wasn't the language that was off-putting but the coldness in his voice.

"I thought I'd drop by and visit my grandson."

"He's asleep." Nikesh crossed his arms, taking the stairs slowly, one step at a time, Becket just behind. "You should have called."

"You might have pretended not to be home."

"I wonder why that is."

A silence followed, and it sent a chill through the air. I glanced over at Ainsley. She was aggressively heating up something in a frying pan, the tongs clanging against the metal in an irregular beat. Her eyes were darting between Nikesh and his father, and I could tell she was trying to understand what they had just said, piece the Punjabi words together.

"We have friends over, Dad," Nikesh said, breaking the silence. "It's not a good time."

"I see that." He looked back at me, again right at the tattoo. "Is your friend here Greek? If your wife can manage the time to cook for her, can she not also learn how to cook the cuisine eaten by her own family?"

"Dad, I've told you. If you're going to insult my wife, then you're not welcome in our house."

Nikesh's dad laughed softly, as if Nikesh had just told him a joke, as if the tension could not cross the language barrier.

"It's no matter." Nikesh's father looked at Ainsley. Still speaking Punjabi, he said, "When MacKenzie is older, he can learn about his culture by going to the Taj Mahal restaurant and ordering butter chicken, *hah*? By watching *Slumdog Millionaire.*" He smiled at Ainsley, as if he wasn't bad-mouthing her right in front of her. "It is such a good film."

"That's enough." Nikesh walked down the stairs, stopping on the last one. From one stair up, he towered over the man. "You need to leave. Now."

"OK then," Nikesh's dad said, switching to English. "I must be off. Enjoy your . . . Greek food."

He turned to me. "It was nice to meet you."

"It wasn't at all nice to meet you, Uncle-ji," I said, in perfect Punjabi.

If he was shocked that I was Punjabi and that I'd understood every word he said, he didn't show it. I guess the yellow mask must have blended out my South Asian features to him. Nikesh beamed at me while his dad grabbed his coat and his briefcase and walked briskly out the door.

The door slammed shut. The house shook. By the time I looked back at Ainsley, Nikesh was in the kitchen, holding her from behind. She was shaking and tears were spilling from her face. I'd never seen her like that.

"Don't let him ruin your night, baby. Please?" he whispered into her ear. He dried her cheeks with the back of his hand, and she closed her eyes, the weight of her head falling into him. My chest hurt watching the tenderness between them, and I had to look away. My eyes locked with Becket, who was still standing awkwardly on the stairs.

"Sorry you had to see that," Ainsley said abruptly in my direction.

"You have nothing to be sorry about." I crossed my arms. "Are you OK?"

She didn't answer me. "So what did he say this time, Nikesh?"

"Don't worry about it." He looked over at me. "I've told her so many times not to take it personally. He's a cranky bastard with my brother's wife, too, and she's Indian."

I laughed. "So at least he's not a discriminatory bastard—"

"Seriously, what did he say this time?" Ainsley interrupted. "Did he say I was too old for you again? Used goods?" She ran her hands through her hair. "I heard the word 'Greek.' Does he still want me to learn make to *daal*? *You* can cook *daal*. Did you tell him that? So why do I have to fucking learn how to make it?"

"Ainsley," Nikesh said softly. "Chill, OK?"

"Don't tell me to chill!"

He puts his hands up in surrender. "Babe, it doesn't matter what he said. Let's just . . . have a nice dinn—"

"Serena, what did he say?" She spun on her heels toward me. "Tell me what he said. *Please?* Nikesh never tells me."

Nikesh's eyes were on the ground, and he was shifting his weight between his heels. Was this why Ainsley was really learning Punjabi? To figure out what Nikesh's father was saying about her behind her back?

To figure out that she was now in an Indian family, and the truth was, she was never going to be good enough? What was the point of trying to make them happy when they never would be?

"I didn't really catch what he said," I said finally. "His dialect is a bit different . . ."

"Well, what did you say to *him*?"

"I said goodbye," I lied again, and Nikesh threw me a look of gratitude. "Anyway, Ainsley, you should really wash off the mask."

Nodding, she leaned over the kitchen sink and turned on the tap. The turmeric had dried to both of our faces. I used the bathroom sink, and when I came back into the kitchen, Becket and Nikesh were both in stiches.

"What's so funny—oh!" I shrieked, bursting into laughter at the site of Ainsley's bright yellow face. The turmeric had stained her skin.

"I look like SpongeBob!" she shrieked.

"My wife," Nikesh said, "the Minion."

"Big Bird?" Becket said.

"Tweety Bird." I giggled, wrapping my arms around Ainsley, and she squeezed me in return. Hugging her, I could feel her unclench. Her body shook—in laughter, in tears, I wasn't sure.

"Fuck him," I said quietly into her ear. "Since when does Ainsley Woods care what anybody thinks?"

25

The whole month of July, I lived and breathed The Fifth Ingredient, and so did Vic, who was not only civil with me but, in a few cases, borderline *friendly*. We'd assembled a motley crew from across the office—creative, accounts, business development, and digital—to do the legwork and prepare sample campaigns to bring with me to Richmond in early August. Jerry had already rented me a car and apartment near the office "indefinitely," and I didn't know if that meant he expected me to stay one week, three weeks, maybe even the rest of the summer. The truth was, it didn't really matter how long I needed to be away. This was the opportunity of a lifetime, and I would do what needed doing until I got it done.

The agency still had to cope with its usual workload, and we were short-staffed even with Deborah coming back with a more active creative role. Baby Spice's internship was coming to an end, so I offered her a position as a junior copywriter, and luckily, she accepted on the spot. Ainsley, Deborah, and I also assigned more work to our roster of freelancers, which now included Becket. With the hot desks full, the office was near capacity, and the entire place seemed to be buzzing with life, excitement.

August arrived like a tidal wave, and suddenly it was my last day in the office before leaving for Richmond. I was proud of myself for helping create this atmosphere, and selfishly, I also couldn't help but wonder if the new business—and challenge—might help allay any doubts Ainsley was having about working here. Her father-in-law was an asshole. So what? Why did his traditional, sexist hang-ups have to get in the way of her working outside the home and doing exactly what she wanted? She'd been rather morose ever since he'd shown up unannounced, but every time I mentioned the incident, it only seemed to make her mood worse, so I'd dropped it. I hoped she could let it go.

I had wrapped up everything I needed to do before leaving, so around lunchtime, Ainsley and I decided to take off a bit early and go on an impromptu picnic with "the guys"—Becket, Nikesh, and little MacKenzie. (Deborah encouraged work-life balance and basically pushed us out the door when she overheard us making plans.) By four p.m., the five us were piled into Ainsley's Jetta and on our way out to Rock Creek, me wedged between Becket and MacKenzie's car seat. But I didn't mind. I'd chosen that seat to sit next to MacKenzie.

"Where'd Bob go?" I asked him, ignoring the others' conversation. I spotted his favorite stuffed hedgehog on the floor of the car and dusted it off on my bare legs before giving it back to him. Perplexed, MacKenzie poked it with his thumb and then, squealing in delight, threw it back on the floor.

"I give up," I said to him. "There's no pleasing you men."

Nikesh laughed from the front seat and said something to Ainsley, who was driving, but I didn't catch it. I was still fixated on MacKenzie. The way his eyes bulged in delight or bemusement or anguish at absolutely anything and everything. The way he now recognized me, sought me out, squeezed my hands and cheeks or around my middle whenever he possibly could.

"I don't think Serena really likes me all that much," I heard Ainsley say loudly. "I think she friended me for my baby."

"You're only figuring that out now?" Becket asked.

"It's been twenty-five minutes. Aren't you bored of my son yet?" Ainsley whined. "Talk to *me*. Hell, talk to your boyfriend!"

"Sorry," I said, looking over to Becket. "I'm hogging the baby."

"MacKenzie looks good on you."

"I can't hear you over this damn music," Ainsley said, turning down the radio. "What did you say?"

"I said a baby looks good on her," Becket said a little louder. Ainsley caught my eye in the rearview mirror, and my stomach curdled.

We arrived at Rock Creek, and Nikesh led us to their favorite picnic spot. I felt my phone buzzing on our walk over to the spot, and I slowed down and waved them on when I saw that it was Mom calling.

"Are you coming this evening?" she asked in Punjabi after I picked up. I furrowed my brow, shielding my eyes from the sun with my hand.

"Where?"

"To the barbeque. The one hosted by Mark's parents."

"What barbeque?" I asked.

"The Hartshorne family is having their annual summer barbeque. Did you not see Natasha's invite?"

"Oh." I vaguely remembered Natasha having texted the family group about a barbeque at the Hartshornes' Bethesda home—one of the few times Mom and I had heard from her this summer—but I hadn't replied. At the time, I thought I'd already be in Richmond.

"Are you coming?" Mom continued. "It will be fun."

I slowed to a halt, doubting that it would in fact be any fun at all for Mom. "I can't today. I'm actually just out with some friends."

"Oh. OK." Mom switched tones, and I couldn't tell if she was disappointed or not. "So how fancy will the occasion be? I tried calling you earlier to ask."

"Sorry," I said, my cheeks heating up. I had a missed call from her that morning while I was in the shower and hadn't gotten around to calling her back.

"Your father thinks I am overdressed."

I heard his voice in the background, and then she giggled. I thought about asking what he'd said to make her laugh, but I didn't.

"Where are you guys?"

"On the highway," she said. "We are nearly there. What do you think of the fuchsia *salwar kameez*? It has the gold detail. It is the one I nearly wore to Ritu's anniversary party."

I nodded, remembering it. "It's very pretty."

"We have also packed the mint green in the trunk."

"That one is beautiful, too."

"It is not too *chamkda*?"

"They're both perfect, Mom."

"Serena, tell me . . ." She paused. "What will the other women be wearing?"

My breath caught. *What would they be wearing?*

They would be wearing designer labels Mom had never heard of, showing off necklines and toned limbs Mom had never dared to display in public. They would be drinking champagne, or gin and tonics with limes, and exclaiming over everything from the climate crisis to Herodotus to lip fillers, depending on which group of their friends she was stuck talking to.

I had never been to the Hartshornes' Bethesda home, but I had met their friends and knew that their version of a Friday night barbeque was different than the average American's. And Mom would be blindsided. Although she understood and spoke English well enough, I knew she had felt uncomfortable in the Hartshornes' world during the wedding and gender reveal party, but at least there she'd had her own group of friends. Other Indians. Allies. *Me.*

Today she'd have no one.

I wanted to tell Mom that she didn't have to go, that the Hartshornes had probably only extended them an invite out of courtesy, which of course my hospitable Indian parents had interpreted as being obligatory. I wanted to tell her that it didn't matter what the other women were wearing or what *salwar kameez* she chose to put on.

Because all the Hartshornes would see was that she'd worn a *salwar kameez*. That she was the overdressed Indian woman adding a bit of color to their party.

I kept walking in the direction the others had headed, and a few minutes later, I spotted them settled beneath a maple tree near a grouping of picnic tables. They'd already unpacked our bags of food, sunscreen, and beach toys for MacKenzie, which he was ignoring, fascinated by a piece of apple as he drove it up and down his chubby legs like a car. They all looked up at me, smiling, ready for the day.

"Ainsley," I said, crossing my arms. "I need to borrow your car."

She furrowed her eyebrows.

"My sister's in-laws are having a barbeque . . . it's not far from here." I shrugged. "Do you mind if go make sure my mom is OK?"

Ainsley gave me a look that asked a lot of questions. I averted my eyes.

"Is your mom . . . not OK?"

No. She never has been OK, and I've never been able to do a thing about it. But I'd promised myself I'd be a better daughter, and today of all days, she needed me.

I glanced up. "I just need to go. For an hour, tops."

Ainsley hopped up from the ground and patted down her behind from any grass. "Then I'll come with you."

I glanced at Becket. "Do you . . ."

I trailed off, wondering if he wanted me to invite him along. What was wrong with me that I couldn't—that I *hadn't*—introduced a single guy to my parents except for Jesse? The past was the past, and I needed to get over it. Put it in a box and push it under the bed. Right? No. I needed to throw the fucking box away.

"Why don't we all go?" I suggested halfheartedly, glancing from Becket to Nikesh to MacKenzie, who was now ramming the piece of apple into Nikesh's leg, squealing in delight as it squished into the hair.

"Crash your brother-in-law's family barbeque?" Nikesh asked, laughing. "I'm good. And I think MacKenzie is pretty happy here."

I glanced at Becket, praying he'd volunteer to stay back, too. By virtue of the fact that Jesse was the only guy to have ever met my parents, he'd stayed on a pedestal all of these years. But as much as I wanted Jesse knocked off, I didn't want anybody else up there, either.

"I'll stay, too," Becket said. Relieved, I crouched down and shielded the sun from my eyes with my hand so I could read his face. He didn't look upset.

"Are you sure you don't mind?" I asked, lowering my voice. I put my hand on Becket's cheek and suddenly felt hesitant to go.

"Of course not." He smiled, playfully pinched my nose. "You'll just be an hour or so, right?"

Ainsley and I listened to the radio on the short drive over, and

I was thankful she didn't ask any more questions about why we were going. I'd seen pictures of their house, so my jaw didn't drop the way that Ainsley's did as we pulled into the driveway. Although, I shouldn't call it a driveway. It was a paved private road at the end of a cul-de-sac that led down a hill toward an expanse of green lawn, a small man-made lake, and a house fitting of *Downton Abbey*.

Rows and rows of cars were parked on one of the lawns, and I maneuvered us into a spot on the far edge. As we climbed out of the car, I suddenly felt self-conscious, underprepared. Before heading to Rock Creek, Ainsley and I had both gone home to change out of work attire, and I'd scrubbed off all my makeup and was now wearing jean shorts, a free tank top branded with the logo of a former client, and my favorite flip-flops with a broken loop that I'd taped in place with duct tape.

"What kind of party is this?" Ainsley asked hesitantly. I looked up, noting the tone in her voice. I could see her bikini top through her pale cotton cover-up, which had questionable-looking stains on the shoulder—even though *I* knew it was MacKenzie's morning oatmeal.

Oh well. There was no turning back now. At least this way, no one would look twice at my mom wearing a *salwar kameez*.

I told Ainsley not to worry about it as I grabbed my shoulder bag from the backseat, and we started walking toward the front entrance. We rounded a corner, and up ahead in the clearing, we saw the party. There was a white tent set up and people milling about. From fifty feet away, everyone was simply tiny specs of color against a lush green lawn. As we drew closer, the specs turned into people—the Hartshornes' fancy friends, servers in penguin-like outfits scurrying about with trays of god knows what, bottles of fermented grapes costing god knows how much.

(I never understood humankind's fascination with wine. Grapes, in their simplest form, tasted so, so much better.)

"Ah, the one percent," Ainsley said dryly.

"*Ainsley.*"

"Sorry." She brushed my arm with hers, and I grabbed onto it, laughing.

Once inside the tent, we got our confidence back, and Ainsley seemed to revel in the looks we were getting from the other guests. No one was rude about it, no one gawked, but we were *definitely* noticed.

"Hello," she said brightly to seemingly everyone we passed. "Nice to see you."

"I'm *obsessed* with your fascinator," she said to another. "Is it couture?"

Meanwhile, as I searched for Mom, I grabbed a glass of fizzy lemonade from a passing waiter and did my best to avoid eye contact with everyone in case one of them remembered me from the wedding. Briefly, I spotted Natasha and Mark around the other side of the house, sitting side by side on some patio furniture. Her belly had nearly doubled in size, and she wasn't sitting normally. She looked uncomfortable, pillows propped behind her and padding her right side. Mark was to her left, and he had his arm wrapped around her. He said something that made her frown.

She looked upset, and I could tell that Mark was trying to cheer her up. A part of me wondered what was going on or if I could help, but a bigger part of me knew better than to put myself out there again.

"Mr. Singh, *hey*!"

My stomach dropped as I heard Ainsley's voice. I shifted slightly and looked in the direction she was waving furiously.

It was Dad.

He was wearing a Lacoste polo shirt he would never have picked out himself, surely a gift from Natasha. I wondered where Mom was.

Ainsley gently pushed through the crowd toward him, and reluctantly, I followed. He beamed at her, and when she leaned in for a hug, he awkwardly placed his left arm across her back.

Lots of Indians I knew were weird about hugging, especially with the opposite gender. Even family members who hadn't seen each other in decades, at the airport, seemingly never got more than an awkward, side-facing, one-armed *pat* that looked more like a country line dance move than a hug.

I sipped my lemonade and mercilessly chewed the ice cube that had slipped into my mouth. I couldn't remember the last time Dad had expressed any sort of affection for me.

"Hi, *beti*," he said, smiling. It seemed forced, but I smiled in return to be polite. It had been a while since I looked at him straight on, and I hadn't noticed how many wrinkles he'd gotten; how his beard and eyebrows were fading from gray to white.

"So good to see you, Mr. Singh!" Ainsley said.

"You, too, dear."

"Some party, huh?" Her eyes skirted over the lawn. "Where's Mrs. S?"

"She was rounded up by Mark's mother. I think she is giving some of the ladies a tour of her new exercise room."

Ainsley nodded, turning to me, as if prompting me to participate in the conversation. Avoiding her eyes, I took another long sip of my lemonade.

"Where's little . . ." Dad paused. "Macaroon?"

Ainsley laughed. "Close. MacKenzie. He's with his dad and Beck—"

"So where's this exercise room, Dad?" I interrupted, cocking my hip against Ainsley's in annoyance. Dad didn't know Becket existed. There was no reason for him to.

"I am not sure," Dad said. "Should we go find her?"

I shook my head, looking away again. The way he put his words together was oddly formal, tense. Forced. I suppose I spoke to him in the same way, when I managed to say something to him at all. I cleared my throat, wishing he would leave or that I could leave, but Ainsley kept chatting away with him.

Ainsley was telling Dad all about Nikesh and how his dirty chai wasn't all that "dirty" when one of the penguins waddled up to us. He straight up looked like one of the servers from the banquet room in the *Titanic*, where Kate and Leo eat the night the ship goes down. He crinkled his nose at the three of us.

"An impromptu tasting, anyone?" Without waiting for us to answer, he continued, "The pinot noir is from Côte d'Or. It's to die for. Medium body but bold. You can really taste the cherries." He took a breath. "And then we have a dry Riesling from the Clare Valley. *New*-world wines are—"

"Sure," Ainsley interrupted, grabbing a glass of white indiscriminately from the tray. "Thanks."

"I'm good," I said quietly, so the penguin turned to my dad. I held my breath.

"Sir?"

"Why not," he said without skipping a beat. Dad had also been drinking the lemonade and set his glass down on a nearby bar ledge. "I'll try the"—he cleared his throat—"pinot noir."

The penguin smiled, lifting the tray up no more than an inch in Dad's direction. Half the glasses had red wine; the other half had white. Dad was meant to select it himself, and I knew he had no idea which one was the pinot noir.

I saw him hesitate, and I opened my mouth to say something, but then I closed it again. A beat later, Dad reached for a glass of the white.

"That's the . . . Riesling, sir."

My heart sank as I looked at my dad's face. His cheeks colored, and his lips trembled, and then a moment later, it was all gone.

"It was closer," Dad said, making a joke of it. He brought the glass to his lips, taking a very small sip. "Yes, of course. Well, this is very nice."

I could tell that he didn't think it was nice at all. Dad was never a wine drinker. He set the glass down on the ledge, smacking his lips. Ainsley laughed.

"Our hosts' sommelier selected it on her most recent trip to South Australia. Can you smell the citrus?" The penguin bent over his tray and did a yoga inhale over one of the glasses. "There's a hint of pineapple in there, believe it or not."

"A sommelier," Dad said, "Why do they not call it a smell-ier?"

Ainsley cackled, while the penguin smiled condescendingly and then moved on to another group of guests. "Smell-ier!" Ainsley said, still laughing. "Fantastic dad joke, sir."

"What is a dad joke?" he asked, picking back up his lemonade.

"Dad jokes are cheesy jokes that dads make."

"Then, aren't all my jokes dad jokes?"

"Are all your jokes cheesy, Mr. S . . . ?"

They kept going on like this, and my stomach knotted. Is this what Ainsley had meant at the gender reveal party when she told me that my dad was hilarious? The kind of joke that made Natasha laugh so hard she cried, always when I was in the other room?

Smellier. I smiled, sadly. It was a great dad joke, and if he wasn't the one who had told it, I probably would have laughed.

"I'm going to go say hi to Mom," I said to them both, before quickly walking away. I pushed through the other guests on the lawn. These were the sorts of people I had to sell products to every day, analyze their psyche to convince them that my client's stuff was what belonged on their wrists and ears, in their kitchens and stomachs. I'd learned to rub elbows and nod and smile and say the right things so I could pretend I was one of them, but I really wasn't. And I didn't want to be.

A much friendlier penguin on the patio pointed me in the direction of the new home gym. I followed the corridor until I reached a flight of stairs, turned left at the bottom, as instructed. I could hear voices now, laughter. I inched forward down the hall. They were just around the corner.

"Look at you go, Sandeep!" someone exclaimed. It sounded like Mrs. Hartshorne.

"You've never tried this before, *really*?" another voice said.

"She's a natural."

"I am, right?" Mom exclaimed, laughing. Her voice rang out, vibrantly, and it shook me. I had never heard my mother laughing like that.

I chanced another step forward and peeked around the corner. Beyond the workout machines was a large flat-screen TV playing an aerobics class, a young, peppy bodybuilder squatting and cheering and kicking. Mom, Mrs. Hartshorne, and a few other women were in front of the TV copying her, facing away from me, fully clothed in their party attire.

I stared at them, incredulous. At *her*. She was bouncing around like a young woman, the loose pants of her *kameez* swishing as she followed the steps on screen impeccably. Her arms were graceful, her neck like a swan, her loose ponytail hanging beautifully down her back.

"You're going to have a tight booty tomorrow, Sandeep," Mrs. Hartshorne said, elbowing Mom. "Just you wait."

"*Uh-ho.* I already have a tight booty, Carol!"

The other women exploded in laughter, and breathing hard, I retreated so they couldn't see me.

I'd never seen Mom dance before. I'd never seen her do anything.

I didn't know she could.

26

Thirty minutes later, we were back at Rock Creek. The picnic grounds were busier than before, and it took a few minutes to find the guys. The shade had moved, and they'd relocated to a new spot down by the sand. Becket was on his back on a blanket, my backpack wedged beneath his head, a book propped on his stomach. Nikesh and MacKenzie were in the shallows of the water nearby, building a castle in the wet sand.

Seeing my family had drained me entirely. Since Ainsley had driven, I'd even dozed during the ride back. I plopped down next to Becket without saying anything as Ainsley walked farther on to her family. I smiled, watching the way MacKenzie squealed in delight as he saw her, toppling the castle as he darted into her arms.

"He's adorable, isn't he?" Becket asked me, leaning his head against my shoulder. "I've been watching him more than reading."

I glanced over at his book. It was my copy of the crime thriller I'd read for book club. The book club that kicked me out for dissing the author.

"I borrowed it when you were in the shower the other day."

"What do you think?"

"I think the carpenter did it."

"Maybe he did." I let my eyes close and tilted my face up toward the sun. "Maybe he didn't."

"You're not going to tell me?"

I shook my head, smiling. "Not a—"

"Oh my god, look at him." Becket laughed, cutting me off, and it made me open my eyes. MacKenzie was bobbing up and down, plugging his nose with his fingers, as if he was trying to plop down beneath the water. He looked like a little rabbit, and it made me giggle, too.

We both watched him for a while, and it struck me that Becket and I were both being silent about the elephant in the room. (Or in our case, the beach.)

Children.

It was an important question, and one that I'd been asked in every single romantic situation that went past a few dates. It was a question that could define or end a relationship. It was a question Ainsley still thought I needed to ask.

"Becket." I sat up cross-legged, stalling for time as I worked up the courage to face him. "Can we talk?"

I had never said those words before, at least not to a guy I was seeing. I had spent more than a decade avoiding those three little words like the plague, and I couldn't believe that I was the one saying them first right now. Maybe seeing my parents had thrown me for a loop.

Or maybe I wasn't going to let myself get away with avoiding everything anymore.

"Do you want to have children?" I blurted. "I mean, I see the way you look at MacKenzie. The way you talk about him."

Becket squeezed my hand. I could hear him breathing. "You look at him the same way."

"I love him, yes," I said, my voice filling with emotion just thinking about Ainsley's little boy. "But I need to be clear about the fact that I don't want children of my own."

"You don't?"

"Do *you*?" I glanced up, and from the look on his face, I could tell that, indeed, Becket did want children. That our relationship was about to come to an end.

"I'm sorry," I said finally. "I thought you knew."

"I didn't know."

"But, you were the one who encouraged me to go out and make friends and regain a social life. You remember the reason, right?" I paused. "It was because almost everyone I know had gotten married, had kids—"

"Yeah, but I thought . . ."

"That I was just jealous of them?"

He didn't answer. Of course that's what he thought, and I didn't blame him, because it's what everyone thought.

"I never pushed you to talk about this stuff, or to meet your family, because I know how independent you are." He scoffed. "I thought we'd get there eventually, you know?"

"Becket . . ."

"I'm such an idiot . . ."

"You're not. It's my fault."

He reached for my hand, and I squeezed it. Our limbs were entangled now, and I could feel his heart beating. Unexpectedly, a tear dripped down my cheek, and I caught it with my wrist. We'd had a good run. Our relationship had been *good*, but it wasn't enough. Even if both of us wanted children, if we had the exact same vision for our future together, it still wouldn't have been enough.

"You said you thought we were going to get 'there' eventually," I said after a while. "Why did you think that? I'm asking honestly."

"You're a catch, Serena."

"You are, too." I laughed.

He smiled, sadly. "So what's the problem then?"

"You don't love me, Becket." I turned to him, pushing my feet farther into the sand. I didn't need to point out that after six months, I didn't love Becket, either, or that, with Jesse, it had only taken us a few weeks to declare our feelings for each other.

"I like you a lot, though," Becket whispered. "You're . . . perfect."

"Untrue, but thank you for the compliment—"

"You're ambitious and thoughtful, *hot*—"

I laughed.

"—who wouldn't want to settle down with you?"

"You can't just 'settle down' with me because we're getting *older*, Becket."

He didn't answer, and I wondered if I'd hit the nail on the head. A lot of his friends were married with children, too, at a totally different stage in life than both of us. Had Becket felt the pressure, too? Had he decided he was ready for something different and gone along with a relationship with the next woman he found? *Me?*

"You're right," he said finally. "This wasn't meant to be. I mean, the truth is I don't even know you that well."

What he said was true, but it didn't feel good to hear those words out loud. Six months and he didn't know me, but it wasn't his fault. I'd never let him in.

A couple of hours later, I woke up to the sound of MacKenzie crying and, a beat later, Ainsley's voice from the front seat of the car.

"Serena, could you?"

I nodded, sleepily gathering myself. I undid my belt and scooted into the middle, nearer to MacKenzie.

"There, there . . ." I whispered, gently stroking his cheeks. "I hate traffic, too."

"We all hate traffic," Nikesh muttered. He sounded irritable, which made sense because he was the one stuck behind the wheel in the traffic jam as we headed back into the city.

Becket had taken an Uber home immediately after our breakup, even though I had insisted he didn't need to leave the picnic early. I think all of us wished we'd gone home when he had. Not only had a major accident caused some of the worst traffic, the breakup seemed to have put everyone in a bad mood, especially MacKenzie, who had been whining or crying nonstop for hours.

It was well past his bedtime by the time we got back to Columbia Heights, so I insisted Ainsley drive straight home and told her that I would walk back to my apartment. By foot, it was only fifteen minutes away. Nikesh hugged me goodbye and then took MacKenzie upstairs. I helped Ainsley unpack the car, and silently, we put away the toys, blankets, and dishes they'd brought along.

With seeing my parents, and now my breakup with Becket, the whole day had thrown me for a loop, but I didn't want to dwell on any of it. I didn't have the time. In just a few days, I was off to Richmond.

"I think that's everything." Ainsley gently shut the trunk. Yawning, she leaned her weight back into the car. "Are you sure you don't want a ride home?"

"I'm sure. I could use a walk."

"How are you feeling?"

I worked the toe of my flip-flop into the pavement. "It was to be expected."

"That's not what I asked you, Serena."

"I . . . I'm fine. Honest."

"Honestly. You're *fine*?"

I shrugged. I was fine. Did she expect me not to be? Did she expect me to feel guilty?

My legs were chapped from an afternoon of wind, water, and sun, and there was still a spot of emerald-green polish on my left big toenail from a pedicure months earlier. Ainsley had been right all along; I should have been clearer to Becket about what I wanted from the beginning.

Becket was thirty-six, but he was also a man. He'd have no problem moving on, finding another woman of childbearing years who would bring him iced tea while he painted their freaking white picket fence. It angered me to think about all the expectations, burdens, and "time limits" that were exclusively placed on women.

But I was tired of being angry. Right then, I was just plain tired.

"I really am fine, Ainsley," I said.

Without saying anything, she started walking up toward the house. We hadn't said goodbye yet, so I assumed she wanted me to follow her, that we had something else to put away. But a few steps later, she turned around and threw her hands up.

"What?"

I recoiled, confused by her body language, her tone. Her eyes were bulged open, creases running horizontal on her forehead.

"Are you OK?" I asked hesitantly.

"Of course," she said, her voice dripping in sarcasm. "I'm *fine*!"

"Oh my god, are you mad that I broke up with Becket?" By her face, I could tell that wasn't it. I tried again. "That . . . That I don't want to talk about the breakup?"

Her eyebrow twitched. So that was it.

"I'm tired, OK? And I'm not . . . touchy-feely like that." I guffawed, and suddenly my frustration with the whole goddamn day came pouring out. "You *know* that. Sorry if I don't want to grab cosmopolitans in the city and talk about *dudes*."

"I'm not asking you to talk about dudes, Serena. You've just broken up with a very lovely man who you've been dating since February. That's not an insignificant amount of time."

I rubbed my face with my hands. It might be weeks until I would see her next, and I needed to calm both of us down. I didn't want to fight.

"Can I ask you something?" she said suddenly. Without waiting for me to answer, she continued. "Why haven't you told me anything about your parents?"

I hugged my arms around my chest, confused by the sudden change of topic.

"Becket told you that after all this time, he doesn't feel like he even knows you well. And it got me thinking. I don't think *I* even know you."

"You could hear us?"

"Of course I could hear you," she snapped. "You were breaking up like fifteen feet away from us."

I didn't respond. I wasn't sure if I was annoyed that she'd eavesdropped.

"I'm asking you something, Serena. Do I know you?"

"Ainsley," I said, exasperated. "Of course you do."

"Well, you clearly hate your dad. And you never talk about him, or why just being *near* him turns you into a completely different person."

"I don't . . . hate anyone."

Ainsley continued as if she hadn't heard me. "I know for a fact that I'm your closest friend right now. So I had to assume, if you're not talking about this stuff with me or Natasha, well, at least you had Becket."

"Ainsley." I hesitated. I knew what she was getting at, and I didn't want to go there.

"But it turns out, you were closed off to him, too."

Closed off.

I hugged my arms over my chest, squeezing so hard my ribs hurt. Who the hell was she to say that to me? To tell me off when she—she didn't know *anything*?

"I just don't understand—"

"What do you want me to say to you?" I asked. I was exhausted. "Should I admit that I'm closed off and nobody really knows me? Fine. I'll admit it. You barely know me, Ainsley."

My words sounded like shards of ice, and I didn't really mean them, but they were out there, and I couldn't take them back. I wanted to apologize, but her face had turned to stone.

"That's . . . not . . ."

"No, no," she said, holding up her hand. She smiled at me, civilly, devoid of the warmth I'd grown used to. "That's absolutely fine."

"Ainsley—"

"I've been trying to find the right moment all day to tell you the news, but if I barely know you, you can find out when Tracy e-mails everyone at the office next week."

A shiver ran down my spine. "What news?"

"I'm going to hand in my notice."

I froze. My feet felt heavy on the ground. I couldn't believe it, and suddenly, I wondered if I didn't know her that well, either. Ainsley was one of the most talented web developers and digital specialists I had ever met. And she was throwing it away—for *what*?

"Carlos can run the show without me. I've trained him well."

I nodded, swallowing the lump in my throat. Her deputy, Carlos, was good, he'd be just fine, but he wasn't Ainsley.

My gut instinct had been right all along. Ainsley was leaving, and I could see and feel and even taste our friendship crumbling around us right there on her driveway.

Love. Friendship. *Happiness.* It was all a fucking mirage. It blindsided you and then left you winded, worse off than you were before.

A part of me was tempted to try to press pause. Somehow, miraculously, make it right between us. But I could feel my throat tightening, and suddenly the anger and my frustration with her came pouring out.

"I suppose you'll need the time to learn to cook *daal*."

Her mouth dropped, but I didn't stop. She needed to know, and I couldn't.

"It doesn't matter what you do, Ainsley. It wouldn't matter if you made a wish to Aladdin's genie and miraculously became Indian. You know that, right? You're *never* going to please him."

"You think I'm quitting because my father-in-law wants me to?"

"You're learning Punjabi so you can eavesdrop on him, aren't you?"

She bit her bottom lip, shaking her head at me. It suddenly occurred to me that we weren't just fighting; we were changing everything.

"I'm quitting my job," she said coldly, "because I need to prioritize my family. Nikesh has been the primary caregiver since MacKenzie was born. It's my turn—"

"Your turn to sacrifice everything you've worked hard for?"

"Give me a break, Serena." Ainsley rolled her eyes. "Do you think you're somehow superior to the rest of us who allow ourselves to feel vulnerable enough to fall in love? To make compromises—"

"Yes!"

Tears welled in my eyes. I couldn't look at her. And without looking back, I walked away.

27

My phone rattled on my bedside table, buzzing repeatedly. I opened my eyes to Natasha's picture on the home screen. There were blond streaks in her hair and purple glitter on her lids. I'd taken it at Osheaga, when we'd driven up to Montreal for the music festival years earlier. It was just the two of us. It was the week before she met Mark.

Where did you go yesterday?

The text flashed up just as the phone stopped ringing. With one hand, I lazily keyed in my passcode and texted her back.

Had other plans and couldn't stay long.

I bit my lip as I watched the text go from delivered to read in a flash.

Ah . . . I see. Well, can we talk?

I didn't respond, and a few minutes later, she rang again. I declined the call.

After another hour, I dragged myself out of bed, put on a pot of coffee, and turned on my favorite Saturday morning talk radio program. I felt hungover, emotionally. I'd tossed and turned all night, going over and over my stupid fight with Ainsley, the breakup with Becket, and a million other things I didn't want to think about. No. I wanted to concentrate on *work*.

I was *positive* that Jerry, Patricia, and their team would love our pitches for the digital campaign, slogan, and sample logos and labels. But I still wasn't confident that either of our two commercial pitches would blow them out of the water. Jerry didn't want another beer commercial about bros watching Aaron Rodgers throw another touchdown; rather, an accessible spot that would speak to an average American, whether that was a beer drinker whose family had lived in Virginia for centuries or were more recent immigrants.

I treated myself to a bowl of Cap'n Crunch and sat on my tiny balcony with a pad of paper and pen to my left, my phone on the seat to my right, and started brainstorming to see if I couldn't think of a mind-blowing commercial to present as a third option. Eating in silence, I wondered if Jerry's vision was even possible. How on earth was I going to come up with something that would entice both a man like Jerry and a man like my own father to buy the same beer? Jerry and my father were polar opposites. I wasn't sure there was any common ground to find.

After an hour of getting nowhere, I welcomed the distraction of my phone again. My heart lurched when I saw that it was a text from Jesse.

Do I get to see you again before you leave?

I let my head fall back as I considered his question and felt a weird lump in my throat when I realized that our weekly lunches would be postponed indefinitely while I was in Richmond.

Are you free now?

He replied immediately, and we agreed to meet outside my building in a half hour and then walk over to the farmers market. And exactly thirty-two minutes later, I found Jesse waiting for me on the stoop outside my building.

"Hey . . ." I trailed off, noticing that he was dripping wet and his chest was heaving. "Did you fall in the Potomac or something?"

He smiled, panting. "I jogged here."

"Oh." I had suggested he come over first because I thought he'd be driving, and there was never any parking near the market. "Well in that case, we could have met there."

"It's fine. I wanted to see where you lived anyway." He leaned back on the railing, and I tried not to stare at the way his T-shirt stretched against his shoulders. "Can I have some water?"

I hesitated. "There's this Aussie coffee shop around the corner. Can we get it there? I'm desperate for a coffee."

Two Americanos and an ice water later, we set off for the farmers market, which was already in full swing when we arrived. I pulled out the foldaway shopping bag I kept at the bottom of my purse and led Jesse around to the stalls where I often bought my bread, fruits, and vegetables for the week. Jesse picked up a jar of pesto from the Italian woman who was just known as "Nona" to all the locals. When he and I had gone all the way down one aisle and were rounding the corner to go down the next one, I caught Jesse looking rather frazzled, picking at some lint on his T-shirt.

"You good?" I asked.

"I'm underdressed," he mumbled.

"For a farmers market?"

"That's what I thought." With his eyes, he gestured to a cluster of people in line at the juice stand. "Everyone here is so cool."

I followed his gaze. Indeed, there was an exceptionally cool-looking group of adults standing around with strollers or dogs on leashes. Their skin and hair were all different shades, tattoos and anklets were everywhere, and they all seemed to be in perfect shape and impeccably dressed in the latest hipster fashion. They belonged in a Fenty Beauty campaign.

"See?" I heard Jesse say.

I tucked my arm through his and started leading him farther down the aisle. "Stop being self-conscious."

We walked by a few stalls, and when I paused to examine some produce, he dropped my arm.

"So this is what your life has been like since college, huh?"

I couldn't read the tone of his voice. "What do you mean by 'this'?"

"I'm Serena *Singh*," he said, putting on a Valley girl accent. "I'm a super swanky advertising executive who, like, lives in the city and shops at farmers market and eats *organic*—"

"Hey . . ."

"—and have you heard how cool I am? I have a *tattoo*!"

I rolled my eyes at him, crossing my arms in front of my chest. "I don't sound like that."

"*Like*, you totally do."

"Oh yeah?" I shoved him playfully and then exaggerated Jesse's gruff manner of speech. "Have you heard of me, bro? I'm Jasmeet Dhillon."

"When have I ever said 'bro'?"

"Man, I'm such a dork, bro. I, like, analyze things and make polling graphs for the *Washington Post*—"

He cut me off, pressing his palm into my mouth. I squealed, pushing him away.

"And do you know I jog now?" I slapped my belly. Somehow my accent had turned Cockney. "Bro, I *love* to jog. I'm so fit!"

Laughing, he put his hands on my shoulders, and as he leaned his weight into me, I started walking backward. I was thankful that his bad mood had been temporary.

"So that's what I sound like, huh?"

I nodded as I backpedaled past Charity's stall, which sold fruit pies and croissants. "You're such a city boy now."

"It's true. I live more central than you."

"You live in a traffic circle, Jesse. That's *too* central."

He grinned. "I'm not *in* Dupont Circle. I'm nearby. I live in the building above the poke place on P Street."

"Poke Pete's?" I asked, and he nodded. "I walk by that building every day."

I slowed to a halt. Jesse and I had been friends for months, and although I knew that he lived in the same neighborhood as my office, I was clueless about such a simple fact.

I could still feel the heat of his hands on my body, and I shivered as I wondered what else I didn't know about him. Had he bought those plaid curtains he'd described months back, when I'd refused to go shopping with him at Home Depot? I wondered what his apartment looked like, what direction it faced, and I fought the urge to ask him about details that really shouldn't have mattered to me. That really didn't matter at all.

Jesse had lived in that apartment for less than a year. There were eleven more unaccounted for. My breath got shallow, and suddenly, I felt drained. Physically. Emotionally. Where did he live before that? Where had he and his *family* been all these years?

I could feel my throat closing in. Sweat beading at my temples. And as we passed by yet another vegetable stand, it hit me, again, that Jesse hadn't just reappeared out of thin air. Anadi and his children weren't just pixels on a screen, an anecdote, or an emotionally charged story. They had been and still were Jesse's life. We had broken up, and we had both moved on. He had been living his life without me.

I watched his face as he examined a peach, tenderly held it in his palm. Was this why he had been grumpy with me just moments earlier? Fleetingly, had he imagined my life all these years without him? Did he think I'd been living in some glamorous *Sex and the City* fantasy, free of a husband, of suburbia.

Did he think I hadn't missed him?

Luckily, Dirty Chai was as crowded as ever, and if Ainsley was at the stall, we didn't see each other. My feelings were all over the place, and I wasn't ready to face her. Still, I steered Jesse in a different direction, and we sat outside on the lawn and ate pastries. After a while, I could feel myself tiring and suggested that we leave. Jesse took my bag from me, ignoring my protests, and carried it all the way home.

"I love this neighborhood," he said quietly, closing his eyes into the sun when we reached my building. I smiled. I wholeheartedly loved it, too. The road was lined with trees, and most of the residents seemed to be amateur gardeners. There were flourishes of color, strong scents of rosemary or thyme every few paces.

"Much better than living in a traffic circle."

He grinned, opening his eyes. "Somehow, I feel like I'm on the set of an indie movie."

"An indie movie or *Indian* movie?"

He set down the bag, and before I realized what was happening, he grabbed my hand and spun me so hard I dropped my purse.

"Jesse!"

"*Keh do na. Keh do na*," he sang, twirling me around and around.

My face was beet red, and I could hear laughter coming from people walking past us on the sidewalk. "*You are my So-ni-ya.*"

"Jesse," I pulled my hand away. "Stop!"

He didn't stop and kept twirling me around and shimmying his hips while attempting to sing that silly song he loved from *Kabhi Khushi Kabhie Gham* . . . I was mortified, but I couldn't help myself from laughing, which only encouraged him more.

Finally, he stopped spinning me, and breathless I picked up my purse, and he gathered up the groceries, which had spilled across the pavement. Although he'd stopped singing, he was still humming, and I rolled my eyes at him. He never did have any shame. When he was in a good mood, it took a lot to embarrass him.

"You think you're Hrithik Roshan, don't you?" I asked as we rose to our feet.

"Yeah, sweetheart!"

He was using "the voice" a few of my favorite Bollywood stars used when speaking English—over-the-top, overpronounced. I set my hands on my hips.

"Done yet?"

He shook his head, shimmying his hips and rising to the balls of his feet.

"Well, I'll leave you to it, then." I took a few steps backward and then spun around when I reached my front stoop. "See ya!"

"Your groceries, Serena."

I could hear him following me up the steps, and my keys in hand, I stopped short just outside the door.

"I can carry them up for you."

I shook my head, grabbing the bag from him.

"Thanks, I'm good."

"Sure?" He leaned against the door, and the corners of his

mouth crinkled upward into a smile. I was waiting for him to leave, and he was waiting for me to invite him inside. My stomach lurched.

"Jesse, what are you doing?"

"Can I use your bathroom?"

I had to laugh, and I ran my hands through my hair. "Dude, you're being *so* transparent . . ."

"Come on." He touched my arm. "What's the big deal? Let me see your place. I'll show you my apart—"

"I don't want to see your apartment!" I said, a little forcefully. He balked. I wondered if he knew I was lying.

"Quit being weird, Serena," he said casually, making me feel like I was the one acting strangely. "Do you still have a Tupac poster above your bed? That's really all I want to know."

"Of course it's there," I deadpanned. "Where else would I have put it?"

"And the Beanie Babies? You were twenty when I met you, and you still had Beanie Babies, for crying out loud—"

"It was a collection. They were a *set*—"

"You were a grown woman with toys."

"I was twenty, Jesse. And I lived with my parents. I wasn't a grown woman."

"So, what does a grown woman's room look like, then?"

"Well, for one, there are sex toys everywhere."

He chuckled, shifting his shoulders back. "Come on, Serena. I know it's against the *rules*. But let me see your place. It's really no big deal."

I sighed, looking at my shoes.

"Come on," Jesse said, laughing. He was standing so close now. Too close. The tips of his shoes were edge to edge against mine. All I would have to do was tilt my chin upward to kiss him.

I cleared my throat, pushing away the thought, and when Jesse gently pried my keys from my fingertips, I didn't stop him. First, he jammed my parents' house key into the hole, and then unsuccessfully tried out the key to my bike lock.

"That one," I said quietly, pointing at the long silver one dangling by his pinky.

I showed him around my apartment as quickly as I could. It wasn't big, but he stalled at every nook and cranny to crack a joke, make a comment, ask a question.

"How long are you going to leave this as a shrine?" He said this leaning into the doorframe of Natasha's old bedroom.

All I could do was shrug. He did have a point. I had closed the door when she moved out and barely opened it except to run the occasional dustcloth over the windowsill or track down my copy of Michelle Obama's book, which Natasha had read and then stuffed into the back of the closet. (I also found my favorite yellow sundress back there, which she'd claimed to have never borrowed.) She'd left pictures on the wall, a dusty rose bedspread on the double mattress, and piles of old books, clothes, and knickknacks that she presumably didn't want anymore and were only collecting dust.

"Tell her to clean it up, Serena," Jesse said softly. "She isn't thirteen anymore."

I didn't answer. He knew all about my relationship with Natasha, and I didn't feel like getting into it. I was getting increasingly annoyed with his presence, his chipper attitude, his probing into my life, and by the time we circled back into the kitchen, I regretted bringing him up here.

I felt weak all over again, like a total idiot. When I looked up, I realized he was babbling away about the artwork on my wall and settling himself into the armchair. My armchair. The one I had bought and paid for, and dragged up the stairs all by my fucking self.

"Jesse," I said quietly, the anger rising in my voice. "I think you should leave."

"I have this blank wall above my stove, right? Are you supposed to hang art above a stove?" He looked over at me, craning his neck as he leaned farther back into my chair. He hadn't heard me. "The heat would ruin it, right?"

"I think you should leave," I said again.

"In a minute. Do you think—"

"No, Jesse," I snapped. "Now."

He stopped talking, although his mouth remained open. Slowly, he peeled himself out of my chair and walked toward me.

"Why?" he asked, stopping short just a foot in front me. "I'll go, but you have to tell me why."

"You know why."

"Because of the rules you made up?" Jesse asked. "Because you wanted us to be respectful of Anadi and whoever it is you're dating? Anadi and I are *divorced*, Serena. Frankly, it doesn't matter what she thinks. And as for your mystery fellow, well, it's hard for me to believe that you made up these rules to be respectful of a guy you never talk about."

"I . . ." I stammered, words failing me. The rules failing *us*. I'd mandated them to maintain boundaries in our friendship, to be respectful of Becket. My palms grew moist as I wondered what would happen if I told Jesse that Becket was no longer in the picture. What would happen if we were standing any closer.

"Becket's a nice guy," I said finally. Jesse blinked, and he looked as confused as I felt. Why was I lying to Jesse? Why was I pushing him away?"

"That's all you have to say about your boyfriend?" I didn't respond, and Jesse scoffed. "You're dating him because he's nice? My Toyota Camry is *nice*, Serena. Jesus!"

"Well, not everyone gets to drive a Ferrari or Tesla or whatever they want." I shook my head. "Sometimes you get a car because you need to get somewhere, it's functional."

"And some people get their dream car, and then they crash it for no apparent reason."

It felt like I'd been punched in the gut. My body clenched, and I felt my eyes go moist, so I blinked until the tears receded. Jesse was staring at me, and when he caught my gaze, I couldn't look away. He took another step toward me, and I felt sickeningly powerless. Completely under his control.

"I . . ." I hesitated. "I don't even know what we're talking about anymore." I let out a stiff laugh, trying to break the tension. "This analogy is falling apart."

He pressed his mouth into the back of his hand, the way a person might when they were about to vomit or cry or maybe both. A moment later, he brought his hand down to his side.

"I forgot to tell you," he said, his voice distant. "I have a date tonight."

"A date," I echoed, my voice wavering.

"She's a teacher, apparently, over in Arlington." He nodded, stuffing his hands into the pockets of his running shorts. "Good with kids. A Democrat."

"You . . . haven't met her yet?"

He shook his head. "It's a blind date. My friends think it's time I move on."

"Good. Yeah." My voice sounded colder than I wanted it to. "You should move on. If you're ready and all that."

Jesse bit his bottom lip. "*If* I'm ready."

I swallowed hard as he toed closer toward me. It was only a few inches, but it was an onslaught, and from where I was standing, I could feel his heat, his presence, his power over my entire body.

My heart, too.

"Say something, Serena," he whispered, and I winced, tearing away my gaze.

"I'm sorry."

His arms were by his sides, his hands just inches from mine. I was looking at my feet, but I was aware of every inch of him.

"For what?"

"For kicking you out."

"Is that it?" He sounded incredulous. I forced myself to meet his eye. "Twelve years, and you still can't say anything more?"

I pressed my lips together to keep them from trembling. My strength was faltering, and everything I'd pushed down was rushing up. What did he want me to say? What truth did he want me to admit?

"Is that it?" he asked again.

I wanted to say more. I wanted to throw my arms around him, press myself against his chest. I wanted everything I wasn't ever supposed to have.

"Serena—"

"Yes," I whispered. I turned around, because if I didn't, I wasn't sure what I would do. "That's it."

Who were these people in movies, even real life, who claimed it was possible to stay friends with an ex? With someone who would know you better than you know yourself.

If only you allowed them in.

I could hear my heart beating in my chest, my ears, my throat. I swallowed hard, concentrating on a scratch on my kitchen cabinet. I wondered what I would do if he stayed, if suddenly I felt his hands slip around my waist.

But it was too late. Because a moment later, I heard the front door slam behind me.

28

I spent the rest of Saturday afternoon on the couch streaming episodes of *Jane the Virgin*. When the show first aired, Natasha and I had watched it together. I'd rolled my eyes at nearly everything our heroine Jane said or did or giggled at, and made sarcastic commentary until Natasha hit me with pillows and I finally shut up. Jane was the ultimate romantic who wore her heart on her sleeve and hung every single emotion up on the laundry line for the whole neighborhood to see. She was *so* romantic, in fact, that she was even a romance writer. (It's a satirical telenovela; it's supposed to be corny.)

But today the TV show didn't feel as ridiculous as I remembered. And as I watched grand gesture after tear-filled monologue after soppy French kiss with either Michael or Rafael (for the record, I am one thousand percent #TeamMichael), I found myself swooning along with Jane. Crying. And more often than not, thinking about what it would have been like if I hadn't kicked Jesse out of my apartment, and we'd had one of those soppy French kisses of our own.

After my fourth episode in a row, I turned off the television and took a glass of water out to the balcony. It was sweltering outside, and my little outdoor space had absolutely no shade in the evenings. I sat down, sinking into my solitary patio chair.

Alone. Always alone.

The moment Jesse left, I wished I'd had the courage to turn around and stop him, and now that I'd stopped drowning out my thoughts with television, it was something I could no longer escape.

What did I want from him? It didn't matter. The bigger question was what did I want for *myself*? Maybe the answers to these questions weren't mutually exclusive, and I was overwhelmed by the need to call Ainsley, to momentarily brush aside the disaster of our crumbling friendship and plead for her advice on what to do next.

I snorted, imagining her response. She'd sigh, like she was totally exhausted with me, and dramatically shake out her hair from her topknot. Then, she'd set her hands firmly on her hips, and in her typical Ainsley way, she would tell me to "just get over yourself already," and "follow your damn heart."

And what would I say in reply?

Damn it, Ainsley.

I would tell her that she was right.

Half an hour later, I was a sweaty, loitering mess in front of Poke Pete's, having speed walked down to Dupont Circle. There was an unmarked black door with a call box right next to it. Jesse's name was the third button down.

"Hello?" he answered, a few moments after I managed to press the buzzer. He sounded tired, even through the static, and as I opened my mouth to announce my arrival, he let me in.

Jesse was waiting on the landing at the top of the stairs, but he was reading something on his phone and didn't see me right away. I smiled, slowing down my approach. He was wearing gym shorts and ugly blue Crocs, and his face was covered with a bright yellow paste. Even though he looked like a total dork, I got goose bumps just looking at him.

"Hey."

He looked up, knocking his shoulder against the wall as he caught sight of me.

"*Hey.*"

I hesitated, noting the surprise in his voice. Was he expecting someone else? Was his blind date supposed to come over *here*?

My sneaker caught the edge of a stair, and I stumbled forward.

"I thought you were the pizza guy—you good?"

Suddenly, Jesse was only inches away, helping me up. He smelled like damp earth and sweat, like he'd just gone for a jog. Then again, after walking around in that heat, I probably didn't smell so great myself.

"Turmeric mask?" I asked

"After you found that pimple, I figured I should get back in the habit."

"Did you use yogurt, too?"

"Yep. And honey."

I nodded approvingly as he led me to his apartment and pushed the door open with his back.

"Would you like a tour?"

I followed him inside. The kitchen was open-plan, overlooking a large sectional and wall-mounted television. CNN was on mute, and there was a basket of laundry on the armchair, a game of Monopoly abandoned on the coffee table. He gestured toward a door, and I peered inside to find bunk beds, a wardrobe, and a smattering of toys and clothes all over the carpet.

"The kids were here this afternoon," he said behind me. I turned around. He was standing above the sink, scrubbing the yellow from his face with a tea towel.

Across the living room, I saw two more doors ajar. A bathroom. Presumably, Jesse's bedroom. I stayed where I was, my eyes skirting around the room. It was strange to see him living like a grown-up. The last time I'd been in his house, he and his roommates hadn't owned a broom.

"I still haven't bought curtains," he said. Indeed, there was nothing covering the windows, nothing to stop anyone in the office building across P Street from peering into Jesse's life.

"You scared me off the plaid."

"Sorry."

"You were right, though. I don't live in a Scottish castle."

Normally, I would have made some quip or remark, but I was exhausted. My head was pounding from the humidity and lack of sleep, and I found myself on the far edge of his sectional, my head on the backrest, my feet curled up beneath me.

I closed my eyes and half heard Jesse moving around the room, a kettle whistling, the pizza delivery guy arrive and then leave. I must have fallen asleep, because when I woke up, the apartment was pitch-black except for the cold blue flicker of the TV. Jesse had put a blanket on me. I sat up. He was sitting right by my feet.

"Hey, sleepy," he said, without looking over.

"What time is it?"

"About ten. I saved you a few slices."

"Shit." I sat forward, massaging my temples. "What about your date?"

"What about my date?"

My heart skipped a beat. "You canceled?"

"No, it's not for hours still." Jesse glanced at his watch. "It's actually a booty call, not a date. Did I not tell you?"

I smacked him on the back of the shoulder, and a huge smile split across his face.

"Of course I canceled," Jesse said, softly. "The moment I left your apartment."

"You knew I'd come over with my tail between my legs, huh?"

He shook his head, and my gut twisted as our eyes met.

"Then why?"

"You mean besides the fact that there was another woman passed out on my couch?"

I suppressed a laugh, and he leaned in, lifting my feet onto his lap.

"You know exactly why I canceled, Serena."

My body ached for him as he drew me closer. My eyelids felt heavy, and when I blinked, I didn't see Jesse and Serena, forever-ago exes with enough emotional baggage to fill a U-Haul.

I didn't see us on the set of a telenovela, making grand gestures or having soppy kisses.

I just saw us. Together.

Ever so lightly, his fingers grazed the back of my arm, my shoulder, the tattooed pattern on my neck. His touch scalded my skin, and I closed my eyes as, silently, the tears fell.

"Hey." Whispering, he gently pressed the back of his hand against my cheek. "What's that about, huh?"

My face was wet, and I tasted salt when I licked my lips. My breath turned rapid, a weight lifting from my chest.

"Nothing."

"Nothing?"

It wasn't nothing. It was everything. Everything I could never say or do or admit to either of us. I tilted my chin to the side, my eyes still closed. With my hand, I felt for his cheek. I grazed his stubble, the rough edges of his jaw, and then pulled his face toward mine.

His lips were dry and soft, hesitant. For a brief, terrifying second, I thought he would push me away, that he didn't want me in the same way I so desperately wanted him. I parted my lips, pressing myself into him, and a shiver ran down my spine as he relented, as he pulled me into him and kissed me back.

I hadn't felt those lips in more than twelve years, but I knew them well. I knew what they were capable of. My knees trembled as his hands moved up my arms to gently cradle my head. I ran my hands through his thick hair, tugging, forcing us closer. He kissed me deeply, a fire igniting deep down inside of me as he groaned into my lips.

I leaned back on the couch, pulling him on top of me. His weight felt good, and I moved against him as he kissed my neck, my collarbone. I slid my hands beneath his shirt and then moved them down, tugging at his shorts.

"Serena." He grunted into my ear. "Are you sure?"

I moaned in response, squirming against him. I felt out of control. I felt alive.

I wanted him to put his hands on me again. I wanted him in every way possible.

"Are you?"

I opened my eyes. Jesse was hovering above me, his weight pressed into his arms on either side of me. I nodded again, and slowly, a sad smile stretched across his face.

I hadn't convinced him. I'd wanted to. I wanted *him*. We were breathing hard, and without saying anything to each other, we both sat up on the couch. My cheeks were hot with embarrassment. I was afraid to look at him, and when I finally made eye contact, the hungry look on his face quickly changed into one of concern.

"I'm so sorry—"

"No, I'm the one who should be sorry," he croaked. "You show up here today with your guard down, and what's the first thing I do?" He pressed a clenched fist into his thigh. "Fuck."

"Becket and I broke up," I blurted. "Yesterday."

"I figured," he said quietly. "Still, I shouldn't have done that. You're not ready."

"And you're ready?"

He gave me a look, and I laughed softly.

We wouldn't be a good idea right now.

Wasn't *that* the truth. Jesse was still processing his divorce, and I was—well, I didn't have my shit figured out as much as I'd thought. But sitting next to him, touching him, tasting the possibility of us getting back together, I . . .

I wanted to believe that maybe, one day, we would be.

"What's on your mind, Serena?" Jesse whispered.

He'd showered while I was asleep, and his hair was a bit wet still, drying awkwardly. I reached out my hand to smooth it down, lingering on a gray patch above his ears.

"I'm going to be completely gray soon."

"That's OK. You'll be a silver fox."

I bit my tongue. I'd nearly said, *You'll be* my *silver fox.*

Around Jesse, I forgot everything. I forgot myself.

I was Serena Singh, badass brown woman and creative director at the hottest ad agency in town. Could I have been her if I'd stayed with Jesse? Right now, did I have to choose between them?

"Ainsley says I'm closed off," I said suddenly. My hand dropped from his hair. "She's right. But was I always like that?"

"Serena, the past is the past. It really doesn't matter." He sighed, tucking his hands behind his head, elbows out to the side. "We were barely into our twenties when we met."

"Jesse," I whispered. "I really want to know."

"Then, yes. *Maybe.* There was always something about you that felt . . . unreachable."

I nodded. I'd expected that answer, but for whatever reason, I needed to hear him say it out loud.

"And yeah," he continued. "Right before you broke up with me, you were closed off. No." He shook his head. "You totally shut down."

I'd had to shut down. Because if he knew how I really felt, he could have convinced me that we should be together. That my fears about falling in love, falling into a trap, were completely unfounded.

"I don't hate you, Serena. I understand why you ended things. Your parents don't have an equal partnership. You saw marriage differently than I do."

"Jesse. I'm sor—"

"Look, we don't need to go there. We were both kids. And Anadi tells me I have the emotional intelligence of a robot." He paused. "So whatever happened, even if you had been *open* with me, it's not like I would have known how to help. Or known what questions to ask . . . You know?"

I nodded, even though I disagreed. Jesse was sensitive and caring and would have known exactly what to say. He still would.

I eyed his gray hairs. "We're not kids anymore, Jesse."

We sat together on the couch for another hour eating cold pizza before I tore myself away from him so I could go home to pack. There was so much to say, but right now wasn't the time.

And it wasn't Jesse I needed to speak to first.

I slept soundly that night, and in the morning, I took my suitcase to the car rental and made for the highway.

Richmond was my eventual destination, but there was somewhere I needed to stop on my way. I could drive there with my eyes closed, and without traffic, it took no time at all. Before I was ready, I arrived, pulling up at the curb next to the house. A few of the neighbors were out and about, mowing the lawn or watering the flower beds. The Sharmas across the street were stretching for their daily run on their driveway, and they waved to me. I waved in return.

I had the key, but still, I rang the bell, shifting my weight between my heels as I heard the floorboards creak on the other side of the door, the dead bolt click open.

"Serena?" Mom opened the door, and her face lit up as she ushered me in. I'd seen her only a couple of days earlier at the Hartshornes' barbeque, yet it felt like a lifetime ago.

The familiar smells and sounds prickled my senses as I stepped into the foyer. The rich, spicy aroma of a *subji* she'd whipped up that morning. The violent humming of the dryer around the corner. The light scent of baby powder she dabbed on her skin.

"Is Dad home?"

"He has gone to wash the car. We are having lunch with the Banerjees soon. Would you like to come?"

I shook my head as my whole body trembled.

"Are you hungry? I can make—"

"Stop it," I said evenly, in English. I had started to cry, and my chest was heaving. I couldn't control it.

"*Beti?*" She sounded afraid. She sounded weak. "What is the matter?"

Today, she sounded like herself. At least, the woman I thought I knew. I pressed my hands into my face, my ring fingers pushing hard against my eyelids. I could still hear it. I could still see it.

I hated Dad for what he did, but I was angry at her, too. Because he did, whatever sort of man he was, she was the one who had chosen to stay.

SANDEEP

Twenty-six years earlier

"*Sweet, sweet fantasy, baby . . .*" Sandeep sang softly, swaying her hips side to side. She trailed off, unsure of what came next in the song. Her daughter Serena had told her the name of the singer once, but she couldn't remember it.

Humming the tune, Sandeep scrubbed clean the final pot, set it on the dish rack, and then fetched a clean tea towel from the pantry. She could have let the dishes air-dry, but tonight, she relished the repetition of the task. The song on the radio.

The fact that her girls were finally asleep, and she had the apartment to herself.

Was it selfish to cherish the few hours of peace before Veer came home in the evening? It was the only time she didn't have to worry about his meals, his mood. That she didn't need to keep her eyes fixated on Natasha, who was now a toddler determined to run rather than wobble. Or fret about Serena, who was always quietly reading, quietly watching television, or quietly doing her homework at the kitchen table.

By the time Sandeep dried the last dish, carefully placed everything where it lived in her cupboards, the song was over. Now, a man's voice bellowed through the radio, and he wasn't so much singing as shouting.

Sandeep didn't used to listen to the radio, didn't know that she *liked* to listen to the radio, until the Singh family (*another* one) moved in on the fifth floor. The family was generous and, within the first month, hosted a dinner party and crammed six couples and seven children into their two-bedroom apartment, all of them South Asians from their complex. It was hot, and the men had taken up the entire length of the balcony while Sandeep and the other women fanned themselves in the cramped kitchen, took turns helping Mrs. Singh chop and garnish and marinate and fry, laughing as they listened to upbeat American music on the radio.

There was so much food, but by the time they'd finished serving the men their third, even fourth helpings, and made sure all the children had full stomachs, there was barely a chicken thigh left to go between them. Mrs. Singh had shrugged her shoulders apologetically and then ordered them all a pizza.

Sandeep smiled just thinking about the evening. How they'd left the men and children upstairs, confident they wouldn't notice if they disappeared for a few minutes, and scarfed down the pizza out in front of the building, smearing it with mango and lemon pickle from the jar Mrs. Singh had brought down.

Oh, how they'd laughed. How the time and the chores flew by. How much *fun* they'd all had.

The dishes done, Sandeep retrieved her workbooks and set herself up in the kitchen with a cup of chai, a bowl of *gur para,* and an extra reading light for her eyes.

She didn't do her homework in front of Serena. It was embarrassing. When her daughter chose to speak, she did so eloquently and would have mastered Sandeep's spelling and reading comprehension exercises years ago. The letters and numbers on Serena's report card were confusing, but Sandeep's English teacher at the YWCA said they meant Serena was intelligent. That she worked hard. That she was "vibrant" and "joyful" in class.

Vibrant. Joyful. Sandeep would never use the translation of these words to describe her daughter, and sometimes, watching her, she got the sinking feeling that she didn't even know her. That, by choosing to raise her daughter here, Sandeep never would.

An hour flew by. Maybe two or even three. Sandeep was determined to finish her exercises for the week, to return to the YWCA having shown some improvement. She didn't hear him come in.

The squeak of the vinyl kitchen tile startled her upright. Before turning to him, she glanced quickly at the microwave clock. It was nearly one a.m. Sandeep knew exactly what it meant.

"Are you hungry?" She pushed her workbooks to the side and then stood up. He didn't answer, so she moved past him to the refrigerator, taking out the Tupperware and Corningware she'd arranged just hours earlier. After she plated his dinner, put it into the microwave, she remembered the radio.

"Leave it on."

His tone was gentle.

"I like this song. It plays on the radio at least fifteen times a day."

"What is it called?"

"It's called 'Waterfalls,' " he said in English. "'Don't go chasing waterfalls . . .'" She didn't understand, and a moment later, he translated the words for her.

"Do you want to dance with me?"

She smiled bashfully, turning back to face the microwave. A beat later, she felt him towering beside her.

She smelled the liquor on his breath.

"Dance with me." He turned her around and grabbed her hands. He was smiling oddly. She didn't like to look at him when he was like this, so instead, she looked at his feet, awkwardly hopping back and forth on the floor.

The microwave beeped, but he held firm on her hands, twirling her in the western style. Veer was excellent at bhangra, but not at this, especially in this state. He spun her around again, but far too quickly, and she laughed.

It wasn't a ridiculing laugh. Nor was it one of joy. Immediately, he stopped dancing.

"Is it funny?"

"Veer . . . It's time to eat."

She fetched his plate from the microwave, set it down on the kitchen table. It made a loud noise as the ceramic clanged against the table.

"Is my dancing funny to you?"

"Veer, stop this nonsense." She set her hands on her hips, gesturing to the table. "It's late—"

The slap was quick, sharp. It smarted, but it didn't hurt. She swallowed hard, pressing her hands more firmly into her sides.

"Eat. Now."

"You think I'm ridiculous. *Hah?*"

There was no reasoning with a miserable drunk. Right now, there was nothing she could do to appease him. There was nothing she *would* do to appease him.

Occasionally, other women at their *gurdwara* would turn up with a conspicuous amount of concealer around their eyes or mouth, elaborate stories, excuses.

But not Sandeep.

The one time he'd hit her so hard as to leave his mark, she'd refused to hide it.

"If you want to hit your wife," she had spat at him, the morning after, as his head throbbed and he begged her for forgiveness, "then the whole world is going to know."

"Are you going to eat or not?" she asked impatiently.

In response, Veer quietly picked up the radio and then hurled it at the wall behind her. She could feel the wind of it as it brushed past her face, just a few inches to the left. She could hear her radio crumble, shatter into pieces, as it slid down the wall.

"Fine. Go to bed hungry," Sandeep said coldly. "I'll put the food away." She grabbed his plate and brushed past him, throwing it heavily into the sink. The ceramic crashed and cracked in the basin, and then suddenly, Veer grabbed her upper arm and pulled her toward him.

Violently, she pushed him away, and then he hit her again. This time it hurt, but she refused to cry.

He was a giant next to her. Easily, without much effort on his part, he could have killed her. Nursing her jaw with her fingers, she pulled away from his grip. She looked him dead in the eye.

"Do you feel like a man now?"

Her voice cracked. He gave nothing away.

"Do you, my dear husband?"

She took a step forward, shoved both of her hands into his chest as hard as she could. He barely moved.

"Go ahead. Hit me again."

"Stop it, Sandeep—"

"*Hit* me, you coward!"

Her voice echoed in the kitchen. How loud had she screamed?

Veer's eye twitched, and she wondered if he would hit her. If this time, it would break her. She stood there, ready to take it, and then his face broke.

He started to sob.

She couldn't support his weight all the way back to the bedroom, so she helped him to the couch. He flopped over, crying and babbling like a small child, and with great difficulty, she lifted his legs up, tucked a pillow beneath his head. Covering him with a blanket, she left him there and returned to the kitchen.

Pieces of the radio were everywhere. She fetched a dustpan and broom from where they lived next to the refrigerator and got to work, hunching over to reach the bits beneath the table. Her breath shallow, she inhaled deeply, trying to calm herself. Now, she couldn't help the tears from coming.

"Mommy?"

Wiping her face, she turned around. Serena was in the doorway. Her braids were still wet from her evening bath, and she had her school backpack with her.

"What have you got there, *beti*?"

Eyes wide, Serena stepped forward and set down the backpack. "Is it time to go?"

Sighing, Sandeep placed both hands on her daughter's shoulders and then kissed the top of her head.

"It's time to sleep."

30

He never hit you girls." Mom was sitting next me on the love seat that faced the front window. We were thigh to thigh, and both her hands were wrapped around mine. She was shaking. "That was enough for me."

I nodded, rubbing my wet cheek against my shoulder. I remembered the night the radio broke; a version of it, at least. I didn't recognize the mom from the story as she told it. And for the first time, I wondered if I knew her at all. Her whole life, she'd been closed off, too.

"Does he still—"

"No." She shook her head. "He quit drinking after that night, and it never happened again."

I nodded. I had thought as much, but I needed to be sure.

"He is ashamed, Serena. Deeply."

"He should be," I muttered.

"I know it's hard to see, from your perspective, why I stayed. That I enjoyed my life." Mom sighed, resting her head against my shoulder. "But I did. There were hard times, but overall, I have had a very happy life with your father, and he changed after that night."

I wanted her to say more. I wanted us to relive every single time it happened so I could scream about it. It had taken us so long to get here, to acknowledge the elephant in the room that had lived among us my whole goddamn life, but now that it had arrived . . .

I wasn't as angry as I thought I'd be. I just felt . . . sad.

Mom was right. I would never understand or agree with her decision to stay, but I knew I was judging her from a place of privilege. I grew up in a different country, a different time, and the choices available to me were ones that my mother, and the generations before her, couldn't even imagine.

I'd ended it with Jesse because I loved him so much I'd started to rely on him. For my own happiness. Sense of purpose. Even my own self-worth. I'd thought our relationship made me weak and dependent and would have turned me into my mother.

"The past is the past, and we learn to forgive," Mom said, suddenly. "We learn it's OK to love the people who have hurt you."

All this time, I thought I was strong despite Mom. But, maybe, I had strength because of her.

"My life is full of happiness and joy and love." Mom turned to look at me, resting the tips of her fingers on my chin. "Two wonderful daughters. We are so proud of you and Natasha."

I laughed, my body tensing.

"Serena, that's enough now. You and your father are the *exact* same." In Punjabi, she told me an idiom that more or less meant "cut from the same cloth."

"I'm nothing like him," I said afterward.

"You are both so funny, when you want to be. You both are *very* stubborn—"

"*Mom . . .*"

"And such hard workers, so loyal, so *loving*—"

I guffawed. *Loving.* My father? The man who could barely meet my eye, silently passing judgment on those parts of my life I had allowed him to see?

"Can I show you something?"

Without waiting for me to answer, Mom grabbed a shoebox from beneath the end table. I'd never seen it before, although I recognized the box. The brand made the same dusty brown work boots Dad liked to wear.

Mom cast the lid to the side and began unpacking. At the very top was a family photograph taken of the four of us and Mark, right after Natasha's Sikh wedding ceremony, and beneath it, her wedding invitation.

"Is this yours?" I asked, and Mom shook her head. Next, she pulled out a hazy photograph of the side of a highway. I leaned in, peering closer as I noticed the billboard, an advertisement for a small kitchen appliance in the background.

"He drove by five, six times, before snapping the perfect photo."

I bit down hard on my bottom lip. That was my billboard. That had been my client.

"And remember this?"

Next, Mom unfolded a few pieces of printer paper. My nose ran as I realized what it was.

"Thirty-five under thirty-five," she said, in English. "Do you know he printed copies of the magazine article for all our friends?"

No, I didn't fucking know that. He didn't tell me, nor had he ever expressed any emotion toward me beyond apathy unless I'd disappointed him. He was proud of me? Really?

All this time, I thought he hated me, too.

"Isn't it time to make amends, Serena?" Mom was whispering, and she tilted her head slightly behind her, a gesture toward the kitchen.

My breath caught in my chest. He was in there. He had come home.

I wiped my face with the back of my hand as I bolted up from the couch. I hated what Dad did, and I pushed him away because of it. I knew that.

But he had let me.

My back was to the kitchen, and I could hear his footsteps. I could feel him hovering in the doorway, looking at me. Waiting for me.

Mom wanted me to make amends. I thought about turning around. I wanted to. But I wasn't ready. I didn't know if I'd ever be.

31

I'd never been more thankful to be away from the city and everyone in it, and except for the occasional text message or phone call to Mom or Jesse, I spent the next week throwing myself into The Fifth Ingredient campaign. On the drive down to Richmond, the perfect commercial concept floated into my head, and I presented it to the team as the third option. I knew even before I pitched it that it would be the one Jerry and his team picked.

"Genius," he told me before I'd even finished mapping it out on the whiteboard. "Let's get to work."

After finishing work on Friday, I decided not to return to DC for the weekend. Instead, I got takeout from a nearby Vietnamese restaurant and ate it in front of the television at my rental apartment. When I couldn't stomach any more food or any more of the news, I grabbed my laptop and caught myself up on what was going on back at the office.

There wasn't a lot for me to do. The Spice Girls were talented and self-sufficient, and it's not like Deborah wasn't there. I scrolled mindlessly through my Slack messages, Asana task lists, and Trello boards, and then, hesitantly, opened my e-mail.

Tracy had sent the e-mail the day before at four forty-one

p.m. I'd been with Kriti touring The Fifth Ingredient facilities when the notification popped up.

It's with great sadness that we announce the departure of our digital director, Ainsley Woods . . .

That's all I could see in the e-mail preview on my home screen, and I didn't bother clicking through. Ainsley had officially handed in her notice, and by the time I got back from Richmond, she'd probably be gone.

All week, I thought so many times about calling her and chickened out every time. I was finally ready to *talk* about what had happened with my parents, with Jesse, and she was one of the first people I wanted to speak with. I wanted her to roll her eyes and tell me how stupid I'd been throwing away all my previous relationships just because I was afraid. I wanted her to sass me until I shoved her about how it was *me* who needed to grow up, move forward, and finally forgive Dad.

But I'd hurt Ainsley. I'd said awful things, projected my own shit onto her, and taken our whole friendship for granted. Would she be capable of forgiving me? Now that we didn't have any reason to see each other, since she was prioritizing her family, would she even bother?

The truth was, I loved her. I loved her more than any other friend that had come in or out of my life. Ainsley was bold and silly and sometimes a little abrasive, and she was also the warmest, most welcoming woman I'd ever met. She always made time and listened to her family and friends, but she was also doggedly her own woman.

She thought I'd been closed off with her, and that was true, but I'd also let her in more than anyone else. She saw me for who I truly was and wanted to be, and as much as possible, as much as I was capable of then, I'd been myself.

Tentatively, I picked up my phone and scrolled down to the last text message she sent me last Friday when we were texting at work, deciding on a playlist for our drive out to Rock Creek for the picnic.

Aqua! And Rage Against the Machine!!

I laughed. I missed her. (And her terrible taste in music.) But did she miss me?

A buzzer startled me upright, and it took me a while to figure out where it was coming from. There was an intercom I hadn't noticed before by the front door, behind a coatrack I'd hung all my laundry on the night before. I pressed the button.

"Serena?" I recognized the voice of Emit, the doorman, crackling through the speaker. "You have a visitor."

I didn't know who it would be at this hour, so I told Emit I would come down and then stepped into a pair of sneakers.

The AC was on full blast in the lobby, and my arm hairs prickled as I stepped out of the elevator. Emit smiled at me and, with his head, gestured toward a small seating area.

It wasn't Jesse, as I'd been hoping. It was Natasha.

If I hadn't been looking properly, I would have walked right past her. She'd cut her hair short around her shoulders, which suited her face—I'd been suggesting she get a bob for *years*—and she was wearing shorts and a tank top, the bottom edge of her round belly exposed. I'd seen her so few times during her pregnancy that it still came as a shock to see her like this.

She stood up when she saw me, and we walked toward each other. I noticed she had her white-and-purple polka-dot overnight bag that she used to take to Mark's. It looked heavy, and when I was close enough, I took it from her.

"Did Mom tell you I was here?"

She nodded. She was breathing heavily. I thanked Emit and then led her toward the elevator.

"I've never been to Richmond before," she said as we stepped inside. "The riverfront is really nice."

"Right?"

She stretched her chest out as she set both of her hands on her lower back. She looked uncomfortable. Then again, I probably did, too.

Back in the apartment, I got her a glass of water and then joined her on the couch. She'd put her feet up on the coffee table and was fanning herself with a magazine. Had Mom or Dad told her about what had happened? Was that why she'd come all the way here?

Natasha hadn't even been born when it started and was only a toddler that night the radio broke, when Dad stopped drinking and the abuse abruptly came to a stop. She'd been too young to notice anything, and I hadn't wanted her to. As much as I still carried it with me, I didn't want her to.

"So why didn't you stick around last week?" she asked, tossing the magazine to the side. "You could have at least said hi."

"I only had a few minutes. Ainsley and I were at a picnic nearby—"

"Who's Ainsley?"

I paused, and a pit formed in my stomach.

"Wait, is she the woman you brought to my gender reveal? A coworker or something?"

I nodded. *Or something* was right.

"I wish you'd stayed at the barbeque . . . I had a terrible time."

Natasha was waiting for me to prompt her, and after a moment, I obliged.

"Why?"

She sighed heavily, lolling her head around to face me. "Because my mother-in-law is a *freaking* nightmare."

I laughed without meaning to, shocked. I hadn't expected her to say that.

"I thought you worshipped Mrs. H."

"Are you kidding me?" Natasha whined. She sounded like what I had just said was the most ridiculous thing she'd ever heard. "Well, maybe I used to. Now." She shuddered. "*Ugh.*"

"You're the one who wanted to live with your in-laws," I said. My tone was serious but teasing, and Natasha cracked a smile.

"Do you know she redecorated our bedroom while we were at work?"

My jaw dropped.

"She showed up at my last ultrasound appointment without being invited and *insisted* on staying in the room—"

"*What?*"

"And then started arguing with the doctor about the advice she was giving me, told her she'd 'read otherwise' in some magazine—"

"She didn't . . ."

"And the last straw was, this morning, she literally grabbed my coffee out of my hand, *mid*-sip, and dumped it down the drain."

"But a little caffeine is—"

"I know, it's fine! The literature says it's fine. But *she* thinks it's going to turn her grandson into a goddamn cocaine addict!"

I laughed until my belly hurt, and although it felt so good to be with her, I knew she wasn't here because she loved me or missed me. She had driven two and a half hours because she needed to vent, to get her own shit off her chest. She *needed* me.

My laughing subsided. I dabbed the corners of my eyes with the bottom of my T-shirt, unsure where the tears had come from this time.

"What did you think of Mrs. H?" Natasha asked.

I shrugged, not wanting to continue the conversation. Recalling how lovely I'd seen her be when doing aerobics with Mom, I also wasn't sure all my judgments about Mrs. Hartshorne had been warranted.

"You can't stand her, either, can you?" She grinned, watching me. "Wow, I had no idea. You're a good actor—"

"Is that why you came all the way here?" I asked coolly. "To complain about your mother-in-law?"

It hurt. It had always hurt, but maybe I had to stop allowing myself to feel that way. Didn't Albert Einstein once say the definition of insanity was doing the same thing over and over again and expecting a different result?

"What's happening to us, sis?" Her words caught me off guard, and suddenly my chest felt tight. I averted my eyes.

"I've barely seen you this year," I heard her say. "You never call me—"

"You don't call me, either."

"True. But I didn't think you wanted me to."

I looked at her, exasperated. She thought I didn't want her to reach out? Show she cared? Still be a part of my life? After years of living together, spending so many evenings and weekends and holidays together, why wouldn't I want her around anymore?

"I'm your younger sister," she said quietly. "This past year . . . me getting married and now starting a family . . . I know it's been hard on you."

"The hardest part," I said softly, "has been losing you."

"Serena . . ." Natasha cried. She wiped her nose with the back of her hand. "I'm sorry, OK? I didn't want to rub it in—"

"Rub *what* in? Your pregnancy? Natasha, how many times have I had to tell you? I don't want kids."

"Fine. OK. But you want a *partner*, don't you?"

I'd convinced myself for so long that I didn't, that it would make me weak, like I thought had been the case for Mom. That loving someone as much as I loved Jesse would mean giving up on my own dreams, even my ability to walk away.

But was it weakness or humanity? A pure, imperfect part of life?

Maybe I did want a partner, and I realized that a part of me had known that all along.

"I'm sorry," I said finally, scooting in closer to Natasha. "If I ever acted jealous, I didn't mean—"

"I know you didn't mean it."

"But you"—I laughed—"you just walked away when, for once, I was the one that needed somebody. After everything I've done for you. It *stings*, Natasha."

"I'm sorry. I know I can be selfish," she said quietly. "You think Mark doesn't casually throw that in my face every time we fight?"

I held my tongue, resisting the urge to say all the mean, petty things I'd stockpiled up over the past few months. But I didn't want to fight, and in that moment, I finally accepted that I didn't want her to be my best friend, either.

I just wanted my sister back.

Gently, I placed my hand on the curve of her stomach. It was warm. I'd never done that before. It was probably in my head, but I swear I could feel him in there. I could feel him smiling at me.

"Does he kick yet?" She nodded, and I beamed. "Really?"

"Give it a minute. He'll get going."

I rested my head on her shoulder, closing my eyes. This could be a new start, a new normal. Whatever had happened between us, I was ready to move on.

"So what are you going to do about Mrs. H?" I asked after a while.

"We're moving out. I don't know what I was thinking. There's no way I would have moved in with my in-laws if they were Indian."

For a brief moment, I thought the baby had kicked, but then I realized it was just Natasha's stomach digesting.

"When?"

"As soon as possible. Before he's born, for sure." She paused. "We're looking at a few houses in Fairfax County . . ."

I grinned but didn't say anything.

"That'll make Mom and Dad happy, won't it?"

"You know it will."

"And you'll be pleased to know I've asked Mom to host the baby shower. Would you mind helping her, though? I don't want her to, like, get overexcited and tire herself out."

I laughed, knowing that scenario would happen regardless. "Sure. No problem."

"And can you *please* make sure she doesn't make *pakoras*? There's no way my baby shower is going to smell like a deep fryer . . ."

We snuggled on the couch as Natasha went on about what she did and didn't want, and eventually, the baby kicked. It was perfection.

Not every friendship or relationship—family or otherwise—could be a two-way street. With some, you took more than you could give, and with others—well, they got your heart and your soul, and you picked up whatever scraps you could find.

Natasha wasn't my best friend. She never had been. But she would always be my baby sister. And honestly, it was enough.

32

Serena!"

"How was it?"

"Tell us everything!"

I grinned, looking up from my computer. It was nine a.m. and I was back in DC, and I watched my team members join me at the pod one by one.

"Excellent. It'll be tight, but we're on track to finish on time. Let's debrief later this morning." I took turns looking them all in the eye. "And Deborah told me you did a fabulous job while I was away. Thank you so much for picking up all the slack. I'm really proud of you guys."

"A crash campaign is such a rush, huh?" Jia asked.

"Better than exercise," Layla added. "Better than drugs!" She clapped her hand over her mouth. She looked over at me, horrified. "I was just kidding, Serena. Oh my god. I was totally kidding. I don't do drugs."

I laughed, my heart surging that they were becoming comfortable enough around me to laugh and to make jokes—to make bad jokes. After three weeks in Richmond, I felt recharged and ready to be back in the office, even though it had hurt my heart to see Ainsley's empty chair that morning. She had been gone for a week already, and her deputy, Carlos, had replaced her on an interim basis, although that was likely to be permanent. Deborah and Tracy had even thrown her a farewell lunch, which I regretted not being at. I had considered taking a day away from Richmond to come back for it but chickened out at the last minute, unsure if Ainsley would even want me there.

While they grabbed their coffee and settled in, I fired off a few e-mails, including one to Becket about another project I'd hired him for. I had reached out to apologize for how I'd acted during our relationship and said I hoped our breakup didn't affect us working together. He was very generous, even upbeat about the whole thing, and said he'd love to still work together, and even be friends. Friends I wasn't sure about, but we could try, and in the meantime, I was lucky to have his help and his talent for my campaigns.

I regretted that I'd been closed off with Becket, with every man I'd dated since Jesse, never allowing them anything that would bring our lives closer together, more intertwined. But that was different now. I was ready to move forward with my life.

"Vic," I said quietly, once everyone had started work. "I need to grab another coffee, but then can I see you in the boardroom?"

Three minutes later, I sat there face-to-face with Ginger Spice. I had craved her respect so badly that her rejection and resistance had nearly broken me in half. Made me question whether or not I deserved this job and even question myself.

But I knew exactly who I was. I was a powerful, empowering boss who had earned this job and wanted to surround herself with people who actually wanted to be here. I wasn't going to be afraid of conflict anymore, and I was capable of making tough decisions. Someone who knew when it was OK to stop giving people more chances.

"This morning I was going to tell you I was taking you off

probation," I said after we'd both settled into our chairs. "I've seen some improvements in your attitude, and Deborah loved the work you did for the Lahiri campaign."

"Thanks." Vic shrugged. "Yeah, it felt very natural. It was—"

"But then I talked to Tracy this morning."

Vic narrowed her eyes at me, and I straightened my shoulders.

"Here's something I don't think either of us knew: We have a state-of-the-art security system. Unusual activity gets flagged."

Vic didn't give anything away.

"Over the past week, it seems that you've shared 3 GB of materials from our company's shared drive with . . . fuzzypeaches101@hotmail.com." I paused. "I take it that's your personal e-mail account?"

"I . . . I wanted to work from home last weekend."

"Why didn't you take your work laptop home? Or log in to the cloud from your personal computer?"

She mumbled something I couldn't really hear, and I waved her off.

"And why did you transfer files for campaigns you're not assigned to?"

She didn't have an answer, and I could see her trembling. I felt terrible, but I also knew what I had to do.

"We take client confidentiality very seriously here, Vic. You've broken at least three conditions in your employment contract—"

"Serena, it's no big deal—"

"It is a big deal. There are trade secrets in those files. Your personal computer could be stolen or hacked." I paused. "And I suspect that you were going to add those files to your own portfolio of work, help convince another agency to hire you on."

My stomach churned as I watched her. I'd never seen her look vulnerable before.

"You were planning to take credit for my work because you're *still* pissed that you didn't get my job. Is that right?"

She didn't respond.

"That's really too bad, Vic, because your own portfolio is outstanding. You could have gotten another job on your own merit." I paused again, feeling sorry for her. "In a few years, with a bit more experience, you probably would have gotten my job."

"I'm sorry, Serena." She started crying, her hands falling into her face. "I'm so sorry. I'd do anything to take it back." She looked up at me, whimpering. "Please don't fire me, OK? *Please?* I'll never get another job in advertising if you fire me."

She was right. It was a small world, an even smaller industry, and it still wasn't easy for a woman to get ahead.

"I propose that Tracy accompanies you home right now so you can get your personal computer, and then our IT department will wipe it clean."

Vic nodded, wiping her eyes. Her makeup had started to run.

"And afterward, you'll hand me your letter of resignation. I'm not going to bad-mouth you to other agencies, but we're not going to write you a reference, either. Does that sound fair to you?"

Fair. Nothing about this world was fair. Vic had screwed up majorly, but I didn't want to be the reason she didn't have a future. She deserved another chance; I just couldn't be the one to give it to her.

Autumn

33

The end of the summer blurred together. Work was busier than ever, especially after Jerry and Patricia announced they planned to assign all future advertising campaigns for all their product lines over to our agency, thanks to our good work with The Fifth Ingredient campaign. Still, I made time to spend the occasional evening with Natasha, to help Mom plan the baby shower. I found a new book club that didn't invite authors and reached out to Jasmine, whom I'd only caught a glimpse of at Natasha's gender reveal. We spent hours on the phone reminiscing about business school, about her *Jersey Shore*–themed bachelorette, and decided to start meeting up for monthly drinks again.

I also finally managed to organize that long-promised brunch with my school friends. What was meant to be a two-hour catch-up stretched out for an entire Sunday as we remembered just how long it had been. How much we truly missed one another. I told them, point-blank, that they needed to try harder. That we all needed to. Misty-eyed, they agreed, and we held hands, reminding one another about the good times, why we were all still worth the effort.

And then there was Jesse.

I couldn't pinpoint the day it happened. That everything changed. One day we were sharing a bento box beneath a sliver of shade by the National Geographic Museum, and the next?

We were having coffee or drinks after work on an overcrowded patio near his office. We were sharing every meal together, walks, even workouts, seeing each other whenever we possibly could, sometimes even twice on the same day.

Eventually, those moments found themselves on one of our balconies, couches, or kitchens. It was a natural shift, so natural that it felt entirely ordinary the first time we cooked chicken curry together, or when my hand lingered on his after we accidentally touched. The first time, while reading the paper, he pulled the pages down and kissed me.

Weeks passed, and the moments became larger, more meaningful. We made love, and I spent two nights at his apartment without going home, without showering. Natasha and Mark invited us over for lunch. Jesse suggested that I meet his children. I *did* meet his children. The very same day, I fell in love with them.

It was painful opening myself up, but I wasn't afraid anymore. And one muggy night sitting on the curb outside of my local Trader Joe's, I finally told Jesse why I'd pushed him away twelve years earlier. I told him about my dad and why I'd always had a confusing relationship with alcohol.

I told him that I was finally ready to put the past behind me.

Labor Day weekend blew in on a cool, welcoming breeze, but the first hint of autumn didn't last an hour past dawn. I was awake and restless, and finally, I did what I'd promised myself I'd do that day. I called Dad.

I'd never seen him in shorts or sandals or even a T-shirt, no matter how hot it was outside. Today was no different. He was wearing his uniform of light khaki pants and a checkered collared shirt rolled up to his elbows. His beard was immaculately groomed. He had a bouquet of flowers in his hand.

He held them up, walking toward me. I smiled, taking them. "What's this for?"

"A housewarming present."

"I moved in years ago."

"I never bought you a housewarming present. It's been weighing on my mind."

I thanked him, leading him into the apartment. My parents didn't come into the city often, and I couldn't remember the last time he'd been over. Dad propped himself on one of the stools by the kitchen counter while I made tea, and he babbled about a traffic accident he'd seen on the drive in. Even though I was paying attention, I couldn't quite get the gist of his story.

When the tea was ready, I joined him on the neighboring stool. I'd never heard him talk so much, at least not to me, and it occurred to me that he was nervous. My whole life, Dad and I were rarely alone together. I'd always made sure of it. I always thought that it was because I couldn't stand the sight of him, that I hated him. But maybe deep down I knew. I knew that if we looked into each other's eyes, if we were honest with each other, we would have to address it.

"So," Dad said, switching gears suddenly. "What is . . . *up*?"

I smiled at his tone.

Should I just get to it? Neither of us were good at small talk.

"I'm sorry, Serena," he blurted.

I looked up. There were tears in his eyes, and his cheeks were bright red, no easy feat for someone with our complexion. Tears welled up in my own eyes.

"I'm sorry, too."

"There's no excuse for—"

"It's OK." I cut him off. "I know. I . . . Let's not. Let's just start over, OK?" My voice cracked. "Starting today. Starting *now*."

"*Hah*. Start over." He nodded, massaging his face with his hand. "How?"

I thought fondly about all those times I'd sat at the dining room table in Jesse's family home, watching them together as a family. I smiled.

"Let's just . . . talk." I hesitated. "Actually, there is something I want to tell you."

"*Hah?*"

"Do you remember Jesse?"

Dad's eyes brightened in surprise. Mom must have kept the news from him.

"Jasmeet? Of course!"

"We've . . . reconnected," I said, giving Dad time to process what I meant. "Jesse's divorced now and has two children." I stopped again, trying to read his face. Divorce wasn't uncommon in our community, but it was still a bit of a taboo. "Would that be OK with you?"

"Well." Dad breathed out heavily. "Does he make you happy?"

"He does." I smiled. I couldn't help it. "He really does."

"Then . . . that's wonderful news."

It wasn't just me who talked that morning. It turned out Dad and I were rather similar; he could be very chatty, too.

He told me about what it was like to move to America when he was in his thirties like me. How much harder it had been to get used to this way of life, his lack of social capital, so unlike his life back in Punjab.

He said he'd been secretly saving up to take Mom to India and then Thailand for a few months when he retired the following year. After, I told him everything about my new job, nabbing Jerry as a client, the ins and outs of The Fifth Ingredient campaign. I even told him my salary; he didn't balk. He told me he was proud of me. That even though it was unattainable to most, that he was happy his daughter had achieved the "American Dream."

"I work in advertising, Dad." I laughed. "It's my job to make shit up and *pretend* there's an American Dream to be purchased."

"Do you really feel that way about your industry?"

I shrugged. "Sometimes. But I do love my job. Deborah's philosophy—and I agree—is that we have to make changes from the inside. That's why we only sign socially and environmentally ethical clients."

"Like this Fifth Ingredient." He nodded, swallowing. "So tell me about this new commercial. Will I be able to watch it on TV?"

"We're buying loads of regional airtime. You'll definitely see it. And an abbreviated clip of it will show up as sponsored posts on Instagram and Facebook."

"What's the commercial about—can I get a preview?"

I hesitated.

"*Kya?*"

"I actually got the idea from *you*."

His face fell, and I shook my head vigorously. I hadn't meant to imply his past behavior with Mom was going to be the commercial. "No. It's not about that."

When he didn't respond, I continued.

"Do you remember that afternoon at the Hartshornes, when the penguin—I mean, the waiter—offered you wine?"

Dad nodded.

"You didn't know if the pinot noir was red or white wine—not that you should have. It's cultural knowledge, right? People who didn't grow up in 'wine country' or who don't drink it or socialize with people who do—why would they know?"

Still, Dad wasn't saying anything. He was hanging on to my every word.

"Anyway, it got me thinking. Jerry wanted a commercial that would sell his beer to today's average American. Like himself before his business took off, or like *you*. Someone who immigrated to this country. And neither of those men would know if pinot noir is red or white."

I flipped open my laptop. It was already open to the script. The commercial would begin shooting that week. "You see," I said, pointing to the scene heading. "It all starts at a wedding. There's an Indian bride, a white groom, and it's a *very* bougie wedding—"

"Bougie?"

"Bourgeois. Like, *fancy*."

"So Natasha's wedding."

I laughed, returning to the script. "Precisely. So anyway, there are lots of shots of the happy couple and their young friends drinking and dancing and enjoying themselves. Their clothes are super modern, nothing about the ceremony is traditional. No *gurdwara*, temple, or church. No white dress or sari. For example, instead of a wedding cake, they eat kimchi cupcakes . . ."

Dad chuckled, and it made me laugh, too. I was surprised he knew what kimchi was.

"And in the background," I continued, "are their dads. Average American guys like you and Jerry, and they look completely lost."

A smile stretched across Dad's face as he caught on. "Like I did ordering the pinot noir?"

"Is it OK that I borrowed from real life?"

"Of course, *beti*." Dad sipped his tea. "So tell me how the commercial ends!"

"Well, the dads' faces light up when they see bottles of The Fifth Ingredient because it's finally something they're *both* familiar with, and they grab two bottles each. One for them, one for their wives." I grinned. "And the best part is the end. When they find them on the dance floor, both wives are already holding their own beer bottles."

"*Acha?*" Dad beamed, and my face flushed. "That's very clever."

"Is it?"

"It's absolute perfection. Maybe it will be showcased at the Super Bowl?"

"A girl can dream."

Without thinking, I touched his shoulder. I could feel his arm tense, but then as he caught my eye, it slackened.

He smiled, pressing his own hand against mine. It was the first time I could ever remember us showing any sort of affection toward each other, and it made my heart so full I could have burst.

Mom was right. Sometimes, it was OK to love the people who had hurt you. And if Jesse could forgive me, and Mom could forgive Dad, and I could forgive Natasha, and Dad and I could forgive each other, and all of us could still go on and move forward, then I knew without a doubt, there was someone else who would forgive me.

"Dad," I said, a moment later. "Have you ever been to a farmers market?"

"Serena," Dad tutted. "I am *from* the village. In Punjab, my father *was* farmer."

"What about a bougie farmers market?"

34

As I suspected, Dad had never been to that kind of farmers market before, but he loved it. And today was the perfect day to bring him.

The market was buzzing when we arrived. And even though the sun was red-hot and the air was still swampy, I could tell it was nearly harvest by the mountains of fresh produce. Kale, beetroot, sweet potatoes, and pumpkins. An abundance of watermelons, apples, grapes, and peaches in every other stall.

Everyone's tote bags, shopping carts, and even strollers were full of fruits and vegetables, pies and pastries, homemade jams and chutneys. Dad loved it, stopping at every other stall to buy a basket of raspberries for their morning smoothies or a loaf of banana bread, because it was Mom's favorite. He was as excitable as one of the free-range children or hypoallergenic dogs roaming around.

By the time we were halfway down the first aisle, he'd filled one of my canvas bags to the brim. We rounded the corner, and I started to feel anxious as we drew closer to Dirty Chai.

There were so many days I'd thought about calling, texting, or even dropping by, but then I would worry about what Ainsley would say, what I would say, and chicken out.

Friendships ran their course all the time. We changed schools, apartments, cities, or jobs, and the people who at one point populated so many waking hours of our lives often disappeared forever. There was never a breakup or a talk. An acknowledgment that we didn't have anything in common anymore or were too busy or simply didn't care enough to make the effort to stay in touch.

The crowd thickened closer to Nikesh's stall, and the sun beat down harder on my forehead. Easily, Ainsley and I could drop from each other's lives now that we didn't work together. We both had our families, our partners, our career paths, the meat and potatoes of a good life. We would be fine without each other, and in some distant future, I imagined us crossing on Fourteenth Street. We'd smile at each other fondly, remembering that silly fight that had put an end to our friendship, and then we'd keep walking, too busy to look back.

Dirty Chai had a long line out front. Nikesh was working the booth, rapidly filling eco-friendly mugs and taking orders and credit cards. There was somebody next to him I didn't recognize. He must have hired an employee for the summer, and my heart sank into my stomach as I realized that maybe she wouldn't be here.

"Dirty Chai," Dad said slowly, stopping short. "Is that not your friend Ainsley's stall? We should go say hello."

"I don't know if she's here, Dad."

"Of course she is. She's right there."

I turned to where he was looking. With all the people around, I hadn't noticed her in the crowd right in front of me, taking preorders on a notepad from the people in line. She had her hair pulled up in a tight bun on the top of her head, a yellow kerchief tied up in a bow just in front, and she was wearing a pair of Birkenstocks and the same faded gray T-shirt dress I'd seen her wear a million times.

I could walk away right now, and we'd both be fine. We'd manage. But I didn't want to. I wanted my best friend back in my life, no matter the effort. No matter what I had to do to win her back.

"Two iced dirty chais, please," I said, when Ainsley walked up to us. She was smiling but had her eyes on her notepad and didn't look up.

"When you get to the counter, that'll be eight fifty . . ." She trailed off when she looked up and saw me. I couldn't read her face. Then she noticed Dad, and her face lit up.

"Mr. *Singh*!"

"Ainsley!"

She embraced him and then ignored me completely while enthusiastically grilling Dad about what he thought about the market, what had brought him to the city.

"Serena invited me," he said, putting his arm around me. The gesture was stiff, awkward, but I could tell he was making an effort. I smiled.

"She invited me to 'hang out'"—he threw me a wry look—"*are* we hanging out? More than thirty years in this country, and I'm still not sure I know what that means."

Ainsley and I both laughed.

"We're hanging out, Dad."

"Ainsley, would you like to join us?"

The line had crept forward, and by now, we were right at the front. Nikesh introduced himself, pressed his hands together in front of his chest.

"*Sat Sri Akaal*, Nikesh," Dad said in reply. "I've been looking forward to trying your dirty chai."

"It's on the house." He pushed the drinks forward, and when I caught his eye, we smiled at each other. It wasn't just Ainsley that I'd missed. It was her whole family.

"Where's MacKenzie?" I asked him.

"With his babysitter a block over." Nikesh looked at his left wrist, even though he wasn't wearing a watch. "Actually, would you mind going with Ainsley and picking him up, Serena? He's a been a handful lately." He turned to my dad. "Uncle, how about you stay here with me. I could teach you how to make dirty chai."

Dad, oblivious to the tension surrounding him, enthusiastically climbed into the booth with Nikesh. He even helped himself to an apron.

"When do we have to grab MacKenzie?" I asked Ainsley, staring at my shoes.

"Not for another hour."

So, Nikesh had made up the excuse so Ainsley and I could talk and make up. My heart sang. Did that meant *she* wanted us to make up, too?

"Well, Nikesh is very smooth."

"No he's not," Ainsley said. "He bit my tongue the first time he kissed me."

I laughed, catching myself. There were a few people in line behind us pushing their way forward, so I grabbed my drink, and then we moved into the shade behind a neighboring stall.

"So how's the office?" she asked coolly.

"Deborah promoted Carlos to digital director," I said, unsure about where to begin. "Just this past week."

"Good. I was worried she'd hire externally."

"And I fired Vic."

"*No.*" Fleetingly, Ainsley seemed to forget that we were fighting as I told her what had happened.

"I'm proud of you," she said after I'd finished. "And I also heard you hired Becket on a six-month contract. That was a really good call."

I looked at her, wondering how she knew.

"He and Nikesh still hang out."

I nodded, glad that our breakup hadn't affected their friendship.

"It's nice that you guys have been able to stay friendly at work. Although, I think the fact that Becket's met somebody already helps."

"Has he? *Good.*"

"Sorry, I hope that doesn't bother you—"

"Not at all," I said, waving her off. "I'm happy for him. And, actually, I've met someone, too."

"*Oh?*"

I wiggled my eyebrows sexily, if that was possible.

"Is it—"

"Jesse?" I beamed and felt a rush of happiness just thinking about him. "Of course it's Jesse."

"I knew it!" Ainsley cheered, grabbing me by the shoulders. "Didn't I call this? Because if I didn't say it out loud, I was thinking it the whole freaking time."

"You called it." I pressed my lips together, ready to say what I came here to say. "Because you *know* me. Ainsley, you're my best friend."

"Serena . . ." Her eyes welled up. Other than that one time with her father-in-law, I'd never seen Ainsley cry. "I'm sorry—"

"No, *I'm* sorry. It was such a stupid fight."

"It was stupid! I didn't even go freelance, in the end." Ainsley laughed. "Now I'm at a tech company with even longer hours!"

"You are?"

"I'm a VP, for Christ's sake."

"Ainsley, congratulations!"

"I need to wear a suit *every* day. Can you believe it? I'm a *suit*!"

I hugged her fiercely as she hugged me back.

"You were right," she said, whispering in my ear. "I was learning Punjabi for Nikesh's dad. Fuck him."

"Double fuck him—"

"And you made up with Mr. S? I'm so happy to see that."

I pulled away from her, wiping my face as I nodded, happily. There was so much to catch up on with each other, and there would be time. If we were lucky, there would be decades of these moments. Impromptu trips to the farmers markets. Dinners at each other's houses. Family holidays. Picnics and poetry readings, maybe even cooking classes.

Although, probably not trips to the sex club.

We'd fight, too. Of course we would. But we would always make up. With Ainsley, I would never stop making the effort to make up.

"I love you," I said. My voice was weird. I'd never said that to a friend before, and I wondered how she would react.

"Serena Singh," Ainsley said, throwing her arms out widely. "I love you, too!"

"I wanted it to be you, Ainsley Woods," I said, clutching her face between my hands. "I wanted it to be you so *badly.*"

"You had me at hello!"

"Yes, yes!" I bellowed. "A thousand times yes!"

It occurred to us, after we'd exhausted our knowledge of romantic movie one-liners, that we had caused a scene. We had fallen over onto the lawn, and there were people looking at us as they walked by, some bemused or appalled or somewhere in between. It didn't matter to either of us. We were getting too old for that shit, to care about what people thought of us.

We knew exactly who we were and what we wanted. And right now, we wanted to be silly thirtysomething best friends causing a stir at the local farmers market.

Author's Note

My parents did not have an arranged marriage. Although they knew each other a bit through the South Asian community, they reconnected at my dad's university graduation party, and the rest was history. My grandparents were progressively minded and wholeheartedly supported their interfaith marriage, and my brother and I grew up exposed to and influenced by the religions, languages, cuisine, and cultural traditions of both sides of my family. We had the best of both worlds. But most importantly, we were part of a family that encouraged us to value where we came from while never letting it limit us.

Every Indian living in the diaspora has a different story to tell about how and who they came to be. But we do share something in common: Our stories all started with the choices and sacrifices of the generations before us.

I'm incredibly lucky to have a platform to tell stories and be a part of the growing representation of South Asian women, and with each book, I draw from a different part of who I am and where I come from.

In my debut novel, *The Matchmaker's List,* I channeled the confusion and disappointment I felt over the double standards about marriage that continue to be felt by South Asian women while also borrowing from the vibrant personality of my Nani to create the main character's loving, meddling Hindu grandmother. In *Grown-Up Pose*, my main character, Anusha, went on a journey that reflected my own desire to break free of the "good Indian girl" label. I also explored my love for yoga, the Punjabi culture I inherited from my father's side, and some of the Hindu beliefs and superstitions I understood from my mother's side. And for the first time in *Serena Singh Flips the Script*, I drew on my Sikh background while also tackling the expectation on women—of any heritage—that we are expected to marry and have children in order to have our own "happily ever after." Because no matter who we are or where we come from, we are in charge of our destiny and our own happiness.

Acknowledgments

I am immensely grateful to my family, particularly my mom and dad, for their love and support, and for giving me the freedom to write and flip scripts as I so please. Thank you to my big brother Jay, to whom I've dedicated this book. You are my role model, my rock, (my former tormenter,) and your words of encouragement seven years ago were what gave me the strength to take a leap of faith and start writing my first book.

Thank you so much to my husband, Simon. You're literally there for me every day, whether it's to make sure I'm well fed and caffeinated, to encourage me to write anyway on the tougher days, or to be my sounding board. Thank you for sharing this with me.

A huge thanks to my Berkley family for being as fabulous as ever, particularly my brilliant editor, Kerry Donovan, as well as Brittanie Black, Dache Rogers, Fareeda Bullert, Mary Geren, Vikki Chu, Kristin del Rosario, and Claire Pokorchak. Thank you to my fantastic agent, Martha Webb, and her colleagues at CookeMcDermid for being my champions, and to Federica Leonardis and Stephanie Caruso for all of your help. And thank you to all of the book bloggers, booksellers, librarians, and more who have recommended my books, and for your incredible support online and in real life. It means the world.

Last but not least, I want to thank my friends for decades worth of love and laughter, and for giving me enough material to write a thousand books on friendship. Thank you to Annie, who captured my heart on the first day of Grade 5 and has never let go, and to my amazing elementary school friends: Emily, Michelle, Molly, and Ashley. Thank you to my high school squad—my sisters and my B's: Beshmi, Fafa, and Steph, and to Liz, Sasha, Nick, Fows, Jazz, and Steve. We helped each other survive those awkward teenage years, and we're still helping each other survive to this very day. And a huge thank-you to all the beautiful souls who have come into my life and whose friendship I am blessed to have, including Anju, Heather, Crystal, Bea, Roseanne, Stephanie, Kyrsten, Cléme, Qi, Katherine, Paige, Laura, Ron, and my wonderful friends and colleagues at House of Anansi Press and Groundwood Books. I love you all to the moon.

Serena Singh Flips the Script

SONYA LALLI

Questions for Discussion

1. At the outset, Serena has a strained relationship with her mother, Sandeep. Why do you think that is, and what motivates her to try to mend it?

2. Becket introduces Serena to the idea that she should go online and make proactive choices to find new friends. Why do you think Serena resists at first? Have you ever put yourself out there in a bid to make new friends, and what was that experience like?

3. Why do you think Serena created ground rules for her friendship with Jesse? Do you think it's possible to stay friends with an ex without crossing any lines?

4. Serena's budding friendship with Ainsley forces Serena to realize that she stopped putting in the effort with her friends as everyone grew up and shifted to different stages of their lives. Why do you think she didn't realize her efforts were lagging, and why is it harder to maintain and form new friendships as adults?

5. Serena and Sandeep often feel like they do not understand each other, and Sandeep worries that by choosing to raise her children in America rather than India, she and her daughter will never truly understand each other. Do you think this is true?

6. During their breakup, Serena suggests to Becket that although he cared about her, he didn't really want to settle down with her and just felt pressured to because he was getting "older." Did that seem true to you? Why do you think both Serena and Becket stayed in that relationship for so long?

7. Serena and Ainsley become close friends very quickly, sharing everything from work lunches to family dinners to spontaneous poetry readings. What do you think draws them to the other person? Do you think the blossoming of a new friendship can be like the start of a romance, and if so, why?

8. Serena and Ainsley have their first big fight when Ainsley tells Serena she's "closed off." Why do you think Serena is the way she is? What barriers must she overcome to truly open herself up to a future that has room for true romantic love?

9. Sandeep tells Serena that "it's OK to love the people who have hurt you." Discuss how this applies to the relationships between the characters in the book.

10. Toward the end, Serena wonders if she would still have accomplished all of her career goals and become the same woman she is today if she had married Jesse twelve years earlier. What do you think?

11. Serena ultimately welcomes Natasha back into her life, accepting that not every relationship can be a "two-way street." Have you ever been in this position and faced this kind of choice with a good friend or a family member?

Keep reading for Sonya Lalli's next novel . . .

A Holly Jolly Diwali

Available soon from Berkley!

"We need to talk."

I paused the television just as Matthew McConaughey pressed his palm against Jennifer Lopez's flawless cheek. Mom and Dad were at the bottom of the stairs, dressed up for the party I'd already thought they'd left for. Their faces were like stone, and when Dad put his arm protectively around Mom's shoulder, my stomach bottomed out as I imagined the reasons for said *talk*.

1. They were getting a divorce.

I sank further into the couch, mentally shaking my head. This was unlikely. Most Indian couples their age, however fluent in English and miserable together, refused to learn the "D" word. Besides, my parents' marriage was, for all intents and purposes, a happy one. Trust me. My bedroom was just down the hall from theirs, and sometimes I could hear how *happy* they still made each other. Ugh.

2. *One of them was sick.*

My hands trembled just thinking about this scenario, but then I remembered they both had physicals the month before, and their doctors had said everything was just fine. I should know. I drove them both to and from their appointments so they didn't have to pay for parking.

3. *Jasmine.*

Yes. *Jasmine.* My whole body relaxed when I realized the most likely scenario was that my older sister was up to something again.

On the verge of a scandal. Had broken up with her deadweight boyfriend du jour. (Oh god. Let it be that!) Or maybe she was just being a run-of-the-mill pain yet again, and my parents wanted to vent to me before they ran off to whatever function they planned to attend that evening.

"Yes?" I asked, ready to hear the answer.

Silently, they trundled toward me, but instead of taking one of the many seats in our living room, they chose to stand directly in front of the TV.

"What is up?" Dad asked cheerfully. "Busy?"

"Very." I laughed. "What is *up* with you?"

He glanced at my mom, who was clearly about to do the heavy lifting. I blinked at her, and although I was curious what it was Jasmine had done to upset them again, I was ready to get back to *The Wedding Planner.*

"We are worried about you, Niki."

I scrunched up my face. Hold on a second. They were worried about *me*?

"You are?" A knowing glance passed between them.

"Care to elaborate?" I asked.

"Niki, it's Saturday night," Mom said. There was a tinge of annoyance in her voice, like when I didn't rinse my plate before putting it in the dishwasher. "Why are you home?"

"Mom, I—"

"Enough is enough." She held up her hand like a conductor, cutting me off. "Niki, you are very . . . very . . ."

"Successful?" I volunteered. "Obedient?"

"Single," she interrupted.

Wow. Mom burn.

Yes, I was single and had been for a while, but I didn't know how the "very" played into that.

I tucked my legs under me. "What's your point?"

"You know," Dad continued. "There are apps for dating. Have you heard?"

"No," I deadpanned. "What's a dating app?"

"*Well*," Dad started, but then Mom interrupted.

"She knows very well what a dating app is. Niki, are you on the Tinder? The Bumble? The Hinger?"

I smiled, even though I was irritated. Clearly, they'd done their research before the big talk.

"I am not," I said flatly. "I don't like the idea of meeting people online."

"So you'd prefer to meet people in person?" Dad gestured at Matthew McConaughey. "I see you are meeting so many good candidates."

Mom grinned, and even I had to laugh.

Dad burn. Very nice.

"Niki, we are not upset with you." Mom started pacing; she always enjoyed the theatrics. "We are *so* proud. But, we think you need to start . . . putting yourself out there. You understand?"

"Like, I need to start dating."

"*Hah*."

"Maybe I'm already dating. How do you know I don't have a secret boyfriend?" I crossed my arms. "Or girlfriend, for that matter? Maybe I have several. *Maybe* I'm a total player."

Mom narrowed her gaze at me. "And when do you see all these boyfriends and girlfriends? On the bus home from work? Do you sneak them into your parents' house after you come straight home every day?"

I groaned, burrowing my face into the pillow. Another Mom burn. But this one stung.

You see, they weren't totally wrong. My friends *constantly* gave me a hard time for not being on "the apps," and warned me that I would never meet anybody if all I did was work, go to the gym, and socialize with our group of friends. All of my colleagues were either in committed relationships or single for a reason, and my gym was women-only, rather inconvenient considering that I was straight. And while there was a time when I'd had ample opportunities to meet new guys while out with my friends, the closer we got to thirty, the more we stayed in, choosing each other's living rooms instead of bars.

Now, I was twenty-nine years old and getting zinged by my parents, the same parents who used to stomp their feet whenever Jasmine flitted in and out with a new guy. The same Mom and Dad who, up until today, seemed *thrilled* that I still lived at home, that I wasn't in a relationship they needed to worry about.

I sighed audibly, glancing up at them. I felt annoyed but not surprised, as far too many of my South Asian friends were starting to sink in an all-too-similar boat. One day, we're practically barricaded inside with our textbooks, "boys" not only not a subject worth discussing but, more often than not, entirely off limits.

And then?

And then, as if overnight, we're of marriageable age. Suddenly, we're not girls in need of protection but women, and being *very single* was our very own fault.

"I'll make more of an effort," I said finally, because I did want to get married one day, and there was no point in fighting the inevitable. "But I don't like the apps."

"Fair." Dad nodded. "Thank you."

I grabbed the remote, ready for the conversation to be over, but they didn't budge. Oh great. The talk wasn't yet over.

"Yes?"

I was looking at Mom because she was the one who clearly

had more to say. Her mouth was weirdly tense, and she was playing with the buttons on her cardigan as if they were puzzle pieces.

"*Beti*," she said affectionately, which was strange because her love language was sass. "Do you . . ."

"Mom, please. Just out with it, OK?"

She nodded primly. "OK. I am *outting* with it. I am . . ."

"*Mom!*"

"Do you want us to set you up?"

My jaw dropped. Like, to the *floor.* I could practically hear it land on the hardwood, shattering every which way.

"But . . ." I sputtered. "*You* didn't even have an arranged marriage!"

Mom and Dad snuck a look at each other, sly and knowing and with so much intimacy they really shouldn't have expressed in front of their own child. They were both in their early twenties when they moved to the US, Mom studying and Dad working, and had met at the local *gurdwara.* It wasn't a saucy meet-cute exactly, but it was a love match, and from the stories I heard, they matched so well that the whole dating process chugged right along. They were both Sikh. Tick. They both valued their Punjabi heritage and family values. Tick tick. So within five months of first laying eyes on each other over plates of *aloo paratha* in the *langar* hall below the prayer room, they were married.

Triple tick.

"We didn't have an arranged marriage, no," Dad said, looking back at me. "And we are not suggesting this for you."

"Exactly." Mom cleared her throat. "We are simply saying *if* you were interested in meeting someone outside of the apps, then maybe we know somebody." She paused, searching my face. "Maybe you could go for coffee, and if you like each other, you can . . ."

"Bang?"

Dad blushed, while Mom pretended not to hear me.

"Niki, you can date *normally.* We will not interfere. We don't even know the boy." Mom sighed. "He is nephew of our friends. Apparently, very sweet. *Modern.* A doctor—"

"Wow, a doctor? Sign me up!"

"We do not approach you with this lightly," Mom continued, ignoring me. Her voice was suddenly small and weak, and it made me feel terrible. Like a terrible daughter who, despite every effort to the contrary, had somehow still managed to disappoint them.

"You know." She had turned to Dad and was sweetly scratching the hairs on his beard. "We were Niki's age when we were married."

Their body language mirrored the romantic cheek-hold going on in the background between Matthew and Jennifer, and for the first time in a long time, I *felt* very single.

Were my parents trying to make me feel worse than I already did?

No, they weren't cruel. They were a little cheeky—intrusive and condescending at times—but they were good parents. The best, actually.

And so I, being the good daughter that I was, told them to give their friends' nephew my phone number.

Photo by Ming Joanis at A Nerd's World

Sonya Lalli is a Canadian writer of Indian heritage. She studied law in her hometown of Saskatoon and at Columbia University in New York, and later completed an MA in creative writing and publishing at City, University of London. Sonya loves to cook, travel, and practice yoga. She lives in Toronto with her husband.